SIN BIN

BLADES HOCKEY NOVEL

MARIA LUIS

ALKMINI BOOKS, LLC

After years playing in the NHL, a guy learns a thing or two.

Rule #1: Don't sleep with your publicist.

I've spent my career dropping gloves and racking up minutes in the sin bin, but even my hard-earned reputation as the NHL's toughest enforcer can't save me.

New team, new city, and an off-ice, bad boy persona I've got to clean up—or kiss my hard stick goodbye.

But then I walk into my new PR firm . . . and find *her* sitting behind the desk.

Rule #2: See Rule #1.

For Tina,
I could list a million and one reasons to say thank you because of
your amazingness - but when it comes right down to it . . . thank
you for enabling all of my Josh Brolin/Deadpool fantasies. There is
seriously nothing better than our meme/picture/GIF threads.

X

Good job, honey.

ZOE

BOSTON, MASSACHUSETTS

I am the Queen of Bad Decisions.

Now, before you start thinking that I'm overly dramatic, let it be known that, boy, do I wish that was the case. But no—I have a problem that's otherwise known as "no self-control." See the following:

1. My freshmen year at the University of Michigan, when I drunkenly professed my love for my English teacher via email. The recipient of that email? My professor. Naturally. The next day, I found myself on a transfer list to another class.
2. My ex-boyfriend, Mark, who apparently had a bad habit of humping his next door neighbor whenever I worked overtime. Discovering them together on our anniversary was just the cliché icing on the cake, and so was the way I stealthily slashed his tires the following evening, à la Carrie Underwood.
3. Andre Beaumont. Sorry, but we're not even getting into this one. I'll only mention that because of my .

.. indiscretion—big muscles and silky smiles that hint at bed sheets and panty-dropping sex are always my downfall—my life has been one downward spiral for the last three-hundred and forty-two days.

But all that changes today. Here. Right now.

I flash a bright smile at the CEO of Golden Lights Media. Golden Lights is Boston's premiere entertainment marketing empire, and hopefully my next place of work. *Believe it and you will achieve it.* That might as well be my tagline. "I can't say thank you enough for asking me in for a second interview, Mr. Collins."

"Zoe." Mr. Collins utters my name the way some might say "Satan," like he's worried he might catch my plague just by sitting opposite me.

My smile slips, just a little. *Think of the job, Zoe. Think. Of. The. Job.* "Yes, Mr. Collins?"

Heaving a big sigh, Walter Collins drops back in his seat to study me with stoic brown eyes. "Zoe. Miss Mackenzie."

This cannot be good.

I gird myself for the worst, flipping my folder up against my chest like a body shield. It's packed with my résumé, cover letter, and three letters of reference. It's also packed with my hopes, which are seconds away from shattering, if the CEO's expression is anything to go by.

"Listen, Miss Mackenzie," he says again, scrubbing a hand over his bearded jawline. "You've got the right qualifications for the position . . ."

I know what's coming. The urge to scream is overwhelming. I bite down on my lower lip and count to ten. *One . . . two . . . three . . .*

"But while I'd *love* to welcome you onto our public relations team, I've done a little research since our preliminary interview, and what I've found . . . . Well, I can't say that I'm all too impressed with your professional conduct."

I'm sure he's putting that mildly, just as I'm sure he practiced that exact line in the mirror this morning. His words have a pre-orchestrated feel to them, and he delivers them somberly, in the same tone that my former employer oh-so-graciously gave me the news that I was fired. You'd think someone had died the way that he'd—oh, wait, that was my career.

Slowly I meet Mr. Collins's gaze, and I make the decision that I have nothing to lose. Not my pride or my dignity, nor am I harboring any longstanding too-high expectations. I know what the score is, and I'm willing to play to this CEO's fiddle, as long as I come out with a job on the other side.

"Mr. Collins," I say carefully, "I understand your reservations. But I can promise you that what occurred a year ago won't be repeated." Nervously I tap my fingers against the folder, internally debating how to approach the situation. I straighten my shoulders. "After my . . . transgression last year, I've had quite a while to think over my faulty decisions."

Mr. Collins does not look impressed.

Panic enters my body. After almost a year of applying to jobs in my field, Golden Lights Media is my last hope. My last hurrah. I'm twenty-seven years old and living with my dad and step-mom. If my dad has it his way, I'll be working at his restaurant full-time like a good daughter, while also babysitting my half-sister on my off-days.

I love Tia, but even my love for my twelve-year-old half-sister can't make up for losing out on my dream —permanently.

Mr. Collins doesn't know it yet, but he's about to offer me this gig as the new Public Relations Coordinator for his firm.

I plant the folder down on the desk with the flat of my palm. "Let's do a trial run."

"Beg pardon?"

Bam. Stifling the abrupt pleasure of throwing the CEO off his game, I say, "A trial run. You want to hire me, but you're not sure if it's a good idea. I'm convinced that you won't regret it. As you told me in our first meeting, Mr. Collins, my résumé intrigues you. I've worked for all sorts of mainstream celebrities, including some of Detroit's biggest sports stars."

Brown eyes narrow on my face. "Including Andre Beaumont."

My knee-jerk reaction to hearing that name is to throw something. Maybe pound back a bottle of Jose Cuervo, because there is *nothing* I would like more than to forget the feeling of Beaumont between my legs, as he proves once and for all that multiple orgasms are a thing.

Or, rather, a thing that can happen with men.

(To be fair, my vibrator does a solid enough job on its own.)

But I digress.

I clear my throat, awkwardly reaching for a small glass of water and downing half for fortitude. "Yes," I murmur, "my former list of clients does include Mr. Beaumont."

Mr. Collins studies me, his brown eyes unblinking. "Let me make sure I'm understanding you correctly, Miss Mackenzie. You would like for me to give you a trial run." He scratches at his perfectly manicured beard. "Does this entail assigning you a client? Do I hold you to the same standard as the other publicists on my team?" He drops his elbows to the desk and leans forward. "Do I draw up a contract that reaffirms that you are not allowed to sleep with a client just to be certain that we're on the same page?"

My cheeks burn with embarrassment, and the words die on my tongue. *It was only one time.*

It just so happens that the "one time" was also caught on camera. Then shared across the Internet.

I promise you, until the day that your step-mom texts you to say that she never knew about the birthmark on your butt, you're not living life hard enough.

When silence steals my tongue, Mr. Collins turns to his computer. His fingers fly across the keys, tap, tap, tapping away with all the speed of a Tasmanian devil on speed. He clicks the mouse, another click, two more, and then he swings back around to face me.

"All right, Miss Mackenzie." He folds his arms across his chest and stares me down over the bridge of his nose. "I'll go along with your trial run."

My heart drops clear down to my feet. "You will?"

Way to sound confident, Zoe.

"Yes," Mr. Collins murmurs, "I will. I'll give you one month, as you suggested. And one client."

I'm not sure whether I ought to cry with relief or laugh at the fact that my desperate ploy is working. I do a little bit of both, and Mr. Collins gives me such a stern side-eye that my sobbing laughter dies an awkward death in my throat.

Straightening my shoulders again, I realize that I'm preening. *Down, girl, down.* I drop my shoulders—lift my chin instead. "Thank you, Mr. Collins. Thank you so much."

Finally, *finally*, I'm catching a break. The first professional break I've been given since the entire world found out that I slept with Andre Beaumont, NHL superstar. The former right wing for the Detroit Red Wings. King Sin Bin, as raving hockey fans like to call him, thanks to his lethal skill set on the ice—a skill set which regularly lands him in the penalty box.

Maybe, if I play my cards right, I'll shed the dreadful nickname the media gave me—Moaning Zoe.

Maybe, if I play my cards right, I can finally get my life back on track.

"I promise that you won't regret this," I say, reining in the urge to gush. "Whoever you assign to me will be perfect, and I guarantee that Golden Lights Media won't have seen a better PR Coordinator."

There's a knock on the closed office door. I don't turn around.

Everything that I want is at this desk. My hands itch to sign whatever contract my new boss might have stashed away in the drawers. My heart stampedes in my chest, overjoyed with the fact that after three-hundred and forty-two days, I finally have the chance to prove myself.

I'm not just the woman whose career took a hard tackle.

I'm not just the woman crashing on her parents' couch, and watching the *Disney Channel* every night with her sister.

I'm not just the woman who threw everything away for thirty minutes of hot sex with the sexiest hockey player in the NHL. A hockey player who had no interest in talking to the media on my behalf. No, the jerk quietly accepted his trade to the Boston Blades and never looked back.

"Miss Mackenzie," Mr. Collins says, recapturing my attention. "You're in luck. My assistant, Gwen James, just signed a new client, and we're pretty eager to get him settled in with an agent who will keep him in line and ensure that his public reputation remains scandal-free."

"Scandal-free is my middle name, sir."

Okay, slight exaggeration. But it *used* to be my middle name, you know, before the whole thing went down with Beaumont. And it might as well be my first name now, since I fled Michigan to Boston six months ago in a life do-over.

If Mr. Collins picks up the irony in my words, he doesn't mention it. "One month, Miss Mackenzie. We'll be coming back around to this in thirty days. But I'm telling you right now—if I hear one sliver of gossip about you, your so-called "trial run" will become null and void. Do you understand?"

Do I understand?

Hell to the yes, I do. "Absolutely. You can be confident that I'll be on my best behavior."

"Brilliant." He gives one short nod, then presses a buzzer on his desk.

The door swings open as I turn around, and a woman with voluminous red hair waltzes in with a spring to her step. "Walter, I've got our new client here."

Her wide-eyed gaze lands on me. Oh crap, I know that look. It's the one I get when people recognize me. And by that, I mean, they've seen the banana-shaped birthmark on my ass, as well as a quick glimpse of my face from the security camera video.

Kill me now, please.

"Miss Mackenzie," she says, coming over to shake my hand. "My name is Gwen. It's great to have you. Walter already let me know that you're on board. I . . . well, let me introduce you to our newest client."

I try not to let my hopes lift. Golden Lights Media is the top public relations company in Boston. From actresses to sports heroes to politicians, Golden Lights has backed anyone who's anyone in the Bay State.

My gaze flicks from Gwen to the empty doorway. Who have they paired me with? I'm hoping for someone awesome like Mark Wahlberg. Maybe Matt Damon. Hey, a girl can dream, right?

When a shadow fills the doorway, an acute sense of dread settles in my stomach. That shadow is familiar and that body even more so. I tilt my head, squinting against the afternoon glare from the sun for a better look.

Leather shoes slip against the marble flooring as the shadow enters Mr. Collins's office. Inch by inch, the body emerges as my sight readjusts. Dark jeans cling to muscular thighs, and a white T-shirt is halfheartedly tucked into the pants.

Something about this isn't right.

I shift in my chair, wishing that I could see his face. I so want to reach into my purse for my sunglasses. Unlike Gwen, who pranced right into the light like a beam of sunshine, this person hugs the darkness.

"Miss Mackenzie," Mr. Collins says, interrupting my thoughts, "might I introduce to you our newest client?"

And that's when The Day from Hell is replaced.

Because out from the shadows emerges Disastrous Mistake Numbers One through Infinity.

"Hello, Zoe."

Andre Beaumont, the Devil himself.

Oh, hell no.

2

ZOE

*H*e looks exactly the same.

For all of his faults (and there are many, trust me), Andre Beaumont is certainly not lacking in the looks department. Perfectly disheveled dark hair is swept back from his face. Dark eyes the color of Italian espresso travel up the length of my body, starting at my no-nonsense red pumps and working all the way up to my equally no-nonsense black dress. That hard gaze pauses at my breasts—not that there's much to speak of, considering that I'm "willowy" at best—before landing on my face.

He doesn't even have the good grace to look ashamed for his thorough once-over.

My hand itches to leave my side and flash him the bird, and I sit on my fingers to keep from giving in to temptation.

Speaking of temptation—it's overrated. Officially.

The sound of Mr. Collins clearing his throat breaks my death glare. "Miss Mackenzie," he says, coming around his desk to greet Andre with a handshake, "I trust that you recall Mr. Beaumont?"

Sarcasm. It's like music to my ears.

Swallowing a hot retort, I smile blandly at my new boss, as well as at the man responsible for my downfall. "Yes, of course." Brushing invisible lint from my dress, I stand and walk over to the two men.

The two couldn't be more opposite. While a gray suit encases Walter's thin frame, "casual" is the name of Andre's ensemble. He's completed the look with a black leather jacket —the same buttery-soft jacket that I remember pooled on the floor as I slipped my fingers over his ribbed abs.

Do not go there, Zoe.

I hold my hand out stiffly, still faking a welcoming smile that might crack my cheeks. "Mr. Beaumont, it's nice to see you again."

Andre takes my hand. Instead of shaking it like a normal person, he gives a sharp tug and pulls me close: so close that I can't help but remember firsthand that his irises and pupils are one synonymous black hue; so close that the fading bruise on his cheek, no doubt from a fight on the ice, catches the light and glimmers purple and yellow; so close that when he drops a brief kiss to each of my cheeks, I catch the scent of sandalwood off his skin. "It's been too long, Zoe."

"Or, not long enough," I mutter under my breath.

"What was that, Miss Mackenzie?" Mr. Collins stares me down, and it's so fierce, so intimidating, that I have to physi-cally push back my shoulders to avoid withering like a dejected wallflower.

Right. Must be on good behavior.

Suddenly I'm not so sure that this trial run idea was a good one.

"Walter, I'm glad that Gwen convinced me to come on board with Golden Lights Media," Andre says, breaking the uncomfortable moment in a rare show of . . . well, hell, I don't think it's compassion. Andre doesn't do compassion— for anyone. "After the work I've seen your firm do for Duke

Harrison, I'm positive that you'll have the media thinking that I've turned a new leaf in no time."

Call me cynical, but I doubt Andre has turned over anything, leaves or otherwise. I've followed mentions of him in the media closely this last year, closely enough to know that he's panicking.

Not on the ice. The big, bad Andre Beaumont is as fast and dangerous in the ice rink as he was on the day that the Detroit Red Wings drafted him from Northwestern University. But outside the rink? That's another story. The tabloids love to dish the dirt on his love life, which generally involves leggy supermodels followed by mentions of little ol' me.

Will Andre Beaumont Finally Move on from Moaning Zoe? Only Time Will Tell!

Or, another recent favorite of mine: A Trusted Source Has Told Us that Moaning Zoe Has Moved to Boston to be with Hockey Superstar Andre Beaumont. Will the Couple Finally Shed Their Dirty Laundry and Come Clean?

You'd think that after nearly a year, the media frenzy over a security camera catching us doing the naughty in the Red Wings' laundry room would have died down. Alas, each new girl that lands in Andre's muscular embrace only adds more fuel to the gossip rags.

I like to think of it as Divine Justice.

Only, I'd prefer not to have my name dragged through the mud in the same dirty swipe.

Retreating to his desk again, Mr. Collins takes a seat. "We're pleased to have you, Mr. Beaumont." He shifts stacks of papers to the side, and then pulls out a thick binder. "Yours is the exact type of case that we enjoy taking on."

Andre's thumbs go to the belt loops of his jeans, and his rugged features tighten. "An easy case, I hope?" he asks. Damn him, but his voice still hasn't lost its sexy appeal—

gritty, raspy. I once asked him if he smoked cigarettes, but he denied it vehemently.

"My body is a temple," and all that jazz, he said.

He's right—his body *is* a temple. A temple he chooses to share with any Jane, Kathy, and Sally who comes his way.

Not, of course, that I pay *that* close attention to the tabloids.

Walter's hand visibly pauses in the midst of flipping open the binder—a binder that I can only conclude holds all of Andre's deepest and darkest secrets. Walter looks to his assistant, the redhead, who visibly blanches and then launches into a flurry of motion.

"Mr. Beaumont—"

"You can call me Andre. The formality is a bit much."

"Right, right." Gwen slides a glance my way, and I arch my brows in a helpless gesture. If she's looking for help, she's come to the wrong place. Andre wouldn't listen to me, even if I hogtied him to Mr. Collins's office chair and threatened bodily harm.

Realizing that I'm no help, Gwen fluffs her red hair like it's her body armor and then takes a deep breath. "Mr. Beaumont—"

His buttery leather jacket creases along the shoulder as he lifts a hand to stop her. "Andre."

"Right, Andre." Another deep breath. "See, the thing is, Andre, you've provided us with a very . . . different sort of case than your teammate. For the most part, Mr. Harrison kept to a relatively low profile over the last number of years. As you might imagine, this made my job easier. With you, however . . . "

"Just tell him, Gwen," Mr. Collins jumps in with a flick of his wrist. A shiny gold Rolex sparkles under the office lights. "You're pussy-footing around the issue."

Gwen mutters something unintelligible beneath her

breath. Then, shoulders straightening, she announces, "You scare people, Andre."

Walter Collins harrumphs his approval.

Gwen looks on the verge of vomiting.

And then the man, who is known for being as impenetrable as finely cut marble, reacts.

His jaw drops open. And I—well, I feel the most ridiculous urge to clap my hands. His powerful shoulders twitch as he sharply glances back at me, and I realize that I've released an ill-timed squeak of delight.

Oops.

Pardon me.

Andre whips back around to face off against Gwen. "It's my *job* to scare people," he growls.

"Correction," Gwen says, lifting her finger like she's checking the wind direction, "the Blades hired you to intimidate other hockey players. On the ice. Not the media, off the ice."

She does have a point. Most players ham up to the cameras after a game, or, at least, they're reasonably polite.

Andre Beaumont is not "most" hockey players. Only the bravest of souls dare approach him in the locker room, and those numbers grow fewer by the game, based on what I've heard trickling down the grapevine. Back when I handled his PR, he'd had a similar, snarly disposition, but he cleaned up the attitude whenever I laid down the law.

"So the fact that I don't smile is a problem." Andre's voice is hard, surly.

Gwen's bright smile cracks, just enough to see that she's trying desperately not to wince. "That's one problem . . ."

"And the other?"

"Women."

Silence descends over the room, tense and oppressive.

Gwen resolutely holds Andre's gaze, though I swear her right eye twitches.

Slowly, as though tasting the word "women," and finding it repulsive, Andre mutters, "So, what? I date. Is that a crime?"

"Frequently," Gwen interjects, still standing strong, bless her heart. "You date *frequently*."

This time, there's no mistaking the way Andre looks at me over his shoulder. His dark eyes glitter with frustration, and his full mouth flattens into a thin line. Without taking his gaze off me, he tells Gwen, "I hadn't heard that it's a crime to test the waters." His gaze dips to my mouth and I fight off a shiver of unwanted desire. "Sometimes it's not what you expected."

This time, it's *my* jaw that slackens.

The . . . the . . . jerk!

Blood centers in my forehead, making it pulse like it's under siege from a bloody stampede of wild elephants. Letting my fury carry me, I meet his gaze and sweetly reply, "That's what happens when you take too many dips in the ocean, Mr. Beaumont. You choke on saltwater."

Walter slaps a closed fist to his chest.

Gwen lets out a scandalized, tinkling laugh.

Andre and I exchange a look that can only be categorized as pure snark. If "snark" had a look, I mean.

I stare him down, refusing to look away until he breaks eye contact first. Back when I was at—ahem—my prime, my clients fondly called me the "barracuda." Like the sharp-toothed beasts roaming the Amazon, I rarely stepped down from a fight. I learned from the very best—my mother, who, despite raising me on her own, worked three jobs and never failed to put food on the table for the two of us.

I count out the seconds that it takes for Andre to glance away. Nine. But glance away he does, and that slight measure of victory sends a thrill dancing down my spine. He may have worn me down a year ago, toppling over my defenses and warming up my girl parts, as well as my heart, but no longer. Nope.

I wouldn't sleep with Andre Beaumont again if he were the last man on earth.

Let me amend that: I *would* sleep with Andre Beaumont if he were the last man on earth, but only because I feel a very ingrained sense of duty to the world to continue procreation and to not let our species die.

You're welcome.

The sound of Mr. Collins faking a hacking fit jars me back to the present. He points at Gwen, as if telling her to take the reins and handle the misbehaving child.

Her eyes drift up to the ceiling. I wonder if she's praying for strength.

After long seconds, Gwen says, "We're aware of your slipping sponsorships. Last week alone you lost both Nike and Gatorade. That's a very big deal, especially for someone already coming off a big scandal." Thankfully, I'm not wearing a scarlet A on my shirt, and no one looks at me. "Whether you choose to admit it or not, your attitude might not be an issue on the ice, but it is absolutely affecting your game play off of it. Unless you're interested in losing every sponsor you have currently, you're going to have to do what we suggest, Mr. Beaumont."

This time, he doesn't even bother to correct her.

Although he's still presenting me with his back, I swear that I can see the wheels turning in his handsome head. Does he realize where I fit into this equation? That, more likely than not, he's stuck with me . . . maybe indefinitely?

The irony would kill me if it weren't for the fact that I'm too busy staving off the panic.

Andre and I . . . we aren't strangers. Far from it, actually—

I handled his PR for nearly a year. While we certainly butted heads on more than one occasion, I haven't forgotten the way that our business relationship slowly converged with a personal one. Snack runs after a particularly long session with reporters. Jogging on early Sunday mornings, whenever he wasn't out of town for games. Double dates when I caught a man's notice. Whenever this happened—and, not to totally throw myself under the bus, but the dating thing wasn't frequent—Andre always agreed to come along with whatever girl he was sexing up that day.

Andre's intimidating demeanor kept the creepers at bay.

Hard as it might be to believe, Andre had my back.

Just as I had his.

Until we let one explosive kiss ruin everything. And it really did ruin everything, because that one spontaneous kiss led to the laundry room fiasco, and obviously we all know how *that* turned out.

Aka that time my birth-marked butt hit every small screen in America.

It's as horrifying as it sounds.

Andre rakes his fingers through his thick, dark hair. "So, what you're saying is that either I take your advice, or I'm screwed. Do I have the gist of it?"

Gwen doesn't wince, but there's no hiding the way her gaze shifts to the floor. "If you want to keep your current lifestyle, then, yes, that about covers everything."

For a long moment, no one says a word. Then, he grumbles, "Fine. Whatever you have to do about this, then we'll do it."

Except that he doesn't say "about" but rather *aboot*, because, naturally, he's Canadian.

A Canadian who isn't all unicorns and rainbows and *nice* —in other words, Andre is practically unrecognizable amongst his own kind.

"Great!" The tense lines in Gwen's face ease. "Then I'd love to officially introduce you to your new publicist."

Andre's back stiffens. "You won't be in charge of my case?"

"Oh no," Gwen says with a flippant wave of her hand. "Golden Lights is expanding to other cities, and I've got about ten different clients right now, one of whom can't complete a sentence without dropping the f-bomb. No, Andre, you'll be paired up with our newest addition to the Golden Lights Media family."

Slowly, as though his body is battling a rough current in the ocean, Andre twists at the waist to look at me. Seeing the realization spark in his expression might be my new favorite memory, right after the time my only pair of Manolo Blahniks arrived in the mail, and I slipped those beautiful babies onto my feet while I ate cereal and watched reruns of *Friends*.

But this moment . . . Oh, boy, it's a good one. I'd be lying if I said I haven't waited a year to see Andre Beaumont look off-kilter and just a little bit scared.

His eyes glitter, but the inscrutable emotion banks as his mouth turns down. The quiet before the storm.

"No."

It's all he says, and yet the two-letter word is everything.

I grin, making it extra toothy just to show him that I am *unfazed*. With a little finger wave, I say, "Hello, Andre."

A pulse ticks to life in his jaw. "No."

"Didn't you say it's been too long? I could have sworn that I heard you—"

"No."

"I think you did," I murmur sweetly, just short of batting my eyelashes at the man who I've dreamed of beating with his own hockey stick—between the legs, where it hurts.

"Walter—" Andre twists around to face the CEO of Golden Lights. He clears his throat, then does so again. "Mr.

Collins, with all due respect, I demand someone else handle my case. Considering my . . . past with Miss Mackenzie, it only makes sense."

Walter tucks his hands under his armpits. "I'm sorry, Mr. Beaumont. We've hired Miss Mackenzie on a thirty-day trial, so unless something momentous happens during the interim, you have her and her only."

"A trial," Andre drawls. I don't like the way he rolls the word over on his tongue, like he's considering the ramifications of his next few words. "And if she doesn't last the thirty days?"

"Then you'll be assigned to someone else, and we'll have to meet with Miss Mackenzie one-on-one to discuss her position with Golden Lights."

I don't like the way that Andre glances at me over his shoulder, a considering look darkening his rugged features.

And I especially don't like the way he turns to look at me fully, crosses his arms over his chest, and huskily says, "Let's hope that she makes it to thirty days, then."

3

ANDRE

*S*he looks exactly the same.

As I listen to Coach Hall mouth off about shitty stick-play at the front of the locker room, that's the only thought running on repeat in my head. *She looks exactly the same.* I'm not thinking about riding the Chicago Blackhawks hard enough that they'll cry themselves to sleep tonight. I'm not thinking about the fact that I've already dropped gloves twice in the last two periods—and subsequently served my penance in the sin bin.

For once, hockey isn't my focus.

She is.

Zoe Mackenzie.

The one woman who I was never supposed to see again.

Jesus H. Christ, she looked good today. Criminally good, even. Slim-fitting dress, her usual. Heels that were painted the same color red as her lips. In the span of one second, I'd experienced a range of emotions that rocked me back like a hard-hitting body check. All at once, I'd wanted to tug her into my arms and inhale what I hoped was still her favorite

19

citrusy perfume just as badly as I'd wanted to turn on my heel and get the fuck out of there.

I hadn't expected to see her in Walter Collins's office. Hell, I hadn't even known that she'd moved to Boston. Zoe was a Detroit girl through and through, and having her here in the same city was like liquid heat in my veins.

"Beaumont."

I lift my gaze from my skates to Hall, whose face is blustery with agitation. "Yeah, Coach?"

His white mustache twitches as he clamps his teeth down on a toothpick. "I need you to get out there, Sin. Do what you do best. We're fucking behind by three, and unless someone's up to scoring a goddamn hat trick tonight, then I'm gonna need you to take control."

No one asks what he's talking about. Aside from Duke Harrison, our main man between the pipes, I'm the biggest guy on the ice. If you believe the rumors, I'm also the meanest son of a bitch to play, too.

The sin bin might as well be my second home. I'll be honest, it's a tough balance to find. Play hard enough that grown men flee in the opposite direction when they see you coming, but don't play so hard that you're ejected from the game. The league doesn't support enforcers anymore—we're a dying breed, thanks to changing safety regulations over the years—but when push comes to shove, we're still expected to step forward and do our job.

It's a balance I've perfected over the years, and Coach Sam Hall knows that well.

King Sin Bin.

Earned the damned nickname when I was twenty-one years old, still scrappy, and grabbing players left and right as we hustled for the puck at the boards. Back then, my aggressive style of play was a bonus. Nowadays, it's more of a liability . . . except for times like now, when we're lagging behind, playing slow, and reinforcements are needed.

In other words, *I'm* needed.

Fifteen minutes later, I'm doing exactly what Coach ordered. Driving my elbow into my opponent's side as I grab him by the back of his jersey. My helmet glances off the Plex-iglas as I dig in.

"Get the fuck back, Sin," Marlow grunts.

We used to play together in Detroit, way back when. My knee slips between his legs as we battle for the puck at the boards. Our shoulders jostle, pads colliding. "Hope your wife won't mind your crying tonight," I grunt back at him. "Maybe grab some tissues on the way home."

"Fuck you, Beaumont."

"You're not my type, Marlow. Told you before."

Over the deafening crowd, I hear him laugh. "You still pining after Moaning Zoe, man? Not that I blame you, her ass is . . . "

I drive my elbow into his pads.

Not enough to cause injury—I play hard, ruthless, but not dirty—but the force of my weight sends him sprawling to the ice. Way back when, Ken Marlow used to fist-bump me for pulling stunts just like this one.

From the way he eyes me through the grates of his helmet, he's had a change of heart. He clambers to his skates, lunging toward me, gloved fists raised, just as one of the linesmen skates over and blows the whistle, indicating to the referee that I messed up and deserve to serve time for elbow-ing. Again.

I skate toward the penalty box without a backward glance. The crowd is a cacophony of boos and applause, as the fans take their sides. It's a sound I've been living for since I was just a kid growing up in the suburbs of Ottawa,

Canada. Nowadays, though, those boos and cheers equal a paycheck, making me the top paid enforcer in the league.

King Sin Bin—that's me. Meanest bastard on the ice. Man with a *heart* of ice.

I fucking wish that was true.

As the second line hits the ice, I think of Zoe from earlier today—her dark eyes flashing with sardonic humor when I connected the dots that she's my new publicist. My jaw clenches. While the position might be hers, I refuse to ever cross those blurred lines with her again.

I like my life. It's simple. Easy.

Zoe makes me think, makes me *feel*.

And that just won't do.

I grind my teeth. Once upon a time, I considered Zoe my closest friend. Before I allowed lust to get in the way, before I was so desperate for her that I ignored all the signs that Zoe wanted more than I could give her, emotionally. Better to keep her at arm's length now than to potentially get back in too deep.

I stare at the rink through the Plexiglas and swallow past the growing lump in my throat. This is the right move, for both of us . . . And if I happen to have saved some of the final texts she ever sent me, that'll just stay with me.

King Sin Bin.

Man with a heart of ice.

My fingers dig into my thighs.

Yeah, we're all better off this way.

If only I could forget the vision of her shocked face the moment she saw me today. Damn it, but it felt good to be in the same room as her.

4

ZOE

I spend the rest of my day half fearful that Andre Beaumont will track me down and throw me into Boston's Charles River. It's March, and still frighteningly cold outside, and the black, murky depths of the city's popular strip of waterfront does not look enticing, thank you very much.

But the look Andre gave me just before I left Walter Collins's office this afternoon? Oh yeah. He's planning something. The *what*, however, has eluded me thus far.

In fact, I'm so wound up after the entire experience that even my dad, who is perhaps *the* most unaware person I've ever met, notices that something is up during dinner.

"Zoe?" he says, as he dumps a lump of mashed potatoes onto his plate. "You okay today?"

Fred Mackenzie isn't the sort to talk about those pesky things called *feelings*, and so I spare a quick glance at Shelby, my stepmother, who only shrugs and mouths, *humor him*. Right. My dad and Shelby married when I was in my teens, but since I've always lived with my mom . . . Well, time spent with my dad has always been on the fly. Random weekend trips here. A full week's school vacation there. The last six months in Boston have proven to be an eye-opening experience, that's for sure.

I'm already planning my escape the moment my first paycheck lands in my bank account.

I gird myself for his interrogation by shoving another slice of meat into my mouth, and use the time spent chewing (Shelby overcooked the pork chops) to prepare what I'm going to say. Finally, after I've managed to swallow the pork and not choke to death, I announce, "Well, I got the job."

My half-sister, Tia, squeals and fist pumps the air. "Ohmigod, I *knew* you would!" I love Tia. With her brown hair and dark eyes, she's the spitting image of me. Just a younger me—with heaps more enthusiasm and a zest for life that adulthood hasn't yet kicked to the curb.

"Thanks for letting me practice my interview on you, T," I murmur, and a wide smile pulls at her mouth.

"What's the catch?" Dad says, pointing his fork at me. "You look like someone ran over your dog, then did it again."

"Fred!" Shelby shoots a pointed glance at their twelve-year-old daughter. "Let's lay off the graphic images. Please."

Dad's gray brows pull down, like he can't quite grasp the concept that maybe his youngest child shouldn't be thinking about dying dogs—hell, *I* don't want to think about dying dogs.

"Well, she does look like it," is all he grumbles. I assume he's referring to the dog comparison, which, you know, isn't the worst non-compliment I've ever received from Fred Mackenzie.

There was that time he "accidentally" said I looked pregnant during one of my visits. I was fourteen, and he followed up that comment with bringing me to the drugstore and handing me a pregnancy test. Mind you, I was still a virgin.

There was also that time that he (drunkenly) told me that he wasn't sure that I was his kid when I was sixteen.

I've since learned to take what my father says with a grain of salt.

Something that Shelby clearly hasn't learned to do, despite the fact that she's been married to him for over a decade.

"How about *sad?*" she prompts, her blue eyes locked on Tia in worry. "Zoe looks sad."

"She doesn't look *sad,*" my dad counters, color infusing his cheeks.

Oh, crap. Here we go again.

I try to catch Tia's eye, but she's too busy pushing the food around on her plate. Wanting to put a smile on her face, I kick her foot under the table with just enough force that she knows it wasn't accidental.

Her dark eyes flick over to me, and she makes a "whaddaya gonna do" face, complete with a slack mouth and half-closed eyes, like she's five seconds away from falling asleep at the table. I return the look, not caring how silly I appear, in sisterly camaraderie.

"She looks pissed," Dad finishes, thrusting his fork in the air.

Now Shelby looks pissed. "*Language,* Fred."

"Shelby, it's my house. If I want to say 'pissed,' I can say it however many times that I want."

Eyes narrowing, Shelby seethes, "Don't you dare, Fred Elliott Mackenzie. Don't . . . you . . . dare."

Well, I think this is our cue. I nudge Tia again with my foot, jerking my head toward the doorway that leads to the living room. She nods curtly in silent agreement. We grab our plates, utensils, and glasses of water, and stealthily escape the fray.

Not that there's need for any stealth, because Dad and

Shelby have erupted into a fight that borders on the nonsensical. I enter the living room just as my dad breaks out into a song that consists only of the word, "pissed." He hits the high notes like a champ, then drops his voice down to an Elvis-Presley-worthy croon.

Back in the day, before he opened an Italian restaurant and lost his soul to meatballs, fettuccini, and marinara sauce, I recall my dad having dreams of becoming a professional singer.

Apparently, this is as close as he gets nowadays.

I follow Tia up the flight of stairs to the second level of the house. Second door on the right is hers, and we quickly settle in on the carpeted floor, picnic-style, with the door half-cracked.

"I'm sorry," she mutters, sounding so morose that my gaze immediately jumps to her face.

"For what?"

She points to the floor in indication of the adults who aren't acting like adults. "You know—about Dad and Mom."

I hide my wince. Growing up, it had only ever been my mom and I. Two women against the world. Marsha Mackenzie (she never reverted back to her maiden name) has never been inclined to date, perhaps because her relationship with Dad was so toxic. Even now, she prefers to go out with her girlfriends for cocktails over spending time with a man.

Sure, I never had the ideal family unit, but I would take my childhood over Tia's any day. In the six months since I've moved in, there hasn't been a day where Dad and Shelby haven't broken out the figurative knives and sharpened them on each other's flesh.

"It's okay," I tell my sister, as I kick off my shoes and tuck my legs under me. I still haven't changed out of my interview outfit, so the slim-fitting dress inches up my thighs. Since it's only Tia, I don't bother to shield her from my black Spanx. "Don't worry about it, T."

Her thin shoulders lift with a shuddery breath. "But you got the job, and I know you're going to leave soon."

As much as I want to get out of this house on a permanent basis, the thought of hurting Tia breaks my heart. So, I go for the slip-around-the-issue option. "What? Where am I going to live if I do that? In the Boston Commons?"

She giggles, just as I intended her to. "Are you going to put up a tent?"

I fake-glare at my half-finished plate of food. "I don't have a tent."

The idea of me being tent-less sparks more laughter from my sister, evil creature that she is. "What if it rains?" she prompts.

"Guess I'm going to be soaked."

"What if it snows?"

I pin her with an expression of pure horror and she howls with laughter. "Are you trying to make sure that I never want to leave this house?" I demand.

"What if there's a tornado and it whips through the park, and you get taken with it?"

"Boston doesn't have tornadoes," I gripe with a half-grin, "and you're evil, you know that?"

"So, you're going to stay?" She swipes a thumb under her eye to catch a tear (she laughed too hard at my expense), and proceeds to shovel the rest of her food into her mouth at top-speed. I both admire and envy her youthful metabolism. Around a forkful of corn, she asks, "Please?"

"Yeah, I'll stay."

For now.

At twenty-seven, I miss my freedoms of being completely independent. Walking around in my underwear and a T-shirt are at the top of the list, as is enjoying the company of men.

But, since *men* haven't really been on my radar for quite some time now, I guess I just miss the underwear/T-shirt bit the most.

The thought of men, however, makes me think of Andre. We're due to have our first meeting tomorrow, and I'm both dreading it, and, strangely, also anticipating the thrill of being in his company.

The thrill of drawing his blood, I mean.

The thirty-day trial at Golden Lights Media looms large like a dark, gray cloud over my head. Whether Andre wants to or not, he's about to become the most clean-cut hockey player the NHL has ever seen.

Game on.

5

ZOE

TWENTY-NINE DAYS LEFT

*a*ndre doesn't show for our meeting.

Walter barks at Gwen, demanding to know where the company's newest bad boy client is. Gwen, in turn, sidles up next to me in the office kitchen, red hair bigger than the day before, to ask if I've heard from him at all.

"Nothing," I tell her.

I feel like I've been stood up at prom.

I spend the first thirty minutes, after our scheduled meeting time, at my new desk, rearranging the pretty flowers I've brought in to force life into my otherwise barren office. The floor-to-ceiling windows allow for a lot of natural light, but the walls are white, the carpet is white, my desk is white, the damn door is white.

I made the grave mistake this morning of wearing a white sweater dress and nude heels, which means that I fit right into the sterile-like environment that now belongs to me. For thirty days. If I don't totally screw up.

After that exhilarating part of my morning, I spend the next twenty-seven minutes organizing the mess in the desk. Whoever had the office before me was a hoarder. Tampons, three iPhone chargers, ten packs of gum, six sleeves of Post-It notes, and four travel books about Paris are all crammed into the top drawer. When my fingers land on a square, tell-tale foil, I cringe and throw the condom packet into the waste bucket with a grimace.

Naturally, the following twenty minutes are spent sanitizing the entire office, starting with my (white) desk chair and ending with the (brass) doorknob. Who knows what kind of debauched crap went down in here—and, no, I don't feel like a hypocrite by saying so.

At least Andre and I did it in the laundry room, where the laundry was *dirty*.

Ugh.

That doesn't make me feel any better.

Gwen pokes her head into my office around two p.m. "Nothing yet?" she asks, and I feel the weight of my twenty-nine-and-a-half days like a guillotine poised over my head. "Did you try the cell phone number in the file?"

"Yes." In fact, I called *and* texted the jerk no less than three times. He must know what this job means to me. Instead of pulling on his big-boy pants, however, he's run scared. This isn't at all like the Andre Beaumont I know, but then again, it's been almost a year.

People change in less.

I have.

Whatever starry visions of Andre I had way back when are now nonexistent.

Gwen's blue gaze flits over the office. "You cleaned?"

I shift on my bare feet, wishing I hadn't kicked off my heels around the time that I started scrubbing the windowsill. "I needed something to do."

"Want to clean my office?" she says, although I'm not sure that she's joking.

With the Windex bottle clutched in one hand and a paper

towel in the other, I say, "Will it keep me at Golden Lights for longer than thirty days?"

Her expression seesaws as she presses her back against the open door. "I'm sorry about that."

I shrug. "I get it."

Because I do—I'm a liability. I place the Windex bottle on my desk and throw the dirty paper towel away into the waste bin. The office smells like fresh lemon, its past sins all but wiped away.

"So, is it weird?"

My heart squeezes. *Here it comes . . .* "What do you mean?"

"You know"—she widens her eyes in that way people do when they want you to pick up the clue that they aren't, actually, putting down—"with *Andre*. After everything that happened last year, it must be weird to know that you'll be working with him again."

Do I go for honesty? Play the oblivious tactic?

Not that I think Gwen would fall for the latter. She may sound like she's interested in my answer as a friend, but her gaze is way too sharp for my liking. So, I do what any woman in my position would do: I play it cool, like seeing my one-time fling hasn't completely rocked me off my train to Happy Land.

"It's fine," I tell her smoothly. "Of course, it'd be better if he showed up for our meeting this morning. But he's a hotshot hockey player. I'm sure he just forgot."

It's unlikely Andre has forgotten anything.

All morning I've toyed with a new suspicion—that he didn't show because he *wants* me to be fired. If that's the case, he's got another thing coming to him. Because I'm not going anywhere. If this is my last chance at a career in my chosen field, then I'm going down with fists flying.

Andre Beaumont won't even know what hit him.

Seeing that she isn't likely to get any information out of

me, Gwen gives me a smile that verges on pitying. She knows. She knows that I'm a half-step away from stalking Andre down and forcing him to do my non-sexual bidding.

"If you want to take off for the day, feel free," she tells me, her gaze falling to the fancy, rose-gold watch encircling her wrist. "You can't really shape up Beaumont's career without Beaumont, so you might as well head home and prepare for battle."

My fingers twitch at that. I feel like I've been in battle for the good bit of a year, but this is something different. I need to be strategic. I need to get my ducks in a row and start my plan to wipe Andre's stained reputation clean.

He doesn't want to lose his sponsorships.

I don't want to lose this job.

In theory, we should be on the same page. In theory, the next twenty-nine days should be easy.

In theory, I shouldn't feel the least bit tempted to want another taste of Andre Beaumont after a year of radio-silence, but I do. What they say about thin lines between love and hate? Well, the line between lust and hate is even thinner, and as I stuff my laptop into my work bag, and stuff my feet back into my stilettos, I'm horrified to realize that I'm just as annoyed that Andre didn't show professionally as I am at the sinking thought that he didn't show for *me*.

And the latter just won't do.

No way am I letting lust get the better of me.

Not even for Andre Beaumont.

6

ZOE

I barely get my foot over the threshold at home before my dad comes flying down the stairs. In his arms, he juggles his striped chef pants, coat, and a set of large-as-my-forearm menus. The moment he sees me, his terse expression breaks like he's seen the Second Coming.

"Zoe! Thank fucking God."

It's Thursday and a school week, which means that Tia is in class and Shelby is at work, but I nevertheless glance over my shoulder. "Aren't you supposed to be watching the language thing?"

"No time," he grunts as he drops his armful onto the entryway table and shoves his feet into a pair of non-slip kitchen shoes. "The GM just called. My chef quit, took half the wait-staff with him, the bastard, and we've got a full house tonight."

I decide to let the language thing slide for the sake of not starting an argument.

My gaze flicks to the menus. "So, you're calling in the reinforcements?"

"I *am* the reinforcement." With that, he snaps to attention and puffs out his chest, and it would have been somewhat adorable-dad cute, except that he ruins the Ideal-Fatherhood image by cursing like a sailor when the menus slip from the table and scatter all over the floor.

Still in my stilettos, I dip low and gather what I can.

"What are you doing home so early?" he demands roughly on my way back up.

"Early day." Still no word from Andre. I'm starting to think that I was right—he's totally sabotaging me. I plan to spend the night with a glass of wine, a heaping of chocolate, and my day planner. He can avoid me for one day; he can't avoid me for thirty.

By tomorrow, I'll have my plan sorted to get his butt toeing the line of respectability again.

"Come to the restaurant with me."

At Dad's random outburst, my jaw slackens. "What? I don't cook."

He rolls his eyes. "I'm not asking you to cook. Remember when you spent a summer or two being a server at the restaurant?"

I remember hating my life when I dropped a hot plate of steaming mussels and clams all over the mayor of Boston. Seafood went flying, smacking the mayor's wife in the breasts and landing in the mayor's lap.

The mussels were hot, the wine-infused sauce even hotter.

Dad promptly banned me from entering his restaurant, Vittoria, until just a few years ago.

You can see why I'm not too thrilled about the prospect of returning.

For the sake of Boston's citizens, it's best if I don't touch anything that threatens with a steaming good time.

Slowly, I say, "I don't think that's a good idea."

Dad doesn't get the hint. "Think of it as father-daughter time."

Ooh, low blow. I suck in a breath. "We can have father-daughter time after you come home tonight. You know, with a movie or something."

"Please."

For the record, Fred Mackenzie does not say "please." The last time I heard him do so, Shelby was giving birth to Tia as he paced the hospital's hallways, alternatively cursing God and also praying for a vasectomy.

No more kiddies for Fred, not after Tia.

Taking a deep breath, I stare at my father resolutely. He may call it father-daughter time, but it's the furthest thing from his mind. He wants help and he wants help now.

And I'm the only one around that he can push into doing his bidding.

✕

Two hours later, I'm decked out in Vittoria's server uniform. Black pants mold to my legs and a crisp white button-down is fitted over my torso. I've rolled the sleeves up to my elbows, and my dark hair is pulled back in a high ponytail.

I don't know how I've managed to get myself into this situation, but I can promise you it's as bad as I remember.

"Do you know the menu?" Manny, the restaurant's general manager, demands when he catches sight of me hiding in the beverage station. I'm seated on a blue rack that's meant to be used to store pint glasses, and not, you know, my butt. Admittedly, it's not the most comfortable, but beggars can't be choosers.

I flip the menu over on my knee, so that Vittoria's logo of the Sicilian countryside stares up at me.

"Zoe?" Manny's polished leather shoes clip across the tiled floor. "How much of the menu do you know?"

My fingers tap anxiously over Sicily. "The specialty cocktails." I sneak a quick peek at the black typography. "If I fake it, I can probably get through the appetizers."

"It'll have to do." The menu slips from my grasp as he steals it, and I feel like he's straight-up taken away my lifeline. "Table 21 is all yours."

I don't want it to be all mine. Sure, serving tables shouldn't be all that different from serving high-end celebrities. I'm a people person. They like me; I like them. Not to sound arrogant or anything, but this shouldn't be a problem —except at the thought of recreating the fiasco with the mayor all over again, the blood immediately seeps from my face.

"Aren't servers supposed to have a training period?" I eye the menu Manny clutches in one hand, wondering how desperate I'll look if I try to take it back.

As if reading my thoughts, he tucks it under his armpit and clamps down. "Our chef quit today and he took most of the serving staff. I don't care if you fake your way through the entire night. Get out there and pretend you know what the hell you're talking about."

His monologue ends in pure silence.

I stare at the menu longingly.

He watches me like he's expecting me to make a break for it.

After thirty seconds, I ask, "Where's Table 21 again?"

His eyes squeeze shut. "Lover's Lane."

Ah.

More silence.

I open my mouth. "Which lane is that?"

In response, all he does is lift his arm and point at the swinging door leading to the dining area.

I stealthily sneak a peek at a printout of the dining room layout on my way out of the kitchen. Lover's Lane— to the right and along the back wall of the restaurant. I've got this.

At this time of night, Vittoria is packed with patrons. When my dad first opened the restaurant about twenty years ago, its first rendition was more pizza-joint and less fine-dining atmosphere. But as the years bled into one another, and as his phone calls to me grew more sporadic the busier he became, thanks to the restaurant's newfound fame, Vittoria slowly climbed the ranks.

Now one of Boston's trendiest restaurants, Vittoria can be found in the historic Italian neighborhood of the North End. The interior is designed with exposed brick walls, wrought iron sconces and chandeliers, and pristine white tablecloths. The menu regularly scores high reviews from top food bloggers, and, from what my dad has told me, it's not uncommon to see celebrities step through Vittoria's front doors.

Sidling up to the hostess stand, I snag a vase of water and count my way over to Table 21 in Lover's Lane.

Eighteen…

Nineteen…

Twenty…

Here we are. I slide my finger into my shirt collar, and subtly straighten my black bow tie. Taking a deep breath, I step up to the table and grin.

"Hi there! Welcome to Vittoria!"

A blonde-haired woman blinks back at me. "My date is in the restroom."

Gotta love the people who *must* let everyone know that they aren't eating alone. Once, I was just like them. Recently, I've learned to enjoy my independence. I can eat when I want, where I want, and thank God I no longer have to worry about a man telling me to lay off the second slice of cheesecake.

My cheesecake, my rules.

My gaze drops to the woman's dress, which borders on Academy-Award-worthy, it's so fancy. While my dad's restaurant is largely upscale, it still doesn't call for . . . . Well, *this*.

The woman is encased in cheetah-print silk.

It's rather stunning, actually.

I almost want to ask where she purchased it.

Her incredibly breathy, high-pitched voice stops me. "Did you hear me? You can come back in five minutes."

"Let me give you some water while you wait," I murmur, lifting the vase. My elbow hikes up as I lean forward, cutting short when it hits flesh.

There's a male grunt.

A gritty curse.

Oh, no.

I whip around to apologize, only to be stilled by strong, masculine fingers.

"Give me a second," the voice growls, and instant awareness hits me. I know that voice way too well.

Andre.

Please, for the love of all things holy, someone just end my misery.

"Oh, my God," the blonde exclaims, her eyes landing on the NHL's best enforcer behind me. "Are you okay?"

With Andre's fingers still locked around my elbow, and my back to his chest, our little position is starting to feel way too familiar. "I'm fine," he says between gritted teeth.

"I'm pretty sure she nailed you in the—"

"Suzanne."

The blonde clamps her mouth shut, sitting back primly in her seat as she shoots daggers in my direction. Like this is my fault. And, yes, *theoretically* I did potentially elbow him in the crown jewels, but I certainly didn't ask for him to swoop up behind me, all stealthy, ninja-like.

With the vase of water still clutched in my hand, I decide there's no other recourse. "Andre," I say evenly, "would you please let go of me?"

"Zoe?"

His hand drops from my arm like I've combusted into fire.

I turn around, water vase clutched tightly. The scowl on his face is the stuff of legends, but beneath the frown, beneath all that bad attitude, I sense his shock at finding me here. And, boy, the glint of surprise in his black eyes warms me considerably.

Andre Beaumont is not the sort of man that one frequently one-ups, and the fact that I've managed to do so . . . . Yeah, it feels good. Mentally I give myself a pat on the back.

I glance down to where his big hand is pressed flat against his stomach. "Did I get you where it hurts?" I ask with a downward tilt of my chin.

The shock evaporates from his expression like a wisp of smoke, and the hard, impenetrable glare shifts back into place. "Are you hoping that you did?" he asks gruffly.

My shoulders lift in a lazy shrug. "Wrong place, wrong time."

Dark eyes narrow on my face. "Is that a dig?"

"On the fact that you stood me up today and didn't bother to respond to any of my calls or text messages?" I offer another shrug, noting the way that each time I do so, his eyes narrow further. Any more of that and he'll be staring out at me through mere slits. The part of me that's still bitter about everything encourages me to do just that, to push him over the ledge and see what happens. "Maybe."

"Maybe," he reiterates stonily.

"Depends on whether you actually had a good reason for not showing, like saving homeless puppies or volunteering at an elderly home."

His arms cross over his burly chest. This time, he isn't wearing a T-shirt, and I can't stop myself from taking in my fill. Black button-down, open at the neck to reveal the tan column of his throat; matching black slacks that do nothing to hide his muscular thighs. He clears his throat and it's enough for me to blink up at his face.

He's totally caught me staring, but I refuse to cower. In the end, he blows out a frustrated breath. "Maybe I was saving puppies *and* volunteering. Maybe I thought that our scheduled meeting could be rescheduled."

"Oh, don't you worry," I tell him with a jovial pat-pat to his hard chest, "We have *thirty* days to make sure that all goes as planned." A tick starts in his jaw and I stifle a victorious grin. "Now, we don't want to leave your date hanging." I shoo him into the booth with my free hand. "Let's try the water thing again, shall we?"

While Andre stews in muteness, his expression one that can only be filed under "pissed-off man," his date flits her hands over his chest and down toward his . . . waist. I assume it's his waist, but maybe she's trying for something else under the table. Andre has obviously made it abundantly clear that public places don't deter him in the slightest when it comes to sex.

But he does surprise me when he captures her wrists and presses her hands to the tabletop.

His gaze still hasn't left me. "Are you stalking me?" he asks, voice low.

I top off his date's glass with water and then do the same for his. "I work here."

Temporarily.

Just for tonight.

Definitely not on a permanent basis.

"So, no," I continue, casually tucking the water vase against my hip. "In order for me to stalk you, I'd have to be emotionally invested."

"And you're not?"

"Emotionally invested?" Ha! I try to withhold my laugh for a few reasons, the first one being that he is on a date with *another woman*. And seeing as how we haven't even spoken for the better part of a year, being "emotionally invested" with the man in front of me is absolutely a no-go. I may have been so at one time—*maybe*—but surely not now.

I know better.

He waits for me to continue, and I've got half a mind to tell him that he'll be waiting forever, but then he reaches for the water I've just filled and takes a healthy sip. His throat works down the liquid, and I'd be lying if I said he didn't look sexy as hell right now. Which really isn't fair, because he doesn't seem the slightest bit affected by my presence—only at the potential thought that I've become his personal stalker.

He places the glass on the table, then leans back in the booth, arm resting along the top, to stare up at me. "I think you are."

My back stiffens. "I think you're delusional."

"Well, *I* don't know what I think," Suzanne cuts in testily, "but I *do* know that if you don't run along now and get us some of that delicious bread, I'm going to request that you be removed from our table."

I don't have it in me to hate her because she's so right. She might be on a date with the man who left me high and dry, but I have no reason to be hanging around like a lovesick fool.

Especially since I'm the furthest thing from it.

I murmur my apologies, take their cocktail orders, and

book it back to the kitchen. Only once I've burst through the swinging doors do I heave in a deep breath. Of all the people who I could be serving tonight, Andre Beaumont is the very last person I expected to find seated in my section.

Lover's Lane. Oh, the irony.

I sincerely doubt Andre has the capabilities to love anything, including a dog, and that's saying something.

Almost maniacally, I shove two loaves of bread into a wicker basket, plop it on a round, black tray, and make my way to the bar. I skim my gaze over my section, and note a new couple being seated.

The stampede is about to start, and there's a good chance my body will be found crushed and flattened by the time the night's over.

"Here," the bartender mutters as she slides a whiskey and coke, as well as a Sex on the Beach, over to me. "Don't spill these." She stabs the printout orders onto a toothpick and barely spares me another glance before heading to the opposite side of the bar.

Well, then.

Gotta love them when they're friendly.

Balancing the tray, I carefully set the two cocktails beside the basket of bread, and then weave my way through the white-clothed tables. I promise the new couple that I'll be right with them, holding my tray against my hip like a pro, and continue on to the Table of Doom.

The moment that I set the basket on the table, Suzanne snags two pieces of bread and digs in with full gusto.

"Sex on the Beach," I say, precariously lifting the brightly colored drink from my tray and placing it before Andre's date. "And"—I turn to Andre—"a whiskey and coke."

His brows furrow. "I asked for only a soda."

My limbs freeze and my gaze darts to his. Mentally I rewind our conversation. Oh. He did ask for only a soda. A coke, to be precise. My mouth opens before I bite my lower lip, because what can I say?

I remember your favorite drink.

Sorry, apparently I haven't broken the habit of ordering for you.

Please don't make this weird.

Yeah, because any of *those* options will go over tremendously well.

Praying that he doesn't read into the situation, I mutter, "I'm sorry. I'll get that coke for you." I reach out to grab the cocktail, but he moves it away from my hand at the last moment.

"I'll drink it."

"But you didn't ask for it."

His gaze lands on my face, and maybe I'm crazy (totally possible), maybe I'm imagining things (also possible), but his dark eyes crinkle at the corners as though he's trying desperately not to smile. "I'll drink it, Zo."

Zo.

His old nickname for me.

Damn, but I wish it didn't feel so good to hear him call me that.

Softly, I say, "Okay." *Do not read into the situation.* Somberly, I take their food order and dart back into the kitchen to input it all into the POS system.

My dad hollers at me from behind the grill, cracking jokes about the Mackenzies taking over Vittoria. The staff don't laugh, as they're deep in the weeds and have that crazed-eye thing going on.

I'm pretty sure that I have it too.

For the next hour or so, I flit from table to table in Lover's Lane. I pour water into glasses, and drop off bread baskets. I manage to correctly bring out food, and succeed in not sending mussels cascading from the sky.

I'm so busy, actually, that I don't realize that the rush has died down completely until there's almost no one left in the restaurant. An elderly couple is seated outside of my section, on the other side of the restaurant, and two four-tops have joined forces to sing Dean Martin at the top of their lungs. Since they're also not in my section, I summarily dismiss them as not my problem.

But not even I can resist the draw of Dean Martin. I sway a little side to side, enjoying the patrons' off-beat tempo, a small smile flitting to my face—until my gaze lands on the sole figure at the bar.

Andre.

Even though he's facing away from me, I recognize his muscular frame in a heartbeat. His dark hair is all disheveled from his fingers (or maybe from Suzanne's?), and his crisp dinner jacket is laid over the barstool next to his. Against my better judgment, I follow the line of his spine, sweeping my gaze down over his athletic body. He's seated with one foot up on the barstool's footrest, while his other is planted on the floor.

As if sensing my stare, Andre glances over his shoulder, and his dark eyes find me watching him. It's too late to run, too late to turn away and pretend that I haven't been standing here ogling him.

The man might be an asshole, but he's the sexiest asshole I've ever met.

His eyebrow quirks up, an obvious dare for me to come closer.

And, damn my feet, but I do just that.

As if tethered to him by an invisible string, the distance between us dissipates, until I'm standing right in front of him. Since he's still seated, we're almost at eye level for once, and there's no hiding the way he studies me intently, not saying a single word.

It's an intimidation tactic I've seen him use on his opponents in the rink. Like a lion after its prey, he sits, waiting, prolonging the moment until I give away my ace and he can swipe in for the kill.

Feeling uncomfortable, I focus my attention on his cocktail—another whiskey and coke.

Why is he still here?

"Where's your date?" I ask, hating how I sound less ambivalent and more inquisitive. I don't *want* to be inquisitive. I don't *want* to care, one way or another.

"She went home."

I squash the ridiculous slice of hope springing in my chest. Hope I have no business feeling because it's not like we're together or ever will be. "Not going for a round two, then, I imagine?"

"Probably not."

I feel my eye twitch. "She didn't do it for you or something?"

"Or something." He undoes the second button of his shirt collar, as though overheated. "It was casual." Shaking his head slowly, he adds, "What I meant to say is, it just didn't work out. No chemistry."

The twitch threatens to turn into an all-out spasm. Once upon a time, I'd had no problem talking to Andre about his women. But now . . . it leaves a sour taste in my mouth. "I was under the impression that chemistry wasn't something you needed in your romantic life," I murmur, "one and done, right?"

The words are out before I can stop them, and my hand itches to clap over my mouth and stop the verbal diarrhea.

But Andre only laughs, the sound emerging as a deep rumble that hints at twisted sheets and scattered pillows. "Jealous, Zoe?"

"*What?* Absolutely not."

He leans in, one elbow planted on the bar. "Are you sure? You've got that look on your face again."

My hand swipes over the bridge of my nose and down toward my chin, like I'm washing away all emotion from my face. "Better?"

"Hmm, maybe." He shifts his big body on the barstool and reaches out to touch the corner of my mouth. It hardly constitutes anything of importance, but my breath hitches at the brief contact, just as he murmurs, "I can still see your frown."

Memories of movie nights and lunch outings flit through my brain, and I bat Andre's hand away. "Don't," I warn him in a low voice, and just like that, as though I turned off a switch, the easygoing expression on his face evaporates.

In its place is one that I've seen frequently—or, I mean, one that I *used* to see frequently. An icy cold mask that won't melt.

He wraps a hand around his cocktail and, ignoring the thin, neon-green straw, drinks straight from the rim. His Adam's apple bobs down, and he looks like something straight out of a soda commercial. My knees lock together. I hate him for doing this, for turning me on with nothing more than a stupid sip of his drink.

Maybe I need another year of no contact with him to really get my brain in the right place.

"So," he says, breaking the terse silence, "your thirty days."

Right, back to business.

"Twenty-nine," I reply instinctively.

"All right, twenty-nine." His tongue flicks out over his bottom lip to absorb a droplet of whiskey. "I've been thinking today—"

I feign shock, going so far as to press a hand to my chest. "So *that's* what held you up this morning? I had no idea that you couldn't think and do at the same time."

46

Though his shoulders twitch, he ignores my taunting. "I think we're going to have to lay out some parameters."

For once, I agree with him. "Yes, that would probably be a good idea. What's first on your list?"

"No sex."

A surprised cough splits my lungs in half, and I double over. He waits patiently for my recovery, ordering another whiskey and coke from the bartender, as well as a bottle of water.

The bartender pops the water bottle on the bar first and Andre immediately slides it over. "A peace offering," he tells me, "for nearly killing you."

"I'm surprised you don't want me dead," I rasp, accepting his offering with as much finesse as possible.

"If you were dead, then who would revitalize my reputation?"

Good point.

When I've fully recovered from my coughing spree, I say, "Can you handle no sex for a month?"

Something in his gaze flickers, something that I can't even begin to understand. "I'm not talking about no sex in general . . . I'm talking about not having sex with *you*."

My mouth falls open, and I'm not entirely surprised when a growl emerges from deep within my chest. "Are you *kidding* me?" I abandon the water on the bar to jab a finger at him angrily. "I wouldn't have sex with you even if you begged me."

The look he gives me would cause a weaker woman to lose her panties upon its delivery, but I stand strong. Been there, done that, and I have no intention of returning to buy the damn T-shirt.

"We both know that I don't beg," he finally says. There's a small pause. His gaze darts down to my lips, lingering, and then he adds, "The same can't be said for you, though."

Oh.

My.

God.

He did not just say that.

From the way his brows arch as he sips at his whiskey and coke, I bet he's feeling mightily pleased with himself right about now. Which is, I decide, the *only* reason I retaliate.

"You're right," I say in a sugary-sweet tone, "I begged you, Andre." I plant my palms on the barstool next to him, crumpling his once-crisp sports jacket, and jut my face close to his. "I begged you to take me, and then, when I realized that you had nothing substantial hanging between your legs, I begged for you to finish as quickly as possible."

Silence swirls around us, and I swallow a flare of satisfaction when his face contorts.

"Did you just say that I have a small cock?"

Folding my arms across my chest, I nod. "If the condom fits. Or, you know—it doesn't."

I smile a little at my play on words, mentally pumping my fists into the air in victory.

But then . . . Andre's dark expression clears, and he laughs. He laughs so hard that his deep, masculine *ha-ha-has* can be heard throughout Vittoria, earning us the attention of the very last couple in the restaurant. He laughs so hard that he wipes tears from his eyes with the pads of his thumbs. He laughs so hard that when he *stops* laughing, all I can do is stare at him, because *why is he laughing when I just said he has a small dick?*

"Oh, honey," he says, his voice still rumbling with buried mirth, "is that the lie you tell yourself at night to feel better?"

Shock spins through me. And the words . . . all words have fled my body. I have no comeback. I have no witty reply to scathingly deliver. I have absolutely nothing, save for an undeniably burning hot face that grows hotter with each passing second.

Because he's *right*, the jerk.

Late at night, when I curl up in bed (aka the couch), three fluffy pillows stuffed beneath the back of my head, I can't help but think about the one day we gave in and had mind-blowingly good sex. Emphasis on the "mind-blowing" part. I don't consider myself a sex savant—I've always been keener to focus on my career—but I'd be lying if I said Andre didn't rock my world that day.

He rocked it one night, and then it all came crumbling down the next.

Andre finally stands, straightening to his full height of six-foot-something. He's taller than me, which is all that matters, though I'm no shrinking violet myself. He pulls a leather wallet from his pocket and drops three Andrew Jacksons on the bar, even though his tab couldn't have run higher than twenty dollars.

"I'll stop by your office tomorrow," he says, sliding the wallet back into his pocket, and snagging his jacket out from under my hands with a sharp tug. "Let you think real hard on what we've talked about tonight."

Aboot.

It's so Canadian, so cute, and I feel the strangest urge to take *my* boot—the one on my foot—and kick him. He's been back in my life for all of two days and *nothing* is going as planned.

"Was that supposed to be a double entendre?" I demand, feeling off-kilter and not at all myself.

"Definitely not," he counters, his dark eyes warm with stifled humor. "Remember, we're not having sex again. Stop thinking about it."

"I'm *not* thinking about it. You're the one throwing out metaphors about things that are hard."

"I have no idea what you're talking about," he tells me as he pulls on his jacket. The sleeves are creased from my hands, but he doesn't even attempt to flatten them out.

"You think you're so sly, Andre, but I can promise you that you aren't."

"I wouldn't dare dream so."

Annoyance flickers through me. "I'm not going home and thinking about you tonight."

"I wouldn't dare dream that either." He turns away, but just before he does us both a favor and actually leaves, he twists back around to give me his parting words, "And, for the record, I distinctly remember you telling me to take it easy because my 'small cock' was too big."

He steps back and lifts his hand in a casual wave. "Have a good night, Zoe. I'll be at your office tomorrow morning. Ten a.m. sharp. Don't be late."

I sag against the barstool, my brain spinning with everything that just went down. I don't even hear the bartender until she's right behind me, gathering Andre's ridiculously sized tip.

"Is he really small?" she asks me. "He looks like the kind of guy who'd be hung like a horse."

I don't even turn around, because I'm not sure I could lie to her face. "He has the smallest penis I've ever seen," I fib. "The smallest."

7

ZOE

TWENTY-EIGHT DAYS LEFT

*B*y 9:45 a.m. the next morning, I am what some would call a "hot mess."

I snoozed my alarm one too many times, therefore losing the opportunity to completely pull myself together for my meeting with Andre. My dark hair is washed, but untamed, and thanks to the very dry March air, the static teased the strands into something unrecognizable during my morning commute.

My coffee decided to leap out of its home—a Styrofoam cup—and splattered my white shirt. I did what I could to clean the stain while I rode the T, Boston's subway, on my way in. But no matter how many napkins I've pressed to the stain, the dark espresso now resembles something that I would rather not talk about.

And, to top it all off, the heel of my favorite stiletto pair broke. Broke! There I was, striding down the street and giving myself a much-needed pep talk, when my poor Manolo Blahnik succumbed to a crack in the sidewalk. I went flying; the toe part of my stiletto went flying, but the damn heel remained wedged in the sidewalk's crevice like a white flag waving surrender.

Walking six blocks through Boston's financial district on bare feet is an experience I never want to repeat.

Honestly, thank God for convenient stores and cheap, plastic flip-flops.

So, like I said, "a hot mess."

This is *so* not my day.

Cracking open my day planner, I scribble in today's key points that I want to cover with Andre. Namely, the fact that we have twenty-eight days to strip him of his bad boy image off the ice.

Having worked with professional athletes before, it's always been a little strange to me as to where the line is drawn. The public loves guys like Marshall Hunt, one of Andre's teammates for the Blades. Since Hunt has just come up from the farm team, he rarely gets the same level of play-time on the ice. But the people love him—they love the way he stops to take selfies with fans after games. They love the way he jokes around with reporters, giving them his full attention whenever he's in the hot seat.

From what I've gathered, Hunt also has a reputation as a ladies' man—he makes no secret about the fact that he dates supermodels, and supermodels exclusively. He's practically the Leonardo DiCaprio of the hockey world. But the public adores him anyway. They adore his boyish good looks, and the way he takes the time to hold open doors for the various women he dates, even when they change every weekend—or every other night.

The public does not adore Andre. He verbally snaps at the media, and, seeing the way he blew off Suzanne last night, it doesn't seem that he's all that kind to the ladies either.

Makes sense, considering the way he treated me too.

I have no doubt that I'm up for a battle today, but I'm

hoping that he'll see reason. Above all else, Andre Beaumont loves hockey. Without sponsors, without a willingness to play like a team-member on and off the ice, this could very well be his last season in the NHL.

Teams will take a risk on a player that's physically injured, but they're less likely to keep a player who is a liability to the structure or reputation of their organization.

A knock comes at the door, and I don't even have to look up to see who's standing there. Cliché as it might be, but the air changes with his entrance. It shifts and crackles and tenses with anticipation.

Or maybe that's just my anticipation to get this over and done with.

I feign nonchalance, still scribbling in my planner. *Play it cool, girl, play it cool.*

"Good morning, Andre."

The chair across from me creaks under the sudden onslaught of his weight. Like most hockey players, Andre is big. A hulking body of pure muscle that is put to the test on a daily basis.

"Morning," he says, the 'o' drawn out in true Canadian flare. "That's a nice shirt you've got on there."

My fingers clench tightly around the pen. "I spilled my coffee this morning."

I glance up in time to see the way he tilts his head in thought. "Very well-placed, eh?"

Perhaps I should have elaborated. When I spilled the Starbucks blend this morning, it somehow—in some stars-misaligning sort of way—splattered me right in the boob area. Specifically, in the left-nipple zone.

My eyes squeeze shut, and I lift a hand to shield the evidence of my embarrassment from his perusal. "I was already running late, otherwise I would have gone back home to change shirts. It's been a rough morning."

"It would seem that way," he murmurs, and I can hear the laughter brimming just beneath the surface.

"Are you going to stare at my chest for our entire meeting?"

"Open your eyes and you'll see I'm not looking at your chest now."

With a deep breath for strength, I glance up to find that what he says is true. He *isn't* looking at my chest.

His gaze is on my face, and for a moment, so brief that I swear I imagine it, I feel like I've jumped back to that second before he first kissed me. In the vacuum of time, I recall his hands lifting to my face to cup my cheeks. His breathing rustling the top of my hair, we stood so close. His mouth moving, expelling the words, *"I need you, Zoe,"* before he closed the distance between us.

Now, in my brand-spanking new office, I'm highly aware of my altered breathing, and also of the way that I'm squeezing my pen so tightly that I'm surprised it doesn't snap in half.

Worry skits through me. *Can I do this?*

The reminder that I'm on a trial run with Golden Lights Media kicks me back into gear. I've submitted so many job applications in the last year, gone on so many interviews that end up with a rejection letter, leading off with, "Thank you for your interest, but we have found another candidate who better suits our needs . . ."

I'm not arrogant enough to believe that I'm the best publicist in existence—I'm not. But during my half-decade of work in Detroit, I certainly made a name for myself within the business. I got stuff done. I made miracles happen to the unlikeliest of clients. But no one wanted to give me another chance in Detroit, which led to my move.

If it doesn't work out with Golden Lights Media . . . I honestly have no idea what will be my next step.

I flatten my hand across my day planner, grounding myself for what's to come next. "We should probably get started."

His wide shoulders lift in a casual shrug. "I'm yours for the next hour."

The words send my brain on a tailspin. "Technically, you're mine for the next twenty-eight days."

He grins, and it's such a rare thing that I almost sit back in my chair in shock. "Who's counting?"

I am—not that I'll ever admit that out loud. "We both should be. I want this job and you want to keep your career. We both benefit from this partnership if we can just work together."

He's silent after that, as if pondering my words. His dark eyes flit to my planner, and then to the document I have pulled up on the shiny new desktop computer that arrived this morning—a white one, because obviously Walter Collins has some sort of weird obsession with the color.

Andre sits back in his chair, and though I can't see his legs beyond the desk, I know his knees must be splayed in that typical hot-guy pose. He looks relaxed, at ease, though his gaze remains sharp. "You're looking mighty comfortable here."

"I want to be here."

"Why Boston?"

At the abruptness of his question, I narrow my eyes. "I'm not stalking you, Andre."

"I didn't say that you were."

"You implied it."

"Well, if the stalker fits . . . "

Reflexively, I cross my arms over my chest. "My dad lives here, if you remember. He owns Vittoria."

Slowly he nods, ignoring my not-so-subtle jab at our past, and a lock of his dark hair falls over his forehead in a ridiculously distracting manner. It's like a calling card for me to push it back, to run my hands through the thick strands. "Ah, so that explains yesterday's appearance."

I don't want to think about yesterday. I don't want to think about last year. I want to focus on the *now*.

"Let's get back to this, shall we?" I tap my pen on the desk impatiently. "I think we need to start with a bang, something big to let sponsors know that you're keen on changing things around."

Andre scrubs a hand over his unshaven jawline. "We talking about charity donations?" he asks, dropping his elbow to his knee as he shifts forward. The new position stretches his gray T-shirt across his broad chest, and I check back the need to salivate. Andre might be an unfeeling jerk, but he is, without doubt, a *sexy* unfeeling jerk.

It's unfair, I tell you, so unfair.

Gathering my wits, or trying to anyway, I select a sheet of paper from Andre's case file and slide it across the desk with the tip of my finger. "Not exactly. Providing assistance to others via charities has never been your problem."

Dark eyes meet mine. "Is there a compliment in there somewhere?"

"I didn't intend for there to be one, no."

He shakes his head with a masculine chuckle, and I swear he mutters the word "ballbuster" under his breath.

"What did you say?"

"I said that I didn't think there was a compliment." He cocks his eyebrow, daring me to question him.

I try a different tactic, mainly because I'm weak when it comes to pretending trash talk isn't the highlight of my day, especially with Andre. "Wouldn't want your head to get too large," I say, throwing down the gauntlet. *Take. That.*

"Are we talking about my reportedly small cock again, Zoe?"

56

Surprised laughter escapes me. I forget sometimes. I forget that under all that broodiness and sharpness is a man with a quick wit.

It's hard to remember when he hardly ever lets that man show up.

"No more talking of . . . penises." I point at the sheet, which he's yet to even look at. "I've signed you up for a few events this week. They work around your schedule and I think they'll do you some good. The first three aren't up for discussion."

He finally drags the paper close, and I see the moment the words sink in because he lets loose a string of curses. "Hell no," he grunts emphatically, running a hand through his messy, dark hair. His finger jabs down at the black ink, and his chin comes up so that he can glower magnificently at me. "Absolutely not."

"Non-negotiable. I called your agent and he agrees."

His mouth falls open, just before he cranks his jaw shut with such force that I hear his teeth crack together. "Joe wouldn't agree to this."

Watching the big and bad Andre Beaumont unravel is now the highlight of my day—no, make that my *year*. Knowing that Joe agreed to this must be killing him. "I asked Joe to reconfirm via email. I had a feeling that you might throw a fit about this."

From behind gritted teeth, he seethes, "I'm not throwing a fit, Zoe."

"I'm sorry, perhaps I should use another word instead? How about 'tantrum'?"

He blows out a big breath, then pushes back off his elbow so he's slouched in the chair again. All he needs is a cigarette tucked between his full lips, and I'd swear I was looking at a young John Travolta, circa *Grease*. Minus the slicked-back hair, of course.

"I'm not doing an interview with *Fame*."

"You've done it before," I point out. *Fame* is a woman's magazine that has popped onto the scene in the last few years, no doubt in an effort to shove *Cosmopolitan* out of the way. I can't say whether their plans for world domination are working, but that doesn't matter. What *does* matter is that they are willing to feature Andre Beaumont, even with his less-than-stellar reputation. "Or have you forgotten?"

"Yes, but—" He breaks off with a sharply drawn breath. "The last time *Fame* interviewed me, it was about the game. *People* named me . . . "

"Sexiest Man of the Year?" I supply, because there's no point dancing around the issue. If he wants his career back on track, then he needs to do the grunt work. And that's proving to the world that he isn't a complete a-hole when it comes to the female sex. "What bothers you more? The fact that you're scheduled for an interview with one of the top women's magazines in the world or the topic you'll have to discuss?"

His palm lands with a *thwack* on the sheet I've given him. "Is it really the best for my career to talk about the various ways I've 'scammed women'? For the record, I don't scam."

"For the record, Joe obviously thinks you need to learn some manners," I tell him. When I notice the way his expression shutters, I forge forth and refuse to feel guilty about going behind his back to chitchat with Joe, the sports agent he's had since he signed with the Red Wings as a rookie. Steepling my fingers, I focus on the gold watch encircling his left wrist. It looks like it costs more than my salary has earned me in the last five years combined.

"Listen, Andre, I'm here to rebuild your reputation." He opens his mouth to counter that, and I head him off, already knowing he's about to take a dip down memory lane. "We can't change your actions in the past, but we *can* work on how you move forward. The first step is talking about your desire to be seen in a different light with a publication that will ham it up. *Fame* will ham it up."

"I don't think it's a good idea."

With a semblance of patience that I don't actually feel, I fold my hands over my knees. "Why's that? Because you might come off as—I don't know—vulnerable and human for once?"

Andre's mouth flat-lines at that, and he shifts in his chair, looking uncomfortable to have his sins exposed under the spotlight. "I can be vulnerable." He pauses, then averts his gaze. "I'm not made of ice, Zoe."

"Sure," I say agreeably with a nod. "You cried after you won the Stanley Cup two years ago. But, again, I'm not talking about hockey here. I'm talking about *you*, and the way you interact with people that aren't decked out in pads, jock-straps, and hockey sticks."

"You just had to add in the jockstrap bit, didn't you?"

I struggle with fighting off a smile and he knows it too. In a voice laden with sexual promise, he adds, "I know you, Zoe. And I know what game you're playing at." He points to my PR plan, then lifts his gaze to my face. "Out of every publication you could have approached, you chose this one, probably with the hope that it'll embarrass me." His hands rest on the desk, and he slowly unfolds his body from the chair. My chin tips up to make sure we don't break eye contact, because if this is a face-off, I refuse to lose.

I mimic his stance, dropping my palms to the desk and leveraging my weight to a standing position. I lean forward, too, until we're in the same breathing space, until we're so close that if I wanted to, if I *dared*, one more inch would land my mouth on his.

Do I dare?

Do I even want *to?*

My eyes drop to his mouth, and for one idiotic second, I wonder if he tastes the same, like the mint-flavored Tic Tacs he used to snack on throughout the day. Can a person change so drastically in a year? I doubt it, but you never really know. Hell, maybe *I'm* the one who tastes different, like a juxtaposing cocktail of bitterness and optimism. The pour of each depends on the day of the week and the hour of the day.

When I'm sprawled out on my makeshift bed at my dad's house, thinking of my old job and the vacations I used to splurge on without second thought, bitterness wins out.

Always.

It's not something I particularly like about the new me. I don't like it at all.

"Zoe."

He says my name like he can't imagine *not* doing so, like he did in that laundry room, right before he pushed me up against the door and set my body on fire. My eyes flutter shut, and I inhale so deeply that I can hear its shuddery crackle in the silence of my office.

"*Zoe.*"

I'm not ready to look at him yet. "What?"

"I'll do this interview on one condition."

"What's the condition?"

His mint-scented breath wafts over my face. "You have to look at me first."

My eyes crack open, and he's right there. Big. Imposing. His dark eyes are centered on my mouth, and I've got half a mind to ask him if what he wants is a panty-wetting kiss. I wonder if he would say yes. Instead, I murmur, "Condition completed."

His head shakes a little, and his dark hair boyishly sweeps over his forehead. My hand itches to push the strands back, but that's my lust talking, and so I close the door on those crazy thoughts.

"No," he says, "That wasn't my condition."

"You can't up it to two conditions on a whim."

The papers under his palms slip as he leans back, away from me, away from the unspoken desire to throw everything to the floor and do it on my pristine, white desk.

Of the two of us, he's probably the only one thinking straight.

Personally, I blame my hormones. The time of the month just came and went, and we all know how that goes.

"Here's my condition." He steps around his vacated chair to the back, so that there is ample space between us. Maybe he needs it just as much as I do. "I'll do the interview with *Fame*, but you've got to come with me. I'm assuming it's not just a phone gig?"

My heart stills, and suddenly it's hard to find air. "Um, excuse me," I wheeze out, clutching my chest like it might give out and fail me. "Did you just suggest that I come *with* you? To New York City? Absolutely not."

He stares me down over the crooked ridge of his nose, broken from countless skirmishes in the rink, and I resist the urge to fidget. The shiner on his cheek from the other day is nearly gone now, too. "You did it when you worked for me in Detroit."

"Yes, well, back then . . . " There's no good excuse here. I used to attend big interviews with him. Largely I did it because my old firm made it a requirement, but the other part of me, the part of me that viewed Andre as a friend and not just as a client, wanted to ensure that everything went smoothly for him from start to finish.

I don't believe that Golden Lights Media has the same protocol, or, at least, it's not mentioned in the training manual. Also, Andre and I are no longer friends.

Which means that this whole "go with me" thing is null and void.

Striving to effuse some hardness into my voice, I say, "Unfortunately, I don't think I'll be able to swing that."

Apparently, that's not going to fly with this pro-hockey player. He points at me with his index finger. "You have one client, Zo"—that finger swivels until it's aimed at himself —"me. The way I'm looking at this, you don't have a viable excuse to get out of this, unless . . ."

Breaking off, he gives me a considering look. It's a look that I can't even begin to interpret, but when he makes a move to tug on his left earlobe, I peel back and shove a hand up. Oh, this is not good. The left earlobe thing is his *tell*— always was, and apparently still is.

"No." I put up my other hand, too, for good measure. "Whatever you're thinking, stop thinking it. Right now."

He tugs again on the same ear, and then a grin, one so sexy it actually hurts, cuts across his face. "Now, Zoe, I'm not the one who said that this job is their last hope."

My hand falls to my side as horror seeps into my veins. "You wouldn't," I whisper.

With his hands shoved deep into the front pockets of his jeans, he saunters toward me, cutting around the desk until he's *there*, right in front of me. My butt hikes back against the lip of the desk, my pencil skirt indecently riding up my thighs. I struggle to appear unaffected, even as I glance down to see if my Spanx are putting on a show.

They're not, thank God, but that doesn't mean anything because he is so close, and I don't know what to do, and every rational thought has fled my brain in favor of one word: *Abort! Abort! Abort!*

There's not a chance in hell of that happening.

He swaggers so close that my hands have no choice but to find purchase on either side of my hips. He swaggers so close that my knees part, the hem of my skirt tightening across my splayed thighs.

Get your mind back in the game, girl.

Get. Your. Mind. Back. In. The. Game!

Naturally, I say the first that comes to mind. With no lead-up whatsoever, I blurt out, "I thought we weren't going to have sex again?"

Ugh, that was *not* supposed to be a question.

Andre's full mouth tilts at the corners, like he finds me hilarious.

I'm not hilarious. I'm panicking.

Mainly because while my brain is shouting for me to take cover and hide, my body—traitorous thing that it is—wants to lean into his touch. Wants to feel his fingers dance their way over my skin.

It's an absolute betrayal, I tell you.

Andre's gaze trails down my body, lingering at my coffee stain, before flicking back up to my face. "We're not having sex."

Oh, oh is that right? He says it so flippantly, whereas I'm over here panting like I've just had the best orgasm all year. Considering that I've been living a completely orgasm-free life since moving to Boston, that's not much of a feat.

Peeling a hand away from the desk, I motion at the scant distance between us. "Then please let me know why you're trying to get between my legs."

"Honey," he murmurs, voice low, "if I were trying to get between your legs for the real deal, you'd know it."

I look down and feel heat swarm to my face. "Then why are you . . . up?"

He follows the direction of my gaze, and then laughs. *Laughs!* I want to crawl into a ditch somewhere and stay there for good.

"Case in point," he tells me silkily. "If I had a small cock, I'd doubt you'd be able to tell that I was . . . up."

Yep, this is the perfect time to go find a ditch. I'll stay there, maybe make it feel quite homey by choosing a spot near an oceanfront view. With some pretty flowers and a fairy garden, because why the hell not?

I throw up a hand to cover my eyes. "Can we not go down that road again?"

His laugh is throaty and too temptingly masculine for my liking. "You brought it up."

I point at him with my free hand, even as the other remains clamped over my eyes. "You cornered me."

"You want me to do this interview? Then you're going to be at my side the entire time." His fingers tug at mine, one by one until his face is there, his dark eyes glittering. "Unless you want me to pay a visit to Walter on my way out of here today . . . "

"You're *blackmailing* me?"

His head cocks to the side. "Maybe I just want your company."

"Now I know you're lying."

Abruptly he pushes away from me, and the space gives me the first opportunity to breathe since he decided to play dirty.

The relief is short-lived.

As his long legs eat up the distance toward my office door, he tosses over his shoulder, "Your schedule from hell has the interview set for this Thursday. Text me your address. We'll take my car."

The thought of Andre running into my family sends me surging toward him. "No! You can't—I mean, we'll meet here. At Golden Lights."

Black eyes land on my face. "Your house, Zoe. Let me pick you up."

As if we're going on a date and not a road trip from hell.

Words flee my brain, and all I can do is watch him as he pauses in the doorframe, one big hand planted on the wood. Thanks to his size, he has to duck a little, probably in worry that he might scrape the top of his head and lose some much-needed brain cells.

"I'll see you on Thursday," he says. With a closed fist, he knocks on the frame and then offers me a brief smile. "Nice flip-flops, by the way. Very chic."

And with *that* parting comment, Andre leaves me to stand there, my feet stuck in a pair of one-dollar sandals and a coffee stain over my left nipple.

8

ZOE

TWENTY-ONE DAYS LEFT

*I*t's the butt-crack of dawn when Andre pulls up outside of my house on the following Thursday. Four a.m.

I'm convinced that the only reason four a.m. should ever be seen is if you're stumbling home after an all-night boozer *and* you've lost both your shoes and your dignity.

While I recently had to put down my favorite pair of stilettos (R.I.P Manolo), my dignity is mostly still intact. Somewhat.

Andre's headlights flash again, illuminating the dark living room where I'm camped out on the couch. I've been ready since two, thanks to the jittery nerves that haven't eased since I first laid down for the evening.

The walls of the living room glow, shadows dancing across its dark expanse as the car lights stress the driver's impatience.

With a groan of displeasure, I roll onto my side, legs slipping onto the floor. My feet go into an old pair of gym shoes, and my hand grapples in the dark for the strap of my oversized purse.

Quietly, so I don't wake my family, I escape out the front door. Since my dad lives in the heart of Somerville, a close suburb of Boston, the street is lit with streetlamps. An ambulance's sirens kick off in the distance, and I swear I can hear Tom Fedd's baby crying bloody murder next door.

But the interior of Andre's car is dark, so dark that I can barely see him sitting in the driver's seat.

His door opens. Like a shadow creeping through the night, he unfolds his body from the car, leaving the driver's side door ajar.

"Want me to put your bag in the trunk?" he asks, his voice still rusty with sleep. I'm ashamed to admit it, but the rustiness does things to my girl parts. Things I would rather not feel when it comes to Andre Beaumont.

I glance down at my bag. "I stocked up on snacks for the ride."

His shoes crunch over the gravel until he's two feet away. In the early morning, he's more silhouette than anything else. His features are a mosaic of slashed shadows stretching over the bridge of his nose and carving out the hollows of his cheeks. His eyes, though, are obscured, thanks to the baseball hat he's wearing.

I want to reach up and tip it back with my finger—get a read on his mood this morning.

In other words—is this drive to New York City going to be as painful as I imagine it will be? God, I hope not.

Andre's chin dips, indicating my bag. "I thought maybe we could stop for some breakfast along the way . . . . I know how you get when you're hungry."

Surprise straightens my shoulders. "Not going to lie—I thought you'd take the starve-me approach this morning."

Eyes still hidden by the brim of his ball cap, I watch the way he swallows, hard. "I thought about it, trust me. Just let you waste away during the drive."

"How sweet of you," I mutter. "What, are you going to toss my body out in Connecticut or something?"

His lips curl up in a wicked grin. "Nah, Zo, I was thinking more along the lines of the Jersey Turnpike."

My heart stutters at the humor in his tone, even as I outwardly scoff. "Always a gentleman, Mr. Beaumont."

"Gentleman? Me?" He lifts his ball cap, teasing me with the promise of seeing his eyes, before resettling the hat over his head, brim pulled low. "I think you've got the wrong hockey player."

"I've certainly got the wrong *something*, that's for sure."

"Already regretting having me as a client?"

"I won't if you promise to behave."

He reaches down and wraps his fingers around my purse strap. "I'm not the best trained pup in the litter."

I roll my eyes at his metaphor, but feel a grin nevertheless pulling at my lips. "I'd venture to say that you're the one still peeing in your crate."

"I have a lot to learn."

"That's an understatement."

With a quick tug, he pulls the purse from my grasp. "Good thing you're the type of woman for the job, eh?"

Damn you, heart, stop pounding like that. Swallowing past my nerves, I ask, "What kind of woman is that?"

His teeth flash white with a grin. "A badass. Now, do you want breakfast or not?"

He thinks I'm a badass.

I shouldn't find that as thrilling as I do. I'm supposed to hate him. Really hate him. But our quick banter reminds me of our friendship back in Detroit, and as much as I should tell him to drive straight to Manhattan, I find myself weakening. Just a little. Maybe.

Then again, breakfast means making pleasant conversation with him, something that neither of us has done exceptionally well with each other since reuniting in Mr. Collins's office. Since then, my days have been spent doing damage control by calling the publications that Andre has ignored like the plague for the last few months. Some places, like *Sports Illustrated,* were amenable to opening the doors again. Some places, like *GQ,* hung up on me after I mentioned Andre's name.

With twenty-one days left, I'm quickly realizing that the damage Andre has done to his reputation might not be fixed within the course of a month. Not without a whole lot of groveling and heartfelt apologies.

Since neither groveling nor heartfelt apologies are his thing, we're left with one option: *Fame.*

Hopefully, today's gig will help on that front. What am I saying? We *need* it to help in every way that matters. Breakfast will probably do us some good—we can talk business, stuff like that. *Only business.*

The sound of the trunk slamming breaks me from my thoughts. "You good with that?" Andre asks.

"Am I good with what?"

"IHOP."

I haven't been to an IHOP in years. "Is there one close by?"

He claps his hand over the driver's door, and even though I can't see his eyes, I know he's giving me an *are-you-serious* expression. "Right up the road. We can grab some pancakes and some of those home fries you like so much, and then hit the highway."

At that opportune moment, my stomach lets loose an unmistakable growl, and I swear; even though I can't *see* him, I practically hear him grin in victory.

"Get in the car, Zoe," he murmurs. "You know you want to."

I get in the car.

Within twenty minutes, we're seated at a booth in the back of the restaurant, which I suppose doesn't really matter, because we are one of only two parties. The group at the other table is definitely wasted. They howl as they eat, utensils flaring through the air, laughter cracking out like a hyena's bark.

Andre and I, on the other hand, seem to have lost whatever mojo we had outside of my house and sit across from each other in near silence.

It's not as uncomfortable as it sounds . . .

Just kidding—the silence is brutal. On a scale of one to ten, our current communication problems are at least a five hundred.

Which is so not how it used to be.

Does he remember the amount of times we hit up restaurants throughout Detroit? Except that, then, conversation flowed like finely poured wine. If anything, we used to have *too* much to say, so much so that there were a handful of times when restaurant staff had to kick us out because it was closing time.

The night hardly ever ended at the establishment's front doors. We continued the conversation by one of our cars—usually mine—so that he could make sure I got in safely before I headed home.

My fingers flatten out a thin, white napkin.

Andre plays with the handle of his chipped mug.

God, what a miserable pair we make.

I open my mouth to speak, and funnily enough, he does the same, so that our words tumble over each other.

I wave to him. "Go ahead. You first."

Shaking his head, Andre readjusts his ball cap. "Ladies first."

It's on the tip of my tongue to make a sly remark, but I hold it back, swallowing it down and shoving it deep where it won't threaten to reemerge again. I fold the napkin in half and then in fourths. "I spoke with *Sports Illustrated* yesterday," I say slowly, even as I wonder if I should hold off on business until after his first cup of coffee. "They're interested in rescheduling a feature piece sometime in the next two weeks."

His mouth quirks, but it isn't a humorous smile. If anything, it looks a little worn, a little frayed. "Somehow managed to swing it within your trial period?"

My cheeks heat at his words, and I return to my napkin, folding it and folding it and folding it, until it's a triangular-shaped football. "I may have told them that it was urgent."

His laugh is short, though not necessarily unkind.

I try again. "They agreed to it, by the way." I shove the napkin to the interior part of the table, against the arrangement of plastic maple syrup bottles. "Why did you flake out on them in the first place?"

Just then, a server approaches our table to take our order. While Andre goes overboard with coffee, OJ, a stack of blueberry pancakes, and two orders of bacon, I opt for a bowl of oatmeal and a single pancake. Tea, not coffee.

Andre snorts as the waiter takes our order back to the kitchen, and it's so sarcastic, that I clap my palms on the table and demand, "What?"

"Oatmeal?" He reaches for a syrup bottle and drags it close. "Zoe, we both know that you can out-eat me, if you wanted."

It's true, and we both know it. But my stomach is a bundle of nerves, thanks to him, and I don't think I could handle more than what I ordered. "Maybe I don't want to," I tell him stiffly, unwilling to admit the truth.

And the truth a muddled space between want and dislike.

I don't like him, not anymore, but my body can't help but

notice his. Notice the way his hair is perfectly disheveled, and the way he's taken a razor to his face and erased the permanent five o' clock shadow he's always got going on. His jaw is sharp, masculine, and I feel the most irrational urge to slide my palm over his face, just to feel the smooth skin.

Yep, I'm officially off my rocker.

The server brings us our drinks, saving both of us the trouble of making more awkward, stilted conversation.

Not that the reprieve lasts long.

Andre downs half of his coffee, then clasps his hands around the mug. His gaze is still hidden by the shadow of his hat, but from the firm set of his mouth, I know he's staring me down. I can sense the weight of it. "So, *Sports Illustrated* said yes. Who said no?"

I fidget uncomfortably on my side of the booth. "Well . . . "

"Zoe, don't bullshit me."

I heave a big sigh. "Pretty much everyone."

"Everyone?" One hand leaves his coffee mug to remove his hat. Without asking if it's okay, he rests it atop my purse, which I had placed on the table. Then, he turns back to me, his brow lifted in disbelief. "'Everyone' is a pretty broad claim. What about *USA Hockey*?"

I shake my head. "Said no."

He lifts his coffee mug to his mouth and blows the steam away, as though buying himself time. Over the rim, he asks, "*Breakout?*"

"No."

His thumb slips down the handle, caressing the white porcelain. It's hard not to imagine that thumb skimming down the ridges of my spine. I slam the brake on those thoughts, and mentally shove them into a metal box with a Never Open Again label.

"Okay, so non-hockey magazines." He lowers the mug to the table a little too forcefully, and the tea in my cup sloshes over the rim. I steal back my football-shaped napkin, unraveling it so that I can wipe up the mess. "*Time Magazine* reached out a few months ago."

"I already called. I spoke to two editors, but after being stood up by you, and then the way you've treated some of their reporters in the past . . . they aren't interested."

"Fuck."

He says it with no prelude, but I can sense his shock. A year ago, I may have even slid onto his side of the booth to put an arm round his shoulder in comfort. In this moment, however, I still myself by holding onto the edges of the booth. Lowering my voice, I ask, "What happened this last year, Andre?"

Once again, the IHOP gods save Andre from having to confess. Our server chooses that exact moment to swing by our table with our feast. Or, Andre's feast, and my small portion.

At the sight of his plate of bacon, I regret my life decisions and shove a spoon into my soupy oatmeal.

He must catch my bacon-ogling, though, because he holds up a crispy piece. "If I give you this, I'll answer your question and then you have to promise not to pry anymore."

My gaze lands on the bacon, and I swear I begin to salivate. "Is this another condition?" I ask, swirling my spoon around in the oatmeal bowl. "Like when you told me last week that we won't be having sex again?"

As if on cue, the bacon gives up on being stiff, and cracks down the middle to dangle limply in the air.

A laugh breaks free from my chest, just before I clap my hand over my mouth. "Oh, God," I whisper from behind my splayed fingers, "it's a sign."

Dark eyes narrow on me, even as Andre drops the bacon on his plate like he's embarrassed to be holding a wilted slice. "A sign of what?"

"Our lives."

Uncontrollable laughter takes hold of my body, because, holy cow, it's so incredibly accurate. Like the piece of bacon, both Andre and I have been broken this last year. I mean, if you really want to look at it, we're *both* still trying to pick up the pieces of our ill-timed shagging at the Red Wings' facility.

There's a beat of breath before Andre, no doubt sensing the irony, gives in. His shoulders don't bounce the same way that mine do, but the corners of his eyes crease, and his mouth ticks up from its permanent frown.

When he's smiling, his features move from broodingly attractive to downright sexy.

Before I can halt the words, I blurt out, "You should smile more. It looks good on you."

His laughter slowly edges into silence. Then, so quietly I almost don't hear him, he says, "Maybe I don't feel like smiling. You thought of that, Zoe?"

And just like that, we've come back full circle. "Tell me what you were going to say. Before the server came around with our food."

I watch him dig into his blueberry pancakes, and I take the not-so-subtle hint. Okay, so, his year is off-limits. I can get behind that, though it does feel a little unfair that he should dangle questions in front of me and then snatch them away. Then again, we aren't exactly friends any longer, so I *probably* shouldn't feel slighted.

Fun fact: I totally do, though.

So, it comes as a surprise when two pieces of bacon land on my plate. Neither piece is the broken, half-dangly one.

My gaze cuts to his face. "Thank you?"

"This is going to be my last season."

That's all he says. That's it. And yet I feel the weight of his depression migrate onto my shoulders. I stare at him openly, trying my best to make the words mean something in my head. "What do you *mean*, this is going to be your last season?"

With a sigh, he pushes his plate away and folds his arms over his chest. "I thought we agreed that you wouldn't pry."

"No, *you* told me that I shouldn't pry, but that was before you dropped that bomb on me." I snag one of the bacon slices he's given me, and pop it into my mouth. Chewing, thinking, I decide I need more time and opt to eat the second slice now instead of saving it. "Why will this be your last season?"

"Zoe, no prying."

"Does this have to do with the sex thing?" I ask, because there's no way I can't at this point. He's made such a big stink out of it that it can only mean one thing . . . "Did you pick up a life-altering STD or something?"

The ridiculous comment pulls a laugh from him. "I don't have herpes."

"I'd hope not," I say primly.

"Even if I did, it wouldn't matter."

"It would *sort of* matter," I tell him, waving my hand back-and-forth in a *so-so* motion. "I have to say, this doesn't make your actions any better. You've still been a dick."

"I've always been a dick."

"Well, this last year you've really upped the ante."

"I try my best."

He says it with such a blasé tone that I roll my eyes. "Maybe you should try your worst?"

He mimics me and rolls his eyes too. "I've been at my worst, Zoe, and I can tell you that this me isn't nearly as bad."

I want to press him for more, but the expression on his face stops me. Sometimes it's best to find a speck of patience —not that I have any.

9

ANDRE

*S*he's planning something.

For the last hour and a half since we hit the road, Zoe has been fidgeting restlessly in the passenger's seat. Which, in turn, makes *me* feel restless.

Although, in full honesty, I've been feeling that way for seven days now. Having Zoe back in my life is both a blessing and a curse. I missed her spitfire attitude, and, if our last few interactions have shown anything, I still get my rocks off on driving her up a wall just so I can see the heat darken her brown eyes and warm her cheeks with color.

Maybe that makes me an asshole, but damn it, it's *fun* to tease her.

But that's also the problem—when I'm knee-deep in our banter, I forget that I'm supposed to be making her want nothing to do with me. That's the goal, that's the mission, and I'm pretty sure that I'm failing seventy-percent of the time.

I cast my eyes over her slim body. She's decked out in comfortable attire, and, for once, isn't wearing stilettos. She looks exactly like the Zoe I remember from our movie nights, when she rested her feet in my lap and cradled a massive popcorn bowl against her stomach. And *that* Zoe is dangerous.

Who am I kidding? Zoe Mackenzie is dangerous to me in every way that matters.

The sound of her nails tapping against her cell phone leads me off the edge. "Do you need to piss?"

Out of my periphery, I see her shoulders jerk. "What? *No.*"

Don't look at her, man. "Do you have to change your pad or something?"

"Oh, my God, Andre. Why would you even ask that?"

This time, I do cut a glance in her direction. Her pink lips are parted in shock, and, fuck me, but I want to kiss them. Of course I do—because when have I ever found Zoe *un*attractive? The answer to that is never; everything about her shines like a beacon only I can see. The thought of pounding my forehead into the steering wheel sounds like a blast right about now. "Because," I mutter, unclenching my jaw, "you keep moving around. My sister does the same thing when she's on her . . . thing."

"*Thing*, Andre?" Her laughter echoes in my car, the sound so fucking sweet it almost hurts. "How old are you?"

I palm the steering wheel, following the curvy Connecticut highway. "Old enough."

"Then say it with me now," she says, poking me in the arm with her perfectly manicured finger. "*Period.* One more time, slower now so you can really work on it . . . *perriooddd.*"

Is it wrong that I simultaneously want to toss her into the backseat and kiss her silent, as much as I want to keep egging her on? I go with the latter, because, fuck it, the kissing thing is strictly off-limits.

Because you *made it off-limits, like an idiot.*

I reach for the car's radio, only for Zoe to swat at my hand at the last second.

"Jesus, Zo!"

At the sound of my displeasure, she leans back in the passenger's seat smugly. Instinctively my hand leaves the steering wheel, heading for ground zero.

"Don't touch the radio, Beaumont."

I jerk my chin toward her. "Are you kidding me? This is my car."

"Well, yes, but we *could* have taken my car, but you wanted to be all high-and-mighty and—"

"You drive like shit," I mutter with a shake of my head.

"Hey! That's not true."

Hell yes, it is. I bite down on my lower lip, debating on whether I should just go for broke. What's that saying again? If you can't handle the heat then stay out of the kitchen? Something like that. If Zoe wants to join the trash-talk train, then she needs to kick it with the best of us. "Let me rephrase that," I tell her. "You drive worse than every senior citizen in the state of Massachusetts combined."

I sense her watching me. Her nails tap the cell phone impatiently. Then, "I think you're just jealous."

A burst of laughter escapes me. "Of your driving skills? Nah, honey. You must have me confused with somebody else."

"Who in the world would I have you confused with? No one else has ever accused me of driving poorly." She trails off with a little gasp, and, damn it, but the sound has me looking at her *again*. The gasp is sexy, the way her eyes narrow is sexy, the way she thrusts her finger at me in an air-jab is sexy. "You're still mad at me, aren't you," she adds, "because of the time I backed your car into a fire hydrant."

Fingers flexing over the steering wheel, I grunt, "No."

She doesn't look away, and I shift uncomfortably in the driver's seat. Flick the air vents toward me, then fiddle with my ball cap. I'm not mad per se . . . but, Jesus, it'd been a nice car. Then again, seeing her shocked expression when she'd realized what she'd done had immediately soaked up the anger. Zoe had looked so damn cute, with her mouth pursed in an O and her brows nearly touching her hairline as she sputtered inarticulately.

Not that I'd ever offer for her to pull a repeat, but the price tag for fixing the damn thing had been well worth having her fawn all over me for weeks.

"You are," she whispers now. "You're totally still mad. It's been almost two years!"

"Zoe, I'm not mad."

I tug on my left earlobe, and she points at me. "You are! You're doing the earlobe-y thing."

"'Earlobe-y' is not a word," I say, struggling to keep my gaze locked on the road when all I want to do is look at her. Damn it, but I've missed this between us. The banter, the laughter, the reminder that one glance at Zoe is enough to make my day feel complete.

"You're sidestepping the issue," she tells me, folding her arms over her chest. "I can't believe you're still holding a grudge."

"Of all the things I could be holding a grudge against you for, the fucking fire hydrant isn't—" I cut off with a curse. Then again, this is what I was worried about. This constant banter, for me at least, sidelines as foreplay.

Not with any other woman, mind you—but with Zoe? Hell yeah. Put me in a room with her. Don't even let me touch her, and I'll be harder than a rock within minutes just thanks to our conversations.

Zoe casually taps the bill of my Blades baseball hat. "So, you're holding grudges against me?"

No. Zoe's not the one to blame here—*I am*. But there's no way for me to explain that to her without giving up details, and the details aren't something I'm willing to share. Not even with her or *for* her. She's better off not knowing . . . or maybe it's that *I'm* better off pretending that parts of my past don't exist. My heart clenches with the memories, and for the millionth time in three years I wish that I was as emotionless as the public perceives me to be.

Hell, if I *was* a block of ice, Zoe wouldn't be getting under my skin right now. I wouldn't notice the strip of skin above her waistband or the way she smells delicious like fresh citrus. I wouldn't be tempted to slip my hand around to the back of her neck and drag her over for a kiss. I wouldn't want to hear all about her year after we went our separate ways.

"Nothing to say to that?" she prompts dryly.

Maybe it's because I'm so worked up already, but her question reminds me that we need boundaries. Concrete boundaries. *Stop thinking about all the ways you want her in bed.*

I make a show of whipping off my hat and tossing it on top of the dashboard. With a sigh of frustration, I drag my hand through my hair and say the words I know will have her wanting to flip me off. "Are you going to talk the rest of the way to New York City?"

She freezes, and I count the seconds as she meticulously crosses one leg over the other and folds her hands in her lap. Her knuckles are white from gripping her phone.

Guilt punches me in the gut.

"Zo—"

She cuts me off with a raised palm. "You're right. I *do* want to talk the rest of the way to New York. Is that so bad?"

"Is this a trick question?" I ask her, easing the car along a curve in the road. "One of those times where it starts out all fun and games and ends with one of us crying?"

"No." From her defensive tone, I gather that she actually means *yes.*

Don't let her see how much she gets to you. In a rough voice, I say, "What if I have nothing to say?"

She shrugs. "I guess we could sit in silence for the next two hours. I mean, if that's what you want."

"I *want* to listen to the radio." Scratch that—I *want* to know if she tastes as good as I remember. Seeing as though that *definitely* isn't an option for more reasons than I can name, I'll settle on listening to the radio and picturing my grandmother in a bikini. Anything to stop thinking about Zoe up against the wall in that damned laundry room.

"Well," she says pleasantly, "I'd rather be in my brand-new office, but you blackmailed me into this trip. Now you have to deal with the consequences."

I tug on my earlobe again, something I've done since I was kid whenever I've felt uncomfortable in a situation. And right now . . . yup, definitely feeling uncomfortable. She's goading me into doing exactly what she wants. There's a reason why her clients in Detroit (including myself) called her the "barracuda." The woman knows what buttons to push and *how* to push them, and I'm convinced she wouldn't get away with nearly half of it if she wasn't so nice.

And, damn it, she knows how to push my buttons, too, because the next thing I know I'm snapping, "Fuck, all right, Zoe."

She clears her throat. "Is that a yes to talking?"

"It's a yes to us getting this over with," I growl, threading my fingers through my hair before clapping my hand back on the wheel again. "Say what you want to say."

She doesn't even hesitate. "Why is this your last season?"

My shoulders flinch. "That's off-topic."

With a little snort, she murmurs, "No surprise there —*everything* is off-topic with you."

"I like it that way." I accelerate the car as we leave the highway-in-the-woods for flatter pastures with gray cement, and walls of rocks on either side of the road. Needing to redirect the conversation, I blurt out the first thing that comes to mind. "You have a boyfriend, Zoe?"

Honestly, I'm not sure which one of us is more surprised by the question. She chokes on air, reaching for the water bottle in the console. "I'm not answering that."

Unfamiliar jealousy pools in my stomach. Yeah, not exactly the answer I was hoping for. And, yeah, I know that makes me a hypocrite because it's not as though I've spent the last year living like a monk. Even so, one-night stands aren't nearly the same thing as relationships. For what it's worth, the only woman I've considered asking out in years is Zoe.

The need to push for more information grows. "So, I'm assuming you aren't dating anyone?"

She's quiet, shifting around again, and the thought hits me that this attraction might be one-sided. Which is good, absolutely—*tell me you're dating someone so I can get over this irrational need to strip you naked and make you mine.*

"Um, you know, I'm *dating*. Just not one person." Her voice emerges as a squeak, and she makes another grab for the water bottle.

She's lying.

"Yeah?" I lower my voice, dropping it to a husky purr. "How's that working out for you?"

"Great!" She sucks down water like she's been stuck in the Sahara for weeks. "It's great. I'm really enjoying it, you know, just playing the field or what not."

This from the girl who used to make me tag along on her dates because she worried that all men were murderers? I shake my head, doing my best not to laugh. "That good, eh? You're just taking over the Boston dating scene and showing these men what Detroit women are made of?"

Something flickers in her expression. "Oh, *absolutely*. I

mean, just the other day I went on a date with this . . . " She swallows. "This—"

"Let me guess," I say, my mouth finally giving up on the battle and curling up into a grin, "he was a doctor."

"No."

"A lawyer?"

She taps her phone against her thigh. "He's a millionaire."

I roll my eyes. "Of course he is. Does he have a penthouse, too?"

"You're assuming I've *been* up to his penthouse."

The thought of Zoe alone with a guy who may or may not be her boyfriend doesn't sit well with me, even though I know she's faking this whole thing. "Have you?"

"Aren't you dating Suzanne?" she counters.

No. "No chemistry, remember?" I pause, deliberately waiting until she's practically on the edge of her seat, and then add, "Doesn't mean that there won't be other women, though. Just like you're not exclusive with your . . . penthouse-owning millionaire."

"You're a chauvinistic pig."

At the frustration in her tone, I smother a grin. "I knew you were lying."

More with the phone tapping. "About what?"

"You dating."

She's quiet, probably deliberating her next move. Then, stiffly, she mutters, "I like my life just as it is."

I hear the seat creak under her weight and then the radio comes back on. It's an old-rock classic. Seems like she's over the whole talking thing, too.

I reach for the radio, prepared to turn the volume up. But my hand wavers, dropping back to the steering wheel, and I hear my voice instead, low and raspy. "Me too, Zoe. I like my life just the way it is, too."

I think we both know that the other is lying.

10

ZOE

"**Why** did we decide to drive again?" I demand two hours later. My legs burn from hobbling in my stilettos for ten blocks. My feet, though I'm too scared to look, have no doubt been torn open and are spilling blood all over the New York City sidewalk—I should have stuck with my sneakers from the morning.

Andre barely spares me a glance as he keeps pace. He's so tall that his long legs naturally bring him farther, but every few yards he lets the gap close between us again. "I hate flying."

I forgot about that phobia of his. It's tough to imagine that the big, bad Andre Beaumont turns scared at the thought of being thirty-thousand feet in the sky. "We could have taken the train," I tell him, pushing my legs to move faster.

We're late for our appointment with the editor of *Fame.*

And, according to my cell phone's GPS, we're still four blocks away.

At this rate, my feet will probably snap off as soon as we get in front of the building.

"We'll be fine," Andre says, then expels a bundle of curses when my ankle wobbles and I go down.

He catches me about the waist, his arm strong and muscular, and it takes every bit of willpower not to beg him to carry me the rest of the way to *Fame's* offices.

"Zoe?" he says, lifting me back up onto my feet. "You good?"

I test my ankle, resisting the urge to wince when a sting flares in the bone. Not wanting to appear a wimp, I shrug off his grasp and wave my hand at him. "I'm good, all good."

He peers at my face, his dark eyes roving over my features. "You look green."

"It's my complexion," I tell him, brushing away his worry. "I'm naturally olive-toned."

"You're Irish. The fact that your dad owns an Italian restaurant doesn't count."

I open my mouth to deliver a hot retort, only to realize that I don't have one. He's totally right.

Over his shoulder, he flashes me one of his rare grins and then beckons me with his hands. "Give me your bag, Miss Italian, before you actually wipe out and I'm not quick enough to save you."

Oouut. He's showing off his Canadian side again.

I don't put up a fuss and hand him my purse. Without thinking twice, he lifts the strap over his shoulder and continues to march down W. 57th Avenue, like he totally isn't rocking a hot pink, faux leather bag.

I trail after him, attempting to lift my feet in a way that doesn't send spikes of pain shooting through the sole of my foot each time the heel of my stiletto meets concrete. "Aren't hockey players supposed to have quick hands?" I call out to him.

Andre turns around, his arms spreading wide in a *this-is-*

what-you-get pose. "Zo, we both know that I have quick hands."

That he does. Coming from a place of personal experience, I can totally attest to the fact that Andre does, in fact, have quick hands.

Thankfully, he takes pity on me and my lack of physical strength by doubling back and taking hold of my arm. I spend the last three blocks cursing high-heeled shoes, hockey players, and my own ambition to reclaim my position as a respected public relations coordinator.

We draw to a stop just inside the rotating glass doors of our final stop. I'm panting, totally out of shape, while Andre only looks like he's been out for a stroll. It's tremendously unfair.

One glance at my reflection in the mirror behind the front receptionist's desk, and . . . Oh. My. God. I look wild. Absolutely wild.

And sweaty.

I feel my humiliation seep from my body and splatter on the floor.

"Can I help you?" the woman at the desk asks politely when we approach her. She cuts me a glance, and there's no way that I miss her brows lifting in horror.

I'm a sight to be had. It's on the tip of my tongue to tell her to stop judging me, but Andre cuts in.

"We're a few minutes late for an appointment with the editor for *Fame* magazine." He casually slings my hot-pink purse to his other arm and extends his hand. "Andre Beaumont," he greets in the most pleasant voice I've ever heard from him. "We had some unfortunate issues with parking."

The woman's expression turns starstruck at Andre's introduction. "It's . . . uh, we don't really have parking here in New York City. It's sort of a thing."

Andre presses a palm to the lip of the desk and leans

forward. "Mhmm, we realized that a bit too late. Unfortunately, we've just driven in from Boston, and since it took longer than expected ... "

"Oh!" She visibly jumps in her seat. "You want to go upstairs."

"That'd be nice."

This from Andre, who has quite literally ditched his moodiness for flirtation.

The receptionist's brown eyes land on me. "Are you his sister?"

Andre lets out a choking noise beside me.

Maybe it's because I'm tired. Maybe it's because I look a fright, and I'm finally coming to accept that my dream of being respected is slipping away again. Maybe it's because of five other million things that I refuse to think about, but I slip my hand over Andre's arm and murmur, "I'd hope not! You don't kiss your sisters."

The arm under my hand stiffens, signaling Andre's surprise. When he tries to pull away, I clutch tighter, refusing to let him go, and widen my smile to scary proportions. "Honey," I say sweetly, "shouldn't we be heading upstairs?"

He responds with silence, and I risk a peek up at his face. Oh man. He is *not* pleased.

In a voice that's tightly leashed, he growls, "Absolutely. *Honey.*"

I pat his hand and turn back to the receptionist. "What floor do we need?"

Her gaze darts between Andre and I. "Um, the twenty-sixth."

"Brilliant." I give a little finger-wave and tug Andre along.

Each step toward the elevator echoes loudly in the marble-floored lobby. The heels of my stilettos puncture the tile, but it's Andre's personal vibration that's off the charts.

We wait side by side for the elevator to descend to the

lobby level. I glance at his reflection in the mirrored doors. A pulse ticks to life in his jaw. With his free hand, he tugs at his left earlobe.

Uh-oh.

With a *ping!* the elevator doors split open, and a group of businessmen in classy suits spill out.

One of them stutters to a stop at the sight of Andre, his mouth gaping open. "Holy shit, man!" He nudges his buddy in the side. "Holy shit, it's King Sin Bin."

Andre tugs his left ear again.

The man's friend reacts appropriately, and echoes, "Holy shit. *Dude.*"

I'm not sure to whom the "dude" is directed, but Andre apparently seems to think it's for him because his face adopts what I would consider a "scary" expression—lip curling and everything—and the men scurry off, their proverbial tails tucked between their legs.

"Seriously?" I demand, pointing to their retreating backs. "See? *That's* what gets you in trouble, Andre. You can't just go terrifying people like that and expect for it all to be just peach—"

"Get in the elevator."

At his high-handed tone, I arch a brow and fold my arms over my chest. "Excuse me?"

His dark eyes flirt over me. "Zoe, get in the elevator."

No *way is* he pulling this sort of stunt. I stare at him unwaveringly. "No."

His big shoulders jolt with surprise, and I actually see the moment he decides to flip the script. The harsh lines of his mouth relax, and the creases fanning out from his eyes ease. In a cajoling tone that would *totally* manipulate a weaker person, he murmurs, "Please, *honey.* Get in the elevator."

My ears twitch at the endearment. It was one thing to say

it in front of the receptionist. It's another thing entirely to say it away from other people, when it's just us . . .

The elevator *pings* again, and this time I step through. I don't do it for him; I do it for me. Because whatever show-down that's about to happen has been a long time coming, and it's probably for the best if we don't have witnesses.

Andre follows behind me.

We take our respective sides at either end of the small box.

Slowly, like in a bad B-rated horror movie, the doors slide closed until they *click* and shut us in. I spare Andre a single glance, then release a breath as I jab at the button for floor twenty-six.

The elevator surges up.

I hear, rather than see, Andre set my purse on the ground. My chin tips his way, my eyes narrowing on his muscular frame.

"Are you over being a high-handed jerk?" I ask, shifting slightly so my back presses against the elevator wall. My hands find purchase on either side of my hips on the wooden railing. "Because I can tell you right now that it is going to be a *long* way home if you keep up the Mr. Testosterone act."

The elevator *pings, pings, pings* quietly with each floor we hit.

"I think we have a problem."

At Andre's confession, I shrug my shoulders nonchalantly and say, "It's called 'ego.' I'm sure you're familiar with it."

Andre comes closer. There's not much room in this eleva-tor, especially not for someone of his size, but that doesn't stop me from staring at him and shoving my butt up against the wall.

"Andre," I say, "you're kind of freaking me out."

His tongue touches the center of his full bottom lip, and

that one caress sends heat down to places I wish it wouldn't. "I'm freaking myself out," he answers.

Ping.

Ping.

Ping.

"Is this where I pretend that you took a crazy pill when I wasn't looking? Just so you know, there's nowhere for you to store my body in here. You can't get away with murder." My breath hitches at his intense expression. I *know* that look. The last time I saw that look, my pencil skirt ended up on the ground, and my panties landed inconspicuously on the door-knob to the Red Wings' laundry room facility.

Andre slowly shakes his head. When the words I suspect are coming actually leave his mouth, my knees nearly crumble beneath me.

"I need to get you out of my system. You're driving me insane. Fuck, you've been driving me insane all day. Forcing me to talk, wearing that sexy skirt. Pretending to fall in the street."

A surprised laugh escapes me. "I did almost fall, actually," I whisper.

"Almost," he returns, just as softly, "but I saved you."

The words yank at my heart. "You don't save people, Andre. You plow into them and take what you need, just like you do on the ice."

"Maybe I need you, have you thought of that?"

He's killing me. He's actually killing me, and now I'm thinking the impossible: *would it be so bad if I let him touch me?* But we've been there before. We've been there, and it didn't work out, and it's quite likely it wouldn't work out now either. There's too much bad blood between us.

"It's been a week."

In a voice husky with insanity—*definitely* insanity—he says, "And we have three more."

"You said no sex."

"I know." His big body closes in on mine, his hands going to the wall on either side of my head. Immediately, I catch the scent of his cologne and it smells *delicious*. Like sandalwood mixed with fresh laundry. "You're dating your penthouse-owning millionaire. I'm dating . . . women. We both like our lives, but maybe we just need to take care of this attraction. Or, at least, prove that it doesn't exist once and for all."

Does he really think it's as simple as that? My chin tips back so that I can meet his glittering black eyes. "This isn't a good idea."

His gaze falls to my mouth. "I know that too."

I curl my fingers around the railing, and try not to notice that in doing so, I inadvertently thrust my breasts forward. Against his chest, like a complete hussy.

I try one last time to hold my ground, to stand strong against the man who wrecked me and then finished me off by leaving. "I don't like you."

My voice isn't quite steady. It isn't all that forceful.

And Andre takes notice. His hand, the one to the right of my head, shifts over to lightly touch my face. The pads of his fingers are rough, abrasive against my skin, and, God, I love it.

"I don't like you either."

For some reason, I don't think he's telling the truth.

I worry that I'm not either.

My eyes flutter shut when his fingers gently trace the slope of my nose, and when his thumb brushes over my lips, I release a shuddered sigh.

"I'm going to kiss you," he tells me softly. "I'm going to kiss you, and I'm going to make damn sure you go home thinking about it tonight. And then we're going to return to our lives that we both like, and get back to what matters."

My eyes snap open at his crude words, just as the elevator jolts to a halt and the doors slide open.

Get back to what matters? Is he serious?

With a hand to his (ahem) incredibly hard chest, I give a good shove. My ankle protests when I swoop down low to gather my discarded purse, and with a sharp tug at my skirt and my loose-fitting pink top, I put myself back in order.

Or, as in order as I can be, considering that Andre was less than thirty seconds away from kissing me.

I don't turn around when he says my name the first time.

I don't turn around when he says it the second time.

On the third time, I whirl back, thankful for the fact that the elevator has exited into a quiet hallway. I strut toward him, all business. Yes, I add a sway to my hips. Yes, I come at him with fingers pointing and at the ready.

I jab him once in the chest, and I'm not surprised when the flesh beneath my attack doesn't budge.

He's as hard as stone.

Now that I think about it, his heart is the same way.

Andre catches my wrist, his gaze dipping down to search my face in overt confusion. "What did I say?"

Unbelievable. See? This is why the man is enemy number one in the hockey world—he's completely incapable of playing nice with *anyone*. I yank my hand out from his grasp. "Let me put it this way for you, Andre." I point at him, then swivel my finger to point at myself. "This? Us? Never happening. You laid down the ground about no sex, and I'm completely fine with that. I don't have sex with men who think that *I don't matter*."

Just like that, his expression shuts down. "Zoe—*Zo*—you know that I didn't mean it like that."

My hands go to my hips. "Then tell me how you meant it."

His eyes go wide, and he reaches up to rub the back of his neck with one hand. "Jesus, Zoe, I have no idea. I'm just saying that it'd probably do us some good. Get the sexual attraction out of the way so we can live our lives."

Fury heats my words when I counter, "I *am* living my life, Andre. I've been living my life since the day you screwed me in a goddamn laundry room, and then never spoke to me again."

Silence meets my words. It's the first time either of us has directly mentioned our past, and the awkwardness is palpable. I almost wish I could snatch them back. Except, no—no, I will not. He can't just *walk* about as if nothing ever happened.

In a voice I wish wasn't so testy, I mutter, "Nothing to say to that?"

His hand leaves his neck to scrape over the lower half of his face. "Let's not do this here."

My eyes narrow. "Are we going to talk about it on the way home?"

I mentally scoff. *Home*—like we share the same house, the same life, the same heart.

Utterly. Ridiculous.

Andre tugs on his ear. "Maybe we should just forget—"

Over the ringing in my ears, all I hear are excuses. I throw up a hand and his mouth clamps shut. "You know what? You're right—*it doesn't matter*. Not what happened then, or what happened after that. I don't care. But don't kiss me, Andre." My heart pounds with adrenaline; it pounds so loud that all I can hear is the blood thundering in my head. "Don't kiss me today, and don't kiss me tomorrow."

I won't survive another round with him between the sheets. Not if he decides to up and leave me again, just like he did last time—not that we were anywhere between a set of sheets a year ago.

But as he stares at me resolutely, with an expression that

borders on hollow, I can't help but wonder if I'm making the right decision. If I've even *read* him correctly.

I remind myself as we silently head toward *Fame*'s office that this is for the best. Andre is a client—*my* client. I can't go back down that road to temptation again. Not even if I'm tempted.

Not even if, for a few minutes today, I remembered the old him, the old us.

I have to be strong, because if I'm not, Andre Beaumont will use me and spit me back out when he's done. Of that I have no doubt.

11

ZOE

TWENTY DAYS LEFT

$\mathcal{O}$ver the next twenty-four hours, I can't shake the sense that I'm missing something when it comes to Andre.

The nagging sensation follows me when I spend three hours on the phone, talking shop with local reporters about considering Andre for a feature piece. It follows me when I email three different charities, all with the purpose of signing Andre on as a sponsor. It doesn't shake off when I end up in a near-argument with one of Andre's dropped sponsors over the phone, either.

I can still hear the man's derisive snort when I mentioned re-signing Andre during the next annual quarter.

"Beaumont?" he sneered at the start of our call. "Not happening. We only took him on because he won the Cup two years ago with the Red Wings, and even that ended up being a huge debacle with the CEO. You'll excuse me when I say I'm not feeling up to another battle."

"I can promise you that Mr. Beaumont has seen the errors of his ways," I told the man, lying through my teeth. Call me Ms. Cynical, but I doubted Andre had seen the light on anything. "Regaining his sponsorship with your organization would also influence the opinion of others." I took a deep breath and went for broke. "You could singlehandedly make a difference in his career, if only you'll say yes."

"A man can't change his stripes when they're tattooed on, Miss Mackenzie. Beaumont is the same way."

My fingers tightened around the receiver because, honestly? I felt the same way. "Shouldn't we refrain from judging others, Mr. Campbell?"

"Perhaps," Mr. Campbell murmured ambivalently.

"So, you'll consider taking him back?"

"No."

"Mr. Campbell," I said, just short of begging, "Give him a chance."

"Unlike you, Miss Mackenzie, my firm has decided that Andre Beaumont is all out of chances."

Something about the way he said that struck me as odd. "What do you mean, 'unlike me'?"

"The fact that you're dating him again after your scandal last year? It doesn't matter, Miss Mackenzie. The answer remains no. Have a good day."

Dating him . . .?

As I stuff my arms into my leather jacket at the end of the day, I deduce that I'm no closer to figuring out the missing link to Andre's unfinished puzzle, but it's pretty clear to me that the people I've spoken to today think that Andre and I are a "thing."

Over my dead body.

We haven't even spoken since our almost-kiss in the elevator at *Fame* yesterday morning. If you're wondering, our ride back to Boston was as awkwardly painful as you might imagine. I'm pretty sure that the only words we exchanged were at a highway-side gas station when he refilled his car, and I stuffed myself into a cramped restroom stall to pee.

"Zoe!"

At the sound of the female voice, I glance up. After a week of working for Golden Lights, Gwen James and I haven't really stopped to chat since that very first day. She's too busy, I think, dealing with clients who actually respect her, and I've been too busy wallowing in Dante's ninth circle of hell with Andre Beaumont.

Sliding my purse strap over my shoulder, I tap a few keys out on the computer keyboard and shut the desktop down. "Heading home?" I ask her, hoping she won't dig too deeply into my epic fail of a workday. The last thing I need her to know is that I'm on the verge of letting down Golden Lights Media in a big way.

With a shake of her head, Gwen's long, red hair bounces like something out of a hair commercial. I'm slightly envious, if only because my dark hair rarely does anything but act like a wild child, completely untamed.

Stepping into my office, Gwen takes a quick look around before settling her hands on her hips. "Actually, I'm not heading home yet. I was hoping to catch you before you left."

That doesn't sound good. Clearly, I'm about to be given the can, and I'll be forced to work at Vittoria for the rest of my life. Bracing myself for the worst, I squeak, "Oh?"

"Do you have plans tonight?"

I blink. All day I'd planned to head home and lick my wounds. Maybe it's been too long since I've been in the field, but after nine hours of working toward a total crapshoot goal, I'm feeling rather sensitive.

Oh, God, I've lost my thick skin.

I wonder if it's the sort of thing you can earn back, or, once you've become a certifiable watering pot, likely to cry at any moment a door shuts in your face, you've lost all hope.

"Zoe?" Gwen prompts, her blue eyes carefully studying my face. "You there?"

"Sorry, yes, I'm here. And, no, no plans." My dad mentioned something about helping out again at Vittoria tonight, but as I'd rather not do so . . . "Did you need me for something?"

"The Blades are up against the Philadelphia Flyers tonight. Through the grapevine I heard that a few prospective sponsors will be up in the box, and I thought that perhaps . . . "

The word "opportunity" flashes before my eyes like an actual slideshow, and I immediately stand to attention, my shoulders pushing back and my chin coming up. "I'll go—this will be great." Casting a quick glance down at my wristwatch, I note the time. "The game is starting in thirty minutes, isn't it? If I leave now, I'll make it with time to spare."

"Great!" Gwen claps her hands together, adding, "Perfect. I really didn't want to go alone."

Alone?

"You're coming along?" This cannot be good. "Is this a test to see how well I do out in the wild?"

"Oh, no!" She waves her hand in the air, dismissing me with just a flap of her slender arm. "Definitely not. You really should be there tonight because it might open some doors up for you. I'm just . . . Well, can I let you in on a little secret?"

Since I see no way out of saying no, and I'd also like to keep my job as long as possible, I shrug. "Sure, of course."

Gwen cuts a swift glance to the door. Apparently satisfied that no one is eavesdropping, she tells me, "I totally made the mistake of dating one of the head guys in the Blades' hockey administration. The General Manager, actually. And since he's definitely going to be there tonight . . ."

"You want me there as a shield?" I throw out bluntly.

Her arms lift in a delicate shrug. "Think of it as being each other's body armor. We can lend each other some much-needed support."

Since Gwen James reminds me of a dolled-up piranha, it's probably not a bad idea to have her around. Plus, if she gets to know me a little better, perhaps this stupid trial run will become a permanent gig. The thought of obtaining other clients besides the NHL's bad boy enforcer brings a smile to my face.

"All right, let's do this."

ONE HOUR LATER, I'M REGRETTING MY LIFE DECISIONS.

Gwen is certainly a body shield, specifically in the literal sense. The woman is practically glued to my side.

We're barely through the door to the owner's box before Gwen bumps my shoulder with hers, like we're suddenly best girlfriends. "Do you see him?" she whispers, except that it's not really a whisper. I'm not sure she knows *how* to whisper. Her hand leaves my arm to point at a group of men in the far corner of the gray-carpeted room. "Right there. The one in the black suit."

Ahem. They're all wearing black suits.

My gaze scours the men, finally stopping on a decent-looking guy with coppery hair and a friendly smile. He looks wealthy, so probably Gwen's type.

"Is that him?" I give him a little nod with my chin. Then I look down, and . . . the man is wearing vibrant red shoes.

"What?" Gwen shakes her head adamantly, then gives me a crushed look. "Absolutely not. Do I look like the kind of girl who'd go for a ginger?"

I blink. "Aren't you a ginger?"

Gwen clucks her tongue. "Girl," she says in that way people do when they're about to school you on life, "it's called hair dye. I'm not a natural redhead. *Anyway*, you didn't hear that from me. *Also*, there are different classifications of redheads. There's me, and I have a *very* deep cherry hue, and then there's a carrot top." Her blue eyes land on the man we've been talking about, and he must sense us watching him, because he glances over his shoulder.

His eyes fall right on Gwen, and I swear he looks like the heavens have opened up and gifted him a goddess. A goddess in the form of Gwen James, who gives the man a bright, white smile—and out of the corner of her mouth, says, "He's a carrot top. Um, no thank you."

I don't even know what to say to that.

Her smile never fades when she points to the guy standing next to the man with the friendly "carrot-top" hair. "*That* guy," she says triumphantly.

That guy turns out to be wearing what most would consider an eyesore: blue leather shoes, a flamingo-pink shirt, and pastel yellow chinos. He looks like Easter, if Easter were a person and not represented to the masses as a cartoon-like bunny bearing candy.

The words stick in my throat, and I cough into my free hand. "He's, ah, very good-looking."

The look Gwen gives me says she doesn't believe me worth a damn. "You don't have to lie. He's not bad, looks-wise, but I *will* say that he is pretty fantastic in bed. What he can do with his tongue should be illegal—"

Nope, totally not going there. "Tell me how you met him!"

As Gwen waxes on about the Blades' GM knocking boots with her between the sheets, I scan the owner's box for familiar faces. I spent the entire cab ride studying important figures within the Blades' organization, but now that I'm here . . . maybe it's my nerves, but I just can't bring to mind anyone that I reviewed.

There's also the fact that for the first time in my career within PR, I feel . . . not quite comfortable. Back in Detroit, I had no troubles mingling. I talked with the Red Wings' owner about his daughters. After the game, I waltzed into the team's locker room to speak with my clients about what was needed from them.

I've seen more than my fair share of dropped towels, and know the exact reason why Detroit's goalie went by the name "Shortie," and I'm not talking about the height of his . . . body.

I was fearless.

And now . . . I run a finger along the collar of my silk shirt, peeling the material away from my flushed skin.

Holy cow, I think I'm having a panic attack.

I've never had one, and so I'm not sure if that's what this is, but it certainly feels like it and . . . I need something to drink. Now.

The food and beverages are laid out on a buffet table along the back wall, opposite the glass overlooking the ice rink below. Members of the media, with press badges clipped to their shirts, walk around with audio recorders crammed below their mouths as they speak in low voices.

I don't walk toward them. Instead, I beeline toward the buffet, leaving Gwen to trail after me or be left behind.

"Where are you—?" She cuts off, releasing a squeal that darts through my skull like pins and needles. "Oh, my God, we have to say hi."

Her fingers latch onto my arm again as she spins me around and drags me toward the other end of the buffet table where a blonde is standing. Poor girl—she has no idea what's coming her way.

Before we even reach the woman's side, Gwen exclaims, "Charlie! It is *so* good to see you."

The blonde glances up, and there's no mistaking the way her eyes go wide at our approach. She looks on the verge of fleeing, but there's no time. "*Heeeey*, there, Gwen." The woman's blue eyes flick to me, before landing on Gwen's shark-like grab on my forearm. "Looks like you've made a new friend?"

By the gods that be, I'm released.

"Charlie," Gwen says, "meet our new publicist, Zoe Mackenzie. Zoe, this is Charlie Denton. She works for *The Boston Globe*."

I hold my hand out for a proper handshake. "It's good to meet you. Have you been with *The Boston Globe* for a while?"

"A little over a month now. It's still pretty fresh, actually."

"She was with *The Tribune* before," Gwen pops into the conversation, as if I should be completely familiar with the newspaper. At my raised brows, Gwen gives a little sigh of disappointment. "I forgot you aren't from here. *The Cambridge Tribune* was a sinking newspaper. It recently closed down."

I look from Gwen to Charlie, then back again. "Is this a . . . good thing?"

"Absolutely," Charlie says, drawing my attention back to her. Just before she stuffs a mini-quesadilla slice into her mouth, she mutters, "I hated that place. Totally soul-sucking."

I have no idea what to say. On a personal level, I can commiserate with her. On a professional level, I have no idea who she is, and the last year has made me wary of reporters. My gaze dips to the forgotten black recorder on the buffet table.

"What Charlie *isn't* saying, is that you probably heard about her on the news. Little fun fact for you, Zoe: Charlie here busted an entire story a little over a month ago about me and her boyfriend, Duke Harrison." Gwen watches me, and I have the distinct feeling that this part *is* a test. "But Charlie is pretty good at keeping secrets otherwise—right, Charls?"

The blonde spares Gwen a narrowed look. "You do

realize that I've known you for nearly a decade, and you've never once called me that. Right?"

Gwen purses her lips. "I thought we were friends?"

"You called me Charlie Sheen two months ago."

"It was obviously a joke," Gwen tells me in a conspiratorial voice, hand curled around her mouth and everything. "Charlie's still feeling a little hurt about it."

"Well," Charlie drawls, dragging another quesadilla off the silver tray, "if it hadn't been for you making Duke see me again, I don't know where I would be today. Thank you for that. But, anyway, I'm an awesome secret keeper." Her blue eyes find my face. "Should I turn off my recorder?"

"You have it running right now?" An itchy feeling catches on my neck, and I briskly rub my palm against it, hating the thought that I'm in a room full of people just *waiting* to bust open the "Moaning Zoe" jokes again.

"Oh, yeah," Charlie tells me, tapping her finger against the recorder. "This baby never gets turned off. You have no idea what you might hear up here. I mean—did you know that the GM was messing around with someone? His divorce papers aren't even finalized yet."

Over Charlie's head, I exchange a look with Gwen. Gwen, mind you, pulls the *least* subtle move in the existence of subtlety, and runs a finger across her throat.

"Gwen," the blonde says, twisting around to stare at my boss in horror. "You *didn't*."

Uh-oh. I shift backward, intent on escaping. "You know, I think I might try to scope out some of those sponsors you were talking about, Gwen. Maybe spend some time convincing them that Andre isn't the devil incarnate—"

Gwen's hand clutches my wrist, stalling my flight. "Body. Shield," she hisses from behind gritted teeth.

My eyes go wide. "From *her*? Seriously?"

Charlie's hands go to her hips. "What's that mean? What are you talking about, 'body shield'?"

"Nothing, Charls."

Charlie makes a theatrical show of flicking off her recorder, before dropping it into the backpack tucked between her feet. "Recorder is away, Gwen. Don't even pretend to play coy. Did you sleep with the *GM?*"

Sensing trouble on the horizon, I lift a finger. "Can I ask how the two of you know each other?"

Charlie says, "She's my best friend's cousin," at the exact same time Gwen mutters, "I've known her for years. Not in a professional setting."

That's all the answer I get before they're verbally lunging at each other again.

"Don't you know how to keep it in your pants, Gwen?" Charlie throws out, looking every inch the disappointed mother.

Gwen, for her part, rolls her eyes. "He's not married anymore."

"It's called settling on a separation. He's still legally married."

"He hasn't slept with his wife in two years."

"Because *that* makes it okay?" Charlie shakes her head, and her blonde ringlets sail through the air with the movement. "Please tell me it was only one time."

When Gwen bites her bottom lip, I decide it's time to make my move. The two women are so caught up in their argument that they barely register the fact that I steal two quesadillas from the silver tray for myself and then make my escape.

Perhaps it's the hockey gods shining down on me, but at that moment, the buzzer kicks off and the announcer's baritone fills the arena: "Alllll rightttt, there, who is ready to watch the game of the season?"

The crowd goes wild, the sound piercing the owner's box, even with the glass enclosing us. My feet carry me over to the window, and, for once, I'm content with knowing that not a single soul knows who I am.

As I shovel the remaining bites of quesadilla into my mouth, I keep my gaze trained on the ice below. Aside from two specks, which look a lot like referees, the players haven't yet entered the arena.

"The Blades are currently 17-23-2 this season," the announcer continues boisterously. "It has *not* been a good season for this Boston hockey team." The crowd appropriately boos, and even a few of the men behind me follow like a pack of lemmings, cupping their hands around their mouths and echoing the *boos*. "The Philadelphia Flyers are currently the leading team in the division, with a record of 38-2-2. I don't know about you, Bob, but unless the Blades manage to pull a rabbit out of a magic hat tonight, it's gonna get bloody down on that ice."

The second announcer, Bob, gives a low, humorless chuckle that revs the crowd into a high-pitched roar. Over the noise, he says, "Don't I know it, Tom. But I think we're going to have ourselves a good one tonight."

"If number twenty-two from the Blades manages to stay out of the penalty box, wouldn't you say?"

"Yes, absolutely. At the rate Andre Beaumont is going, he'll have his name scrawled on the Plexiglas of the sin bin by the end of the season, Tom."

"Any idea on what's gotten into him lately? 'King Sin Bin' nickname aside, Beaumont has always been a hard player, but recently, it's been a different game he's playing. If he keeps it up, he might not even find himself playing for Boston for another season."

"I hate to do this, but I have to agree with you on this one. If Andre Beaumont can't find a way to get out of his head and back into the game, then there is a very good chance he won't be sticking around for much longer."

As the announcers move on to talk about the other players and their predictions for tonight's game, my brain is hardwired on one person: Andre Beaumont.

This is way worse than I thought, and I already thought the situation was pretty bad. It's one thing for him to be messing up off the ice, but for him to be bringing that same mindset to his career? We have a problem—a huge problem that I don't think is going to be solved by earning back some key sponsors.

This is going to be my last season anyway.

His words from yesterday have haunted me all night, and now they push back to the forefront. I hate to put it this way, but it seems like a pretty solid chance that Andre is actually *throwing away* his career.

Which is idiotic.

Even after our incident last year, he remained a first-round trade pick. The man is damn good at what he does, regardless of his other . . . faults.

Wishing that I was down in the crowd, I press my hand to the cool window. The buzzer sounds off again, and then, one by one, the players take to the ice. We're so far up that they appear like little dots, circling around the marked arena like buzzards after their prey.

I find myself searching for Andre. Back when I worked for the Red Wings, I attended almost every home game. In the beginning, it was only so I could slowly learn the nature of the sport. My mom wasn't a hockey fan, and phrases like "deke" or "icing" were totally beyond my comprehension.

Ask me what shoes are the must-haves this season, and I totally have you covered, though.

But then I met Andre, and slowly, so slowly that I barely even realized what was happening, my attendance at the games had less to do with learning and more to do with supporting my client and friend.

I wore his jersey with pride, sitting up in the nosebleeds or wherever I could find an empty seat.

I could have easily sat up in the owner's box, but what was the fun in that?

Sure, there was food, but the life—the *soul*—of hockey was found in the hundreds of rows of seats stretching up from the ice.

By this time last year, I had fallen into a routine: watch the Red Wings play; meet Andre by the locker room, just before he spoke with the media about the game. Following that, we'd head out and grab late night dinner before heading home.

Or, you know, to our own homes.

No kissing, no touching.

Just two buddies hanging out and grabbing a beer. Or, in my case, white wine.

The memories hurt, and I rub my hand against my chest. Heartburn, maybe. I totally shouldn't have scarfed down that quesadilla, and I refuse to believe that I might be feeling anything else . . . like *emotions*.

I felt more than enough of those last year, and I'm still topped off at my lifetime quota.

"*Woo-yee!* Bob, tell me you saw that body check!"

Bob, the announcer, howls in delight. "Boy, did I? You think maybe Beaumont is out to play tonight?"

"I just think he might be, Bob, I just think he might be. Let's watch a replay of that, shall we?"

I lift my gaze to the Jumbotron, and sure enough, there's Andre bulldozing a Flyers player into the boards. The Plexiglas shakes from the force of his hit. And, even though I'm watching a playback, my heart catches in my throat at the sight of Andre jabbing an elbow into the other player's ribs as they fight for the puck.

Sweat beads down Andre's face, and his black eyes shine like the devil, narrowed and unholy, as he battles for his life. The Flyers player takes a jab back, striking Andre beneath the chin. I physically wince, as though *I* were the one to get clocked in the face, but whereas I'd end up on the floor in the fetal position, Andre does what he does best.

He angles his big body in such a way that he hooks the puck with his stick. With a forceful tug, the other player tries to draw Andre back by his jersey. It doesn't work. In the blink of an eye, Andre escapes the illegal holding.

Just like that, he's plowing down the ice, light glinting off his navy-blue helmet. With a sharp motion, he draws back and fires the puck toward his teammate. A half-second later, the buzzer sounds and red lights key up in the arena.

One assist down for Andre Beaumont.

If only he played with that much heart off the ice, too.

ZOE

*C*all me crazy, but I have no idea what I'm doing here.

And by "here," I'm talking about the fact that I'm lurking outside of the Blades' locker room like a total stalker. Thanks to my position with Golden Lights Media, getting past security was a breeze.

I flashed my work I.D., the security guard gave it a once over, and with a low grunt, he gave me access to the narrow hallway that looks like something out of a horror movie.

Lucky me.

"Follow the hall, hang your first right," the guard told me.

Easy, no problem.

But now that I'm standing *outside* of the locker room, it's a bit of a different story. Through the door, I can hear raucous, masculine laughter. The Blades put up a hell of a fight tonight, and it paid off, since they won against the Flyers 3-2. But the laughter and cheering only make me wonder if I'm out of my mind—of *course*, Andre will go out with his teammates to celebrate. Of *course*, he's going to think I'm weird for standing out here, waiting for him.

My eyes squeeze shut and my back presses against the

cool wall. "You're crazy, Zoe Mackenzie," I whisper to myself. "Go the hell home before he catches you out here."

Great idea. Don't know why I didn't think of it sooner.

I twist around and barely make it two steps before I hear a female voice call my name. Looking over my shoulder, I guess I shouldn't be surprised to see Gwen's friend Charlie out here, since she's a reporter and all.

I fake a smile, hoping it doesn't look pained. "Hey there!" I flash a little wave, already backing up to prepare for my escape.

Charlie hooks a thumb over her shoulder. "Did you need to see one of the guys?" she asks, her curly blonde hair bouncing as she approaches me. "They're almost done in there, but someone broke out the vodka, and I can't guarantee any one of them will remember that they were supposed to meet you."

Drunken hockey players? Yeah, that's totally my cue to leave. "I thought, maybe, I should link up with one of my clients before heading home, but if they're partying in there . . ."

"Who are you meeting?"

Crap, crap, crap. I fake a slap to my forehead. "You know, I totally forgot that he mentioned we'd just meet tomorrow! Silly me."

Silly me? Who even says that?

You do, apparently.

Charlie's head tilts to the side. "Gwen mentioned that you're working with Andre Beaumont."

I'm not sure if that's a question or a statement, and I go with shrugging my shoulders and pretending that pools of sweat aren't taking up residence under my armpits. The longer I stand here, the likelier it'll be for Andre to find me waiting for him, and if that happens . . . Cue the panic, for real.

"We're teamed up for the interim," I finally say, stealing a glance over my shoulder. All I have to do is just inch a little bit back, say farewell, and beat a hasty exit out of the rink.

Charlie totally doesn't get the hint. "Seriously, you've got to tell me—is he as terrifying as he seems?"

Worse, I want to tell her. He's cocky and rude, and there's a small part of me that wishes I hadn't turned down his offer to kiss me in the elevator. *Not*, of course, that I want him. Okay, maybe I do, just a little. But I only want his body—not *him*. Crap, that's not quite true either . . . Out loud, I say, "He takes some time to get used to."

Her brows lift with interest. "And you've gotten used to him?"

"I don't think anyone could ever get used to Andre. He's not exactly . . . "

"Cuddly?"

My gaze shoots to the blonde's face. "He's my client."

Yes, Zoe, he's your client—not that it mattered to you before.

But Charlie just laughs warmly. "It was just a figure of speech. I didn't think that you were actually cuddling *with* him."

Right, of course. She doesn't recognize me—and, you know what? It feels *good*. So good that I open my mouth and ruin it all: "Yeah, the one time we—you know—there wasn't much cuddling involved."

My eyes fall shut at the same time that Charlie claps a hand over her mouth. I let out a groan, and it's pitiful. So damn pitiful. "I didn't . . . I mean, I'm not . . . "

"You slept with Andre Beaumont?" Charlie whispers after a moment. But to my surprise, she doesn't sound disgusted. If anything, she sounds . . . intrigued?

I open my eyes, and sure enough, she's staring at me as though I've delivered an early Christmas. "I'm sorry," I say, backing up, "this is totally unprofessional. Just ignore me. In fact, I'm going to head on my way."

"I'm dating Duke Harrison."

The words stop me in my tracks. "Gwen had said something earlier about that?"

Charlie nods. "Yeah, long story. In any case, Duke and I slept together when I was a reporter stalking him down for a story."

There's nothing for me to do but gape. "Wow." I'm impressed. From what little I know of Duke "The Mountain" Harrison's reputation, it's that it has always been ridiculously clean. Sleeping with a reporter, well, obviously there's a reason why they're dating.

A blush stains Charlie's cheeks. "Yup. We did it on a hotel rooftop. It was *glorious*."

"That's impressive." Duke Harrison is a legend, both in the looks department and also in the goalie's net for the Blades.

"Yeah, well, *he's* impressive, if you know what I mean." She opens her bag and pulls out her audio recorder. With deliberate motions, she clicks it off and drops it back into the cavern of her backpack. "Okay, you *know* I'm not recording anything, so you have to tell me everything."

Something about her open expression and friendly demeanor encourages me to do just that. I mean, it's not like I have any friends in Boston, save for Tia, and she has *her* own friends. I'm the uncool older sister camping out on the couch until I move out.

"I, well . . . "

"You don't have to give details. But since the first time I met him, I figured he'd be, like . . . Okay, total confessional here." Charlie holds up a hand like she's taking an oath. "I feel like he would be the worst lover in the existence of lovers. He's so cold and stiff—"

Before I can stop myself, I mutter, "Well, he's certainly stiff."

There's a small pause before we both erupt into laughter, and it actually seems to break the ice (pun unintended) because the next thing I know, I'm telling her everything. And, I do mean, *everything*.

"Wait, you did it in the laundry room?" she asks, gasping for air as we sit on the floor ten minutes later, our backs against the wall and our legs outstretched. I've kicked off my stilettos so my toes can enjoy their freedom. "That's insane."

"It was hot," I tell her with a small sigh. "Hands down the best sex I've ever had. Well, until it was over."

"And then he went back to being cold?"

"Or, to use your other word, he went back to being stiff."

"Insane," she mutters again, shaking her head like she just can't believe it. She's a good egg, the kind of person I'd kill to have as a friend. Propping her elbow on a bent knee, she picks at a torn hole in her jeans. "But, hey, of the two of us, I think your story takes the cake."

"Yeah, well, you're at least *dating* the guy you hooked up with. I'm back in the same position I was in the first place, with him as a client. It's like *Groundhog Day*. I swore that I woke up from this dream a year ago, and now I'm right back in it again."

"Maybe you should shag him one more time. Do it and be done with him."

She sounds just like Andre.

Without warning, the locker room door slips open and the Blades exit in groups. It's a sight to see, really. Hot man after hot man files out. For the most part, their hair is wet, slicked back, and they're decked out in jeans and T-shirts.

"You hitting up The Box after this, right?" one guy says, and I recognize him instantly as Marshall Hunt, Ladies' Man Extraordinaire.

"Yeah, I'll be there," another guy responds. "Going to swing by my old lady's house first, though. Want to say g'night to her and the kid before I meet you for a beer."

Hunt snorts derisively. "Jesus, man, you're whipped."

"No. I just love my girls."

"Yeah? Then when are you going to put a ring on it, dude?"

They move out of earshot before I can hear the rest of the conversation. Beside me, Charlie jumps up, swiping at her jeans as she cranes her head, no doubt looking for her hotshot boyfriend.

Time to get out of here.

With a prayer on my lips that Andre will be the *very* last player out of the locker room, I snag the straps of my stilettos and begin stuffing my sore feet back into them.

"Zo?"

Dammit.

A pair of boots enters my peripheral, and then my gaze is climbing his legs, pausing at the noticeable bulge at his crotch (don't judge me!), and skating upward. I don't make it past his broad chest because his knees *pop! pop!* as he crouches down in front of me.

Black eyes meet mine. "What're you doing here, Zoe?"

Setting myself up for inevitable heartbreak, it seems.

I drop my head back against the wall in defeat. "Gwen invited me to the game."

"And you came?" He sounds surprised, not that I blame him.

"She promised me that there might be sponsors around to preach my cause to, but, alas, no one was there."

Andre doesn't laugh at my theatrical tone. "That doesn't explain why you're down here, by the locker room."

"Would you believe me if I said that I had something important to discuss with you?"

"No." His damp head ducks as he reaches out to touch my ankle. But my ankle is bare, my stiletto still dangling from my toes, and I feel that one brush of his finger like he's wrapped his entire hand around my heart and not my foot. "How is this?" he asks, not going so far as to tap the bone, though he does apply slight pressure. "Did you put ice on it like I told you?"

My breath hitches. "I-I didn't have any."

"Your dad owns a restaurant," he says, his mouth barely lifting into a smile. His eyes, though, gleam with amusement. "You really going to tell me that he had nothing available?"

"Yes," I lie, shamelessly turning my foot so that he has more access to touch me. If he wants.

Shameless.

I know. It's bad.

Maybe he catches my not-so-subtle signal because his palm skims my foot and then clasps my ankle. The heat from his hand has my toes flexing, my fingers digging into the floor on either side of my hips. I look up, meet his gaze, and—

"Yo! Beaumont, my man, are you coming with us?"

The spell, if there even was one, breaks.

Andre's hand falls from my foot, and he straightens to his full height. "I planned to head home," he tells his teammate, a guy I don't immediately recognize from the roster pages. "Get in an early night before we hit the road tomorrow."

Another player comes up beside the first guy, and slings an arm around his shoulder. "Don't bail on us, Beaumont." The man's blue eyes dip to where I'm still sitting on the floor, trying to lace up my heels. "Ah, I see. You have a lady friend for the evening."

Finally, I manage to hook myself back up. I'm struggling to my feet, clutching the wall, when Andre claps a hand around my elbow and pulls me up. Which doesn't help my case at all when I say, "I'm *not* his lady friend."

Andre's teammates exchange a look. "Yeah, sure," the first one says.

"She's my publicist," Andre says in a hard voice. "That's it."

If my heart does a weird little squeeze at his words, I do my best to ignore it. I duck my head. "I should probably be heading out anyway. Andre, I'll see you on Monday?"

Another voice enters the fray.

"Zoe!" Charlie calls out, bouncing over to me with Duke Harrison trailing behind her. I stare at him, a little stunned. He's more attractive in person than he even is on TV. Blond hair, blue eyes. A solid build that speaks of hours spent in the gym. No wonder Charlie did him on a rooftop—I would have too.

Charlie's hand waves in front of my face, and heat rises to my cheeks. "Why don't you come with us?" She snags my hand and gives it a little tug. "We're hitting up The Box. It's a tradition."

"Zoe is heading home." This comes from Andre.

Something about his remote, icy tone snaps my back straight. "I'd love to join," I tell Charlie. "Are you guys taking a cab?"

Masculine fingers wrap around my wrist. "I thought you were heading home?" Andre's thumb brushes the center of my palm. "Remember?"

I slip my hand from his grasp. "Sure, I do. But Charlie and I are new friends, and it'd be rude of me to say no." I lean forward, waiting until he does the same. "Now, aren't you heading home so you can see one of your women? Don't let us stop you."

"Jesus, Zoe." He rears back, scrubbing a hand over his hard jawline. Mouth flattening, he growls, "All right. Fine. I'll go."

My eyes narrow on him. "That wasn't an invitation."

"It is now," he tells me stiffly. Before I can even get another word in, he adds, "You'll ride with me."

He doesn't even give me an opportunity to say no.

"ANOTHER ROUND OF WINE, PLEASE!" CHARLIE SHOUTS TWO hours later. She's seated next to me at The Box, which is a hole in the wall if I've ever seen one. Dark walls and dim lighting give off the impression that the bar is smaller than it is. Seated at the end of a long hallway from the main part of the establishment, this area of The Box is apparently exclusive only to the Blades and their guests.

If we're being honest, it's pretty much a quarantined area for hot-as-hell hockey players. They mosey about this way and that, lounging on couches or shooting pool. Some stick around the bar, talking loudly as they argue who had the better stick play for the evening. One guy comes up to me and, without prelude, begins to show me pictures of his baby daughter.

Cute kid, but I still have no idea who he is.

One other thing is for certain about The Box—the liquor selection is good. Maybe *too* good.

I push my empty glass away with a groan. My skin feels sticky, and my throat scratchy from one too many glasses of chardonnay. "I think I've had too much wine."

Charlie waves away my worries. "One more," she sing-songs, before tapping me on the nose with the kind of familiarity that comes from bonding while being tipsy. "Do you really want to go home with Andre right now?"

At the mention of him, I twist around and find him seated with some of his teammates at a table. Poker chips are laid out before them and empty tumblers litter the table. Even though I can't quite make out his expression, I have the sneaking suspicion that he isn't focused on the game . . . he's watching me.

I sigh. Probably because he feels responsible for my safety.

On the way over, he said no less than three times not to trust any of his teammates. "They're all cold motherfuckers, Zoe. Unless you want to wake up tomorrow morning alone and naked, I'd suggest avoiding them."

Something tells me that he's the coldest motherfucker of them all—excuse my French.

In my attempt to get a good look at him, my butt inches a little too close to the edge of my barstool. There's a split-second moment where I'm convinced I'm about to go sailing to the ground. My arms pinwheel, hands searching for purchase. At the very last second, I catch myself on the bar just as I see Andre lurch to his feet, like he's prepared to come to my rescue.

How cute.

I offer him a two-finger salute and turn to Charlie. "I have a problem," I announce.

"Do you?" Charlie scoots her butt around on the barstool so she's facing me. "Tell me."

"I'm not sure . . . "

She pats my hand consolingly. "You'll feel better."

"Well, it's just"—my hand gestures in the air frivolously —"how do you teach someone to be more . . . *open*?"

"Like, emotionally?" Charlie asks, studying me carefully. "Girl, you're speaking to the choir. Duke is like a clam." She darts a glance over her shoulder and then whispers behind one hand, "Don't tell him I said that. He's doing much better, and I don't want to ruin his progress."

That makes me smile. She and Duke are the kind of couple you can't help but love and hate at the same time. He was quick to purchase her a drink, and just as quick to press a kiss to her forehead and murmur, "Have fun with your friend, sweetheart," before heading off with the guys.

Like I said, cute.

Andre Beaumont isn't cut from the same cloth.

Snagging the stem of my wine glass, I swivel around and slouch against the bar. Swirling the wine around, I take a small sip and wait for the man I'm watching to notice me.

It doesn't take long.

Andre's chin jerks up as if sensing my stare. For a moment, it's like no one else exists in The Box. I sip my wine, and he mimics my move, wrapping a hand around his tumbler and drinking what I know is likely to be a whiskey and coke.

I don't break eye contact as I primly cross one leg over the other.

He doesn't break eye contact as he says something to the guys at his table and then scrapes his chair back.

Neither of us breaks eye contact as he draws closer, his long-legged gait eating up the distance to my barstool. As he does so, an idea brews in my head. It's perfect, perfectly ridiculous, and when Andre stops in front of me, I burst, "Where's Marshall Hunt?"

Andre's brows furrow and an unnamed emotion darkens his gaze. "Excuse me?"

I peer over his shoulder. "Marshall. Is he here?"

There's a small pause, and then, "He's in the back. I think."

Brilliant. "Will you grab him for me?"

"Will I—" Andre cuts off, downing the rest of his cock-tail in one smooth move. He plants the glass on the counter by my elbow, and he's so close that I can smell the sandal-wood off his skin. "You know what? Fine, I *will* go get him.
"

I smile brightly at him. "I'll be here waiting!"

Though he looks on the verge of strangling me, he gives a

curt nod and stalks away. Beside me, Charlie leans so far over, I worry she might topple from her stool.

"You're baiting the lion," she whispers in a voice that's not at all a whisper. "Do you know what you're doing?"

"Not at all," I tell her truthfully.

I am, what some would call, flying by the seat of my pants. But I wait anyway, making small talk with Charlie and the bartender until a sullen Andre comes strolling back toward the bar, Marshall Hunt in tow.

Up close, Hunt looks just as American Golden Boy as he does on TV. Light brown hair, indeterminable colored eyes in the muted bar room. He's big without being massive like Duke Harrison or Andre. When Hunt meets my gaze, the corners of his eyes crease with humor, and he leans in for a kiss to my cheek.

"I heard I was summoned," he says, "though Beaumont here wouldn't tell me why."

Andre says nothing, and Marshall Hunt visibly shudders.

Yes, this will be perfect.

I take another long pull from my wine, then pop the glass back on the bar top. Turning back to the men, I say, "That's because I didn't tell him. Marshall, I've heard you're a bit of a player."

His eyes go wide. Andre thumps him on the back. "Hell," Hunt mutters after a moment, "warn a man before you catch him off guard."

"Sorry," I say without being all that sorry. No, this is perfect. *He* is perfect. "My point is that you're a ladies' man. But the ladies *love* you. The media loves you. You're like . . . a unicorn."

Andre lets loose a groan. "I think you've had too much to drink, Zoe." Softly, he presses his inner wrist to my forehead, as if checking my temperature. It feels . . . well, dammit, it feels quite lovely actually. "You're hot."

Charlie leans over, one hand outstretched for a high-five. "You got that right, Beaumont. Our Zoe is *beautifulll.*"

Andre slides her a hard glare, and I leap at the opportunity he's presented me. Batting his hand away, I announce, "See! That look right there. You have to stop scaring people, Andre. This is why Marshall is perfect."

"Because I *don't* scare people?" Hunt asks, his voice sounding every shade of confused. "Should I be insulted?"

"No!" In the far, far corner of my brain, I realize that I've had *way* too much to drink. But whether it's the wine or the fact that, for the first time in months, I'm hanging out with people my own age, I feel happy. Even if I am earning myself a spot on Andre's mile-long shit list. Pressing my shoulders back, I say, "Marshall, I need you to teach Andre how to be the kind of guy everyone loves."

"Jesus, Zoe."

No surprise on who says that, but I ignore the man simmering beside me. This is for the greater good—*Andre's* greater good.

"Andre, pretend that Marshall is a woman you're hitting on."

For a moment, there's only silence, but boy, is it substantial. Hunt comes up sputtering from his beer, Charlie keels over the bar, rolling with laughter, and Andre . . . Andre turns to me, his dark brows drawn when he growls, "Are you serious right now?"

"Yes," I tell him. "Charlie and I will be the judges—right, Charlie?" Beside me, Charlie throws up her hand to order another round of wine. I take her silence as confirmation. I fold my arms over my chest, trying not to wobble too hard in my seat. "We'll be the judges. Then, once you've gotten it exactly right, we'll head up to the front part of the bar and let you loose on real women."

"I'm gonna need another fucking beer for this," Hunt mutters.

Less than five minutes later, we're all in position, and, sure enough, we've gathered a crowd of eager onlookers. Duke sits behind his girlfriend, his hand clutching Charlie's on top of her knee. A few of the other players have pulled up chairs, the poker game forgotten in the face of watching Andre make a fool out of himself. The chalkboard that sat behind the bar now sits in my lap, so that I can tally the number of times Charlie and I feel as though Andre has done something right.

Clapping my hands together loud enough to end the chatter, I say, "Okay! Our first round will begin . . . now! Andre"—I point a green piece of chalk at him—"you've just walked into a bar and noticed our beautiful, lovely lady right here. What do you do?"

Andre cuts a glare at Hunt, who is now fully invested in the scheme. He presses his chin to the tops of his clasped hands, and flutters his eyelashes outrageously, making his teammates roar with laughter.

"Find someone better looking," Andre grunts.

"Wrong!" I make a *bzzing* sound with my teeth. "Try again."

With a little sigh of defeat, Andre pinches the bridge of his nose. "I would walk up to her."

"Baby steps," Charlie says, "very good baby steps. Now, if you were doing this as your *regular* self, what would be your next step?"

Andre doesn't have the chance to defend himself.

One of his teammates, Jackson, I think, points his beer in Andre's direction. "He'd ask if she had a boyfriend or a husband."

My nose scrunches. "You ask that? That's the first thing you say?"

"It's not—" Breaking off, Andre rakes his fingers through his hair. "I don't say that *every* time, but sometimes it helps to know whether I'm barking up the wrong tree. It saves time."

"Because all you want to do is get into her pants?" With a shake of my head, I look over to Hunt. "What do you do?"

Marshall Hunt seems only too pleased to offer his take on picking up a girl. "Well, it's a bit of a science, y'know? First, I try to get her attention, see if she's even interested. Then, once we've been staring at each other for a bit—"

"Did you have to choose fucking Romeo for this shit?" someone shouts from the back of the bar. "We'll be here 'til morning!"

"Dude!" Hunt shouts back, pointing his finger at where the voice came from. "She asked. Don't be jealous that you get laid once a year, McDermott. The only stick of yours getting action lately is sure as hell not the one attached to your pelvis."

Everyone laughs, throwing up beers and cocktails in a toast.

"Fuck you, Hunt!"

"You're not my type, McDermott!" With that Hunt, turns back around, his handsome face once again a mask of pleasantness. "*Anyway*, now that we've got McDermott's virgin status out of the way, what I was saying is that I make my move slowly. It's methodical. I want this woman to know that I'm coming. Let the anticipation build and all that. When I finally approach her, she's practically begging for me to sit down."

Huh. That *does* sound very methodical, which I suppose is the reason it works. Even just sitting here, *I'm* feeling a little turned on by Marshall Hunt. It's his eyes, I think. Now that he's closer, I can see that they are a pewter gray, slightly mysterious, but open and guileless. Unlike Andre's black-as-night gaze that hints of unspoken secrets.

I reach out and poke Andre in the side. "What do you say to that?"

"I think I'm in my own version of hell," he tells me, lifting his whiskey and coke to his mouth. "You seriously want me to play this up?"

I meet his gaze. "I want you to be nice."

His mouth flattens and the emotion in his dark eyes turns unreadable. Have I hurt his feelings? I wouldn't think it possible, but from the way he stoically sets his tumbler beside me . . . maybe I have. It's on the tip of my tongue to apologize, to blame the wine, but then his fingers wrap around my bicep as he gently tugs me off the barstool. The chalkboard goes to the bar top.

"Fine." Releasing me, Andre steps back, already turning toward the door. Over his shoulder, he says, "But you're my target, Zoe, not Hunt."

My sloshed brain realizes that this is a bad idea. A very, very bad idea. "Andre! What do you mean, *I'm* your target?"

"Exactly as I said." He twists around but doesn't stop moving. He casually walks backward, as if arrogant enough to believe that nothing will trip him up. "When I come back in here, I'll be coming straight for you. Be prepared."

Just like that, he walks out of The Box.

I think I may need another drink.

13

ANDRE

I'm going to fucking regret this.

Zoe Mackenzie has been a thorn in my side for two years. She was a thorn when she was my PR agent back in Detroit; she was a thorn when she wasn't even *in* my life, and all I had was the memory of her to haunt me every night. And now that she's back in it? Now that we've come full circle, like the last year of radio silence never even happened?

She's driving me crazy.

Every last rational thought in my brain is telling me to walk out of the bar. To go home and get my ass to bed before I do something I'll regret.

But the irrational part of me, the part of me that doesn't care about professionalism or emotional boundaries wants to storm back into the bar and prove that Marshall-fucking-Hunt doesn't have what it takes to satisfy her.

I do—*only* I do.

And just like that night a year ago when I kissed her like it was the last thing I'd ever do, I'm tempted to pull a repeat and do it all over again. That night a year ago, it sure felt like my life depended on her kiss, on *her*.

And right now . . .

I drop my forehead against the door that leads into the exclusive area of The Box, and inhale sharply through my nose. I shove aside the ridiculous slice of disappointment that she doesn't want *me*. She's smart on that score. Damn smart. Unlike me, the King of Bad Decisions, she's making a good one by choosing a guy who isn't running from his own shadow. Zoe will always be better off without me—not that she ever realized that fact.

She's the woman who'll bring you Advil when you're hungover. The kind of woman willing to shoot the shit over a game of pool. The kind of woman who'll make you forget your own name.

The kind of woman who doesn't need to be dragged down by excess emotional baggage like mine.

Curling one hand into a fist, I push away from the door. She wants me to be nice? She wants me to be like Marshall-goddamn-Hunt?

Done.

My fingers grasp the doorknob and yank it open. I force myself to slow my gait as I enter the backroom where my teammates are waiting for me to make a damn fool out of myself. Any other day, and I'd give that to them—but not tonight, not when the woman I've been dreaming about for a week straight wants me to be someone else.

"Here he is, ladies and gents," Jackson, a left wing, hollers from the bar, "King Sin Bin!"

The nickname rubs raw. While enforcers in the league are certainly a dying breed, the stigma hasn't quite faded. Goon. Meathead. Impulsive. Only the impulsive bit rings true for me, and it's something I've worked on over the years. *Think before you drop gloves. Think before you smash a guy into the boards.* For the most part, I'm leashed tight on the ice, only breaking into a fight when the situation calls for it.

Still doesn't matter—guys see me coming for them and they immediately turn tail. My reputation for having a quick temper and even quicker fists precedes me.

My mouth twists. If they think that I'm terrifying, then they don't know shit.

But Zoe isn't scared of me. Against all odds, the dark-haired, dark-eyed girl from Detroit chooses to push me instead. She never stops; she never quits. It's what drew me to her before, and it's sure as hell what attracts me to her still.

One taste will be enough.

Yeah, right. When it comes to Zoe Mackenzie, I'm running myself in circles trying to keep to the plan, to stay out of her lane.

I zero-in on her seated at the bar. As usual, she's decked out in a form-fitting skirt and a top that makes her look like she's got bigger breasts than she does. Her legs are crossed demurely at the knees.

She looks pristine, despite her tipsiness. Pristine and oh-so-innocent.

The innocence is a lie.

She lifts a brow, as though daring me to come forward.

The lanes blur, becoming one.

Just one taste.

I school my features, force a casual smile to my face as I saunter toward her.

"This stool is taken," she tells me when I step up next to her at the bar. My eyes narrow on her. Doesn't she realize she's playing a dangerous game?

My foot hooks the wooden rung, and I tug it away from the bar anyway. "Is that so?" I ask, voice low, only for her. "Girl's night?"

Her gaze darts to Duke's girl and then flits back to my face. "Yes."

"I'm sure they won't mind if I steal their pretty friend for a few, eh?" Without giving her time to argue, I take a seat. My elbow rests on the bar, my hand hesitating dangerously close to the curve of her breasts.

She sucks in her bottom lip, and I feel that one breath all the way down to my cock.

"Celebrating anything tonight?" I ask. "A birthday or a promotion?" My thumb brushes the fabric of her shirt. "Maybe an . . . engagement?"

For a second, so brief I can't be sure it happened, she presses into my touch. She's definitely wearing a padded bra —not that I give a shit. Back in Detroit, I'd never had the chance to see her fully naked. Not the top half of her, anyway. And since I've always been a bit of a breast man . . . it's my turn to suck in a deep breath.

What would she do if I leaned in and kissed her? Same as the other day in the elevator, probably—I deserved that rejection, even though I hadn't meant to insult her.

But then she arches away, her attention skirting past me to my caveman teammates who are watching us.

She leans in, crooking her finger. Her breath is hot on my ear when she hisses, "Don't do that."

"Do what?"

"You *know* what."

Do I? Maybe I'm totally reading her wrong. In the elevator, before she jumped away, she'd wanted my touch. I know it. Maybe it's the fact that we're in front of the Blades—understandable, as they're a bunch of assholes and I *am* her client. But they're all two sheets to the wind right now, and I doubt they'll even remember this little episode.

Another thought hits me, and this one packs quite the punch. Not in a good way. "Am I not acting enough like a gentleman for you, Zoe?" The words come out huskier than I intend them to. "Not living up to the charming hype of *Marshall?*"

She rears back. "You're not even *trying*. You just waltzed over, used your sexy voice—"

I feel a grin pull at my mouth. "I have a sexy voice?"

Zoe promptly ignores me. "This is your problem," she rages, fisting her hands in her lap. "You can't bother to drop the macho act for even five minutes. It's all, *I'm too much of a badass to be vulnerable* or *emotions are overrated*. Newsflash, Mr. Beaumont, not everyone is an emotional ice block like *you* are."

I freeze—just like the ice she accuses me of being.

My vision blurs. Images I don't want to see. Memories I don't want to recall.

No one realizes that I've been living in a self-made penalty box for years now. Since Hannah walked out on me. Since I gave in to the temptation that was, and still is, Zoe Mackenzie.

And when I take a desperate, steadying breath, I act strictly upon an impulse formed by anger.

I wrap a strong hand around the back of her neck, gently tugging her close, until our lips are nearly touching. Her eyes are wide and blinking rapidly, and I take advantage of her momentary silence by adjusting my grip, cupping her face, gently caressing her cheek with the pad of my thumb.

"Is this why you didn't want me to kiss you the other day?" I murmur softly, skimming my gaze over her features. "Because I haven't spilled all of my secrets to you?" I take her chin, shifting it up so that I can press my lips to her neck. She shudders under my touch. "Do you want me to tell you my fears and my worries? Rip open my wounds so that you can take pride in healing them, in healing the big, bad Andre Beaumont?" I release her chin. Drop my fingers to her collarbone, where I peel her shirt away from her skin and dust another kiss to her neck. "Is that what you want, honey? What you've *always* wanted?"

"*Yes*," she breathes out, her eyes squeezed shut, "yes."

I don't think she even realizes what she's said, and, with an acute pang, I know that I've taken this too far. The jeering from my teammates has quieted to crickets. My heart thunders in my chest, an identical twin to Zoe's pulse leaping to life beneath my palm.

The part of me that's been craving her presence, her spirit, *her,* for a year, demands that I apologize for my asshole behavior. For exposing her like this in front of strangers or even potential future clients.

Fuck, fuck, fuck.

I pull back at the same time her pretty, dark eyes peel open. There's no hiding the embarrassment swirling in their depths, nor the hatred.

I am the worst kind of asshole.

Fuck.

"Zoe—"

"Don't touch me." Her voice is a quiet crack in the otherwise quiet bar. "D-don't—" Her lids slam shut, her chin turning away. "I have to go. I have to go right now."

I reach for her purse off the bar. "I'll drive you."

She gives a sharp shake of her head. "I don't . . . I don't want to go anywhere with you, y-you *bastard.*"

Little does she know that's a more accurate term for me than she could have ever chosen. Bastard. Asshole. Cold. I've heard it all. To be balls to the wall honest, the words don't bother me when it comes from the general public. But falling from her lips . . . it's a sharp knife to an already festering wound.

Tears bloom, turning her eyes bloodshot red. Another stab—this one right to the heart. "Let me drive you, Zoe. We can sit in silence. We don't have to say a single word. Just let me take you home."

Let me atone for my sins.

Whether it's the fact that we're currently the center of attention or something else, she agrees with a short, barely-there nod. It's all I need to rise from the stool and to quickly pay our tab.

In silence, we walk out of The Box side by side. None of my teammates reach out to fist bump me good-bye, and not a single soul gives even a short wave. They know I've gone too far this time. Hell, *I* know I've gone too far this time.

I meant what I said though—if she wants to sit in silence during the drive to her parent's house, that's what we'll do.

She steals in front of me as we exit the dark hallway that leads into the main area of The Box. But instead of moving toward the front door, she swivels unexpectedly and struts straight over to the bar.

I catch up to her as she two-finger salutes the bartender and orders a vodka and tonic.

"What are you doing?" My voice is low, because I have no interest in attracting the attention of the bar's patrons. While The Box caters to Blades players all day and every day in the back of the establishment, this general area of the bar is not our scene.

There are puck bunnies galore, all hoping for the chance to slip into the rear and into one of our beds.

"Zoe."

Dark eyes snap in my direction. "What does it look like I'm doing, Mr. Beaumont?"

On any other day, I'm a diehard fan of her sass. Today it worries me. "It looks like you're drinking to forget something."

She touches her finger to her nose, as though indicating *you got it*. "You'd be correct on that."

I shouldn't ask. Doesn't mean I don't, though. "What are you trying to forget?"

Her gaze leisurely eats me up. She pauses at my mouth,

and I'd be lying if I said that one look doesn't turn me on in five different ways. I can still recall her taste as vividly as though I were kissing her now. And I can sure as hell remember what it felt like with her legs wrapped around my waist and her nails biting into my back.

I lost myself in her that night. Drowned my emotions and the memories and all of the fear into the feeling of her body moving against mine.

Zoe's gaze leaves me completely. As she plucks her tumbler of vodka off the bar, she murmurs, "You, Andre. I'm trying to forget *you*."

My stomach lurches.

This woman—she's the only one who can wreck me. One reason of the many that I've stayed away from her for so long. My life in the last year and a half has been nothing but turmoil, and I don't need more.

But neither does she need my drama.

"Let me take you home, Zo." I pull the tumbler from her hand, returning it to the bar, far out of her reach. "You're going to regret drinking so much in the morning."

Her dark eyes are pure fire when they touch on me. "You don't have a say on what I do with my life."

"I know."

"If I want to do five more shots, I can do that, too."

I nod slowly. "I know."

She heaves a sigh. "I don't *really* want to do five more shots, though."

This time, I stay quiet, giving her time for the anger to dissipate.

Our stand-off feels like it lasts minutes, but probably only exists in actual seconds. She rises from the stool, gathering her things, and without a backward glance to see if I'll follow, stalks out of the bar.

But I do follow.

I'm hot on her heels, wishing that I could notice anything besides the tight curve of her backside in her slim skirt. Does she recall the way I removed her skirt a year ago, so slowly that by the time the material hit the floor, she was begging for me to take her?

I do.

I remember every last bit of that night.

"Where did you park again?" she asks, pausing just outside of The Box's front door.

"You don't remember?"

She bites down on her lower lip in consternation. "I'm drunk, Andre."

Enough said.

Clasping her elbow, I steer her the opposite way, to where I parked two blocks over. In her defense, she doesn't wobble on her heels. The street is dark, thanks to a lack of working streetlights, and the farther we walk from The Box, the sounds of life become muted, too.

By the time we make it to the car, there's only the sounds of her heels clipping against the cement and the thundering of my heart in my chest.

"I can get it myself," she snips, when I try to open the passenger's side door for her. She wrestles her way into my car, plopping down with little grace, so that the hem of her skirt lifts up her slim thighs.

I swear, this woman was put on this earth to tempt me.

"No problem," I mutter, closing the door after her, and then getting in on the driver's side.

I'd like to say that we launch into conversation after that. That we somehow find ourselves as we were before we kissed, before I knew that her body was my version of heaven.

Not the case.

Instead, we spend the next ten minutes in silence on the

way to her house in Somerville. I palm the wheel, and pull into her driveway. There aren't any lights on in the house.

"I'm sorry."

In the shadows of my car, I see her head whip around to me. "What?"

I shift uncomfortably in my seat. Apologizing has never been my "thing."

"I'm sorry," I reiterate, my fingers tightening on the steering wheel. "For what I did back at The Box . . . for embarrassing you."

"Andre, want to know something?" She doesn't wait for me to answer, just plows forward. "Your little stunt in front of your teammates is *nothing* compared to what I went through last year."

I know.

The words almost leave me, but I damn well know that they're inadequate. I have no excuses for leaving her out in the cold the way I did in Detroit. My only defense—and it's a weak one at that—is that I was so consumed by what was going on in *my* life that there was no room to consider everyone else.

More than that, though, was the underlying realization that I was no good for Zoe Mackenzie. Not then and certainly not now.

But you want her.

Always. I've always wanted her.

And that makes me a shitty person.

Her echoing laugh is caustic. "Still nothing to say to that?" She chuffs harshly. "Of course you don't. King Sin Bin would *never* lower himself to talk about emo—"

Fuck that.

"You really want to talk about this *right now*, Zoe?"

"You're never going to talk about it otherwise," she snaps

in return. "Maybe if you think I'm too drunk to remember, you'll finally open up for once."

Too drunk to remember . . . ?

That sentence right there tells me that she isn't as wasted as she'd like me to believe. Which is fine. If she wants to do this right now, then we will. I twist the keys out of the ignition, then throw them up onto the dashboard. The interior of the car plunges into darkness. Her sharp intake of breath reaffirms what I already know: we need the shadows, the darkness.

In the sunlight, we risk too much of ourselves.

"I couldn't stay, Zo."

She doesn't react to the shortened form of her name. "No," she says stiffly, "you *wouldn't* stay. We both know that you got exactly what you wanted from me. As soon as you got it, as soon as it blew up in your face, you dipped out."

As much as it hurts to know she thinks that, I'm firmly aware of the fact that I never gave her a reason to believe otherwise. "It wasn't just sex between us, Zoe. We were friends."

"Friends don't have sex, Andre, and they certainly don't leave the moment things get rough."

Rough didn't even begin to explain it. My life had been torn at the seams. Zoe had been the balm I needed, the balm I craved. But sex had complicated that—and my life had already been too complicated.

"You're right," I tell her, because it's true. "I'm not going to defend myself and tell you lies." I lower my voice. "I shouldn't have left you to deal with everything alone. You were my friend and I let you down."

The passenger's seat squeaks as though she's dropped down. "Can you tell me why . . . " She swallows, then clears her throat. "There was one day . . . you were home, your car was outside, after everything. I came by to see you, and you didn't answer when I rang the doorbell. You just let me stand out there like an idiot. Why?"

Because I was too busy having my heart ripped out.

I must hesitate too long because she gives a deep sigh that speaks to her disappointment. "Never mind. Just . . . never mind."

Her hand goes to the door to open it, and panic hits me like a freight train. The thought of her leaving steals my breath. "I can't—" I shake my head, needing the words and yet finding none. "If I could tell you, I would, Zoe. I would. But it isn't . . . Something happened and I can't relive it. I don't *want* to relive it."

"Even if it meant we could get back to where we were? Even if it meant that I no longer looked at you like a cold-hearted asshole?"

Knowing that she feels that way about me makes me feel lower than scum. I rub my chest, hoping to ease the growing ache. "I'm sorry, Zo," I tell her softly, "I just . . . can't."

She doesn't respond.

Instead she cranks open the door, and clambers out, her fingers going to her skirt to hold it in place.

She leaves me, alone.

I laugh, low and miserably.

Because the irony is a killer. The man who everyone thinks is a stone-faced emotional ice block . . . isn't. I lower the window, seeking the cool air to hit my face. I'm holding onto a thread here, and I have the sickening feeling that I just cut loose my last hope for happiness.

14

ZOE

SIXTEEN DAYS LEFT

*Y*ou know what I think?

Fuck Andre Beaumont.

Yup, I said it. I'm living the no-regret lifestyle over here, and thus far, it's utterly fantastic. In the three days since I've seen Mr. Sin Bin himself, I've taken out a new meaning on life.

No more living in the past.

No more waiting, hoping, that Andre will one day open his eyes and realize that he ruined a perfectly good friendship (or something more) with kissing me like he never wanted to stop.

No more hoping that we'll ever get back to the place that we were.

Nope, I'm living life to the fullest for *myself*, and it feels great. Magnificent, actually.

I've had dinner with Charlie, helped my dad out at Vittoria (willingly), and taken Tia to the mall to stroll around and have some much-needed girl-time. Hell, I even dragged Shelby along to look at apartments in the area, and I think I may have found the perfect one.

Is it as large as my old condo in Detroit? No. Does it have nice features like marble kitchen tops or stainless-steel appliances? Negative.

Do I care?

Not one bit.

After work tonight, I'll be putting in my "offer." To get on Tia's good side, since I had originally agreed to stay at the home-front with her, I promise sleepovers for her and her girlfriends every weekend for the next three months.

I don't think I've been so happy in a long time.

And that in itself feels . . . amazing.

"Hey, Zoe?"

I glance up at Gwen, who is hovering in the doorway to my office. Since the game the other night, she's taken to popping up here and there to chat. Never about work-related stuff, though. Instead, it seems she's found a "friend" in me, which is both nice and also terrifying at the same time.

Gwen is, after all, a terrifying woman.

I hastily click out of the listing for the apartment on my desktop, thankful that she can't see the computer screen from where she stands. "Hey, Gwen. Everything okay?"

Her usual confident composure slips as she sways side to side on her heels. "Mr. Collins would like to see you for a moment."

My heart drops.

Oh, God, I'm about to be fired.

Does he know that I've been apartment hunting on Craigslist during my lunch breaks? *Idiot.*

With that thought in mind, I shut down the desktop completely. "Sure," I squeak, "yeah, absolutely." I throw a notebook and pen into my bag, hooking the strap over my shoulder. "Any idea what it's about?"

Gwen averts her gaze, and then I know.

I'm doomed.

Done for.

Fired.

Good-bye not-so-beautiful apartment that isn't even mine yet.

Good-bye excitement about life.

Am I being melodramatic? Yes, yes, I am.

With lead for feet, I follow Gwen down the bright hallway to Walter Collins's office at the opposite end. She gives a quick one-two knock, and then slips the door open.

"You have her?" Mr. Collins calls out from the interior of his office.

I suck in a deep breath and pretend that I'm not about to pass out.

Gwen and I quietly enter the office, and it's with a jolt of shock that I realize Andre is already seated across from my boss.

Déjà vu, but reversed.

His dark head twists as he turns to look at me, and his equally as dark eyes pin me in place. I wish I could read the emotion swirling there. Wish I could do more than just stand here, my feet cemented to the floor, my hands slick with sudden nerves.

"Come on in, come on in," Mr. Collins says, waving Gwen and I in. "Pull up two chairs."

Before I have the chance to do just that, Andre jumps up. "I've got it," he says, voice low, "Zoe, take mine."

My gaze cuts to Walter, who is watching me like a hawk. He thinks he knows what's up, that Andre and I are knocking boots again. Ha! Little does he know that he couldn't be further from the truth.

Andre's biceps flex under his T-shirt as he deposits two chairs, one on either side of his original one. "Take whichever one you want."

Why is he being so nice?

139

Maybe it's wrong for that to be my first thought, but after our last confrontation, this . . . cordial version of Andre Beaumont has me raising my hackles and wondering what he has planned up his sleeve.

"Sit down everyone."

At Mr. Collins's no-nonsense tone, both Gwen and I drop into the nearest chairs, leaving the NHL's sexiest bad boy to practically clamber over my left armrest to retake his seat.

Then, we're all sitting, waiting, like naughty school children who have been caught in the wrong.

"All right." Walter snaps his binder shut and touches his computer mouse to bring the desktop to life. "We need to have a discussion."

God help us all.

My fingers twitch on the armrest, just as Andre shifts his weight, leaning close to me. His elbow brushes my hand, and I *so* wish that I didn't feel that immediate connection throughout my body.

"What I think Mr. Collins is trying to say is . . . " At Walter's sharp glance, Gwen falls silent.

Then, he looks at me. Yeah, that warm tingly feeling from when Andre accidentally touched me? Gone. Nonexistent. If anything, I'm feeling a sudden chill.

"Miss Mackenzie," Mr. Collins murmurs, "when you first began, you assured me that you had everything under control. That fixing up a celebrity's failing image was something you've done on the regular."

"Yes," I answer slowly, "I did say that."

As much as I want to defend myself, the situation calls for me to keep quiet and listen. Men like Walter Collins get off on their power trips—there's no way that saying anything at this point will do me any favors.

"If that's the case, then I would like for you to look at something and let me know why you thought this would be even *reasonably* acceptable for our client." With a few clicks of the mouse, he pulls up a file. With stiff motions, he flicks the volume up on a miniature stereo, clicks on the mouse another time, and then angles the desktop so that we can very clearly see what's going on.

Music blares from the speakers before the video starts to roll.

There's no mistaking the upbeat voice of Justin Bieber. Andre's knee lurches into mine, and at first, I think it might have been an accident, but . . . no. It's not. I inch my leg away, and he spreads his right leg over, so his right thigh is pressed to my leg. The cat and mouse game ensues, but dies a quick death when the otherwise black screen cuts to its first shot.

Oh. My. God.

"Motherfu—"

With a kick of *my* foot against his, I quickly shut Andre up.

Gwen giggles hysterically on the opposite end of our lineup, and I don't even know what to say aside from the fact that Andre *seriously* makes a speedo look good. Damn.

The B-roll of Andre standing about in practically his birthday suit pans to an image of him causing hell on the ice. His gloved fists clench the hockey stick, before he drops it to the ice. Then it's him against his opponent as they grapple for a hold of each other's jerseys. His helmet goes flying, and a trickle of blood starts at the corner of his mouth. But his eyes . . . his eyes are as black as the nighttime sky as he pummels the other player with his fists.

"I've been playing hockey since I was four," Andre says in the clip's voiceover. *"My dad handed me a stick, told me to get into the net. Man, I sucked there. Never found my stride until I was allowed to fly down the rink."*

The camera cuts back to him wearing nothing but the speedo. This time, however, he's holding a hockey stick behind his head, clamped against the back of his neck. The posture elongates his sturdy torso, ripples his abs, and clenches his thighs.

His thighs.

I gulp at the massive bulge at the *apex* of those thighs.

I need air. Maybe some water. Maybe a new set of panties.

Please don't judge me.

The video goes on for at least another minute—more scenes from the ice, more close-ups of Andre wearing next to nothing as he swaggers around *Fame's* studio. All the while, the magazine's editor coaxes information out of him.

"First time I kissed a girl?" He chuckles low, and weird as it is that he's sitting beside me, I'm rooted to my chair, watching him on the small screen as his lips quirk up into a devilish smile. *"Kindergarten. I traded her a packet of Skittles for a kiss. Pretty sure I got the better end of the bargain, but she didn't complain."*

"Crazy thing I wished I'd never done?" His gaze casts down, a big hand coming up to rub his bare chest. *"Nipple rings. Had them done when I was reckless and nineteen. I thought they'd be a chick magnet. Unfortunately, I got a bad infection and had to take them out before anyone had the chance to appreciate them."*

"A time when a woman broke my heart? I . . . " His Adam's apple bobs down his thick neck. *"That one is too personal. I hope you understand."*

The idea of a woman breaking Andre's heart makes *me* feel a little sick. I swallow against the lump in my throat. I guess that I didn't . . . Well, I guess I didn't think he'd ever allow a woman close enough to break his heart.

The video—and Justin Bieber—ends in acute silence.

I wonder how obvious it would be if I launched myself out the window behind Mr. Collins.

"Did you approve of this video, Miss Mackenzie?" Mr. Collins asks, breaking the quiet.

The window is looking better with every second that passes. "To be fair," I start awkwardly, "*Fame's* editor was adamant that I remain in the waiting room."

Which now makes sense.

At the time, I'd only been too happy to get away from Andre after our little elevator incident. Sitting in a separate room which overlooked Manhattan's skyline with a cup of tea in hand had been just the slice of reprieve I'd needed.

"You're his *publicist*," Mr. Collins seethes. "Your entire job is to make sure he doesn't come off in a bad light."

I cringe. "I wouldn't say that Mr. Beaumont looks *bad* in that video." No, if anything, he looked way too good. Delicious, even. Trust me when I say that the entire female population would say he looks bad in the best way possible. Since I can't say that, I settle for, "And I was under the impression that everything was well-received by Mr. Beaumont, otherwise he would have said something."

Mr. Collins's accusing gaze swings to Andre.

Andre, mind you, only shrugs his big shoulders. "The speedo was tighter than I liked, but other than that, it was fine."

"See?" I murmur. "Everything was fine. *Fame's* team did a fantastic—"

"Mr. Beaumont, I hope you won't take offense to this, but you looked ridiculous."

My mouth falls open. "Now, wait a second, Mr. Collins. Andre *opened* up in that interview. He—"

Andre's hand lands on my own, and I'm so shocked by the sudden contact that I grow quiet. His dark eyes roam my face, searching, seeking something I don't understand, before he glances away. His hand, however, remains on mine. Oh, boy.

"Mr. Collins," he says stiffly, "I get what you're trying to say. Honestly, I agree with you. I put up a hell of a fight because I *didn't* want to do something with *Fame.* Stripping down to a speedo that can barely hold my junk isn't my idea of a good time. With that said, I knew exactly what Miss Mackenzie aimed to do when that interview was scheduled."

My boss's eyes narrow. "And what, exactly, is that?"

"To strip down my walls and to make me look vulnerable to the public. Something that I don't do." He pauses, and his thumb traces the back of my hand. "That's what Miss Mackenzie wanted with this interview. Is it fucking ridiculous? Absolutely. Do I want the world to see me in a bathing suit that barely fit? No. But this *openness* is what my career needs."

I don't know what to say.

I've never . . . I press my free hand to my lower belly. Right now, it feels like old times. All those times Andre had my back. All those times I had his. Desperately, I want to flip my palm over and squeeze his hand in return. To show him that I'm *here*. Hell, I've been here.

Maybe this is what we needed to come back together.

Mr. Walter-effing-Collins.

Who knew that he would be the tie to unite us?

15

ANDRE

THIRTEEN DAYS LEFT

*I*f there's one thing that I hate in life, it's lifting weights—even if I'm doing so in my personal gym in my own house.

Give me a running track any day of the week. Hell, drop me in the godforsaken Berkshires out in western Massachusetts, and I'll be happier than I am while pumping iron.

It's the repetitive motion that kills me. The repetitive breathing techniques and the repetitive number of reps. It's the fact that I'm stuck in one singular spot, driving myself up a wall since my thoughts can never be silenced.

And right now? Yeah, my thoughts aren't so sweet.

They aren't so holy.

Having Zoe Mackenzie back in my life is certifiably making me insane.

The heavy iron dips to the right as my thoughts simultaneously go off-kilter, and I'm forced to realign my balance or end up with another broken nose. Not that it would do all that much damage, since the damn thing has been pummeled by gloved fists and Plexiglas boards for the last nine years of my life.

Shoulder blades clenching against the cushioned bench, my muscles tighten into balled coils as I inhale and allow the bar to skim my chest.

Stop thinking about Zoe.

Exhale.

Stop thinking about her naked and riding you.

Inhale.

Stop thinking about her naked and not *riding you.*

Exhale.

My steadied breathing breaks its rhythm, and I shove the iron up and onto its slot. Sweat gathers on my skin, like droplets of verified success for a job well done. Ironic, because for the last year of my life, nothing has gone as planned.

And, from the looks of things, shit isn't going to turn around anytime soon.

I ignore the familiar pain that settles in my chest with a brisk rub of my palm. Nothing I'm not used to, but since the pain is emotional and not physical, it's not like a couple trips to physical therapy can axe the feeling and put my world back to rights.

Honestly, I don't even think I know what "right" feels like any longer.

Then again, "right" was sticking up for Zoe the other day in front of Walter Collins. "Right" was touching her hand and hearing her sigh of relief. "Right" was having her back, and being the support she needs.

As a friend.

Whatever recent thoughts I've been having of us together —crazy, insane thoughts—need to be cut loose. I was right to call the "no sex" rule between us at the start of the month, but I should have added another—no wondering what it might be like to be with Zoe Mackenzie. Full-time. Unprofessionally.

Coworkers. Friends, at the most. That's all.

Throwing my legs over the side of the bench, I straighten into a seated position.

I need protein, a shower, and a beer—not necessarily in that order.

With slow, tempered movements, I come off the bench and stretch my beaten limbs. *Pop! Pop!* My shoulders creak, the tendons snapping back into position like an elastic band that's seen better days.

Which is a fair assessment of my body's status quo.

At thirty, I feel more like I'm sixty on any given day. Snagging my discarded T-shirt from the floor, I shrug it on over my head and head down the hallway of my two-story house. I don't own the place, preferring instead to rent it out. When my career has been as unstable as it has been for the last two years, there's no reason to shore up with a mortgage.

My feet pad down the carpeted steps, the echoing *pop! pops!* alerting me to the fact that, like my shoulders, my knees are hating life too right about now.

One more season.

After that, I'll take my ass down to the Caribbean and set up shop on a white-beached island, drinking Jose Cuervo until I can obliterate my thoughts for good.

I'm busy picturing my life in Turks and Caicos when my doorbell rings. Feet slowing to a stop, I turn and head for the door instead. I had no plans for company—not that I usually do. The night at The Box with Zoe was an anomaly.

My teammates tend to leave me be, unless I voluntarily place myself in their path. Once a week, I strap on my big boy pants and head down to The Box. It's my three hours of bonding time, usually spent drinking one too many whiskeys and cokes, and pretending that I'm fine.

That everything is fine.

But none of the guys ever come to my house. To be

honest, I'm not even sure they know where I live—unless they've turned Chatty Kathy with one of the white shirts and asked for my personal records.

My hand clasps the doorknob, and with a single tug, I blink against the startling sunlight.

Lust hits me straight in the gut.

Goddammit.

My eyes focus on Zoe's face, and it takes everything in me to keep my expression neutral. Blank. *Don't let her see how much you want her here.* If I scare her a little bit, that's probably for the best. In a voice more husky than I intended, I say, "What are you doing here?"

Her heart-shaped face tips up in defiance. It's so like her, to go down arms swinging until she's already six feet under. "Can't I come to say hello?" she says, sounding sweet and demure and everything else that I know she isn't.

Zoe is as tough as I am, and just as sharp-tongued. Sure, she might play the innocent girl next door, but I've seen her in action. I've seen her work a crowd to get what she wants— I've experienced her working *me*. And while my cock might like to see her working me for another round, I know that sex isn't the reason why she's here.

Not even after the way I stood up for her to her boss. The way he'd accused her of failing at her job had lit a fire inside of me. Zoe works harder than anyone I know—hell, since she's taken me on as a client, she hasn't *stopped* working.

My hand lands on the doorframe, blocking her entry into my house. "You don't say *hello*, Zoe," I say, in reference to her greeting. "The last time you popped up unannounced we were in Detroit."

Her long black hair, which is tied back in one of those female hair clips, slips over her shoulder when she tilts her head. "I have some news."

"Yeah?" I murmur, my fingers digging into the wooden

framework. "Have you decided that I'm a lost cause? I hear another sponsor pulled out."

It sucks, especially since *Fame's* video has hit the national media circuit. While everyone fans over and points out my crotch in the speedo, there are less people commenting on the actual interview. On my attempt to be more personable, to open up for once. If Zoe sees the disappointment in my expression, she doesn't mention it. Instead, her lips tip up in a smile that I don't quite trust. "You did lose another one this morning, but I have a plan."

Zoe and "plans" go about as well together as kindling and fire. Straight up, her plans are more likely to combust than to put out the already blazing flames.

I comb my fingers through my hair, and I tug at the strands in frustration. "Not another feature piece with *Fame*, right? My masculinity can take only so much blush, foundation, and concealer."

"Don't forget the speedo."

Laughter climbs my throat. "Pretty sure there's a certain part of me that will never forget that horror."

Her cheeks bloom with a pretty blush, and I'm not surprised at all when she changes the topic slightly. "I'm surprised you even know what concealer is."

I don't, not really, but I know enough that it's supposed to hide the dark circles under your eyes. I figure I'm a lost cause on that front, but only because sleep eludes me on a near-nightly basis.

"Is this where I pretend I have no idea what you're talking about to preserve my masculinity?" I say, leaning my shoulder against the frame to stare down at her. "I'd offer to prove it, but I'm not up for rejection today."

Her cheeks turn even more pink, and satisfaction flares through me. It never fails—teasing Zoe is the highlight of my day.

Shifting side to side on her mile-high stilettos, she purses her lips. "Can we be professional for a moment?"

I lift a brow, knowing it'll drive her crazy. "I'm professional, Zoe."

"When it suits you."

"Is there any other way?"

"You could, you know, try being pleasant for once."

I can't help it—she's so buttoned up, so Miss High-and-Mighty, despite the fact that her childhood was anything but. And, Jesus, but her snippy attitude turns me on as much now as it did when we first met two years ago.

Maybe that's the only reason that I shift my weight and let my hands rest on the top of the doorframe. I see her hollowed out breath the moment that I feel my T-shirt rise above the waistband of my shorts. "How am I not being polite? I didn't slam the door in your face. We're having a perfectly nice conversation. Am I supposed to start whipping puppies out of thin air next, or what?"

She steps near, edging closer, until she's right in front of me. And then, because Zoe Mackenzie is nothing if not an unbreakable hard-ass, her fingers find the hem of my shirt and tug down. "You're trying to distract me, Andre. I know your game. But it's not going to work. Let me in the house."

The feminine scent of citrus accosts my nose, and it's so strong and so fresh, that I'm tempted to throw caution to the wind and wrap my arms around her in a hug. My fingers dig into the frame, and I fix my gaze on her face. "You gonna say the magic word?"

"Abracadabra," she says dryly, her fingers still tangled in the cotton of my shirt. "Open sesame."

I let go of the frame with one hand, then close my fingers over hers. "Those weren't the magical words I was talking about."

"Please."

"As much as I like to hear you say that word, Zoe, that's not it either." She jolts when I use my hold on her to tug her close, closer than she expected, until her willowy curves press against my chest. The hitch of her breath rings like victory in my ears. "How 'bout we try this one more time, eh? Repeat after me."

"I'm not repeating anything," she mutters, the words muffled thanks to the fact that she's speaking into my clavicle.

"Sure you will." My fingers release hers. "Now, repeat after me—Andre, you are a god among men."

Her laugh is just as contagious as I remember it. "There's no way I'm saying that."

"Don't make me encourage you. I just worked out and I'm sweaty."

"Now *there's* a threat," she says, still laughing. Her dark eyes fix on my chest, and the close scrutiny makes me uncomfortable. I'm good with everything as long as it remains surface-level. No drudging up the past. No deep talks about the future.

But then Zoe leans in close, and her free hand lands on my chest, just over my heart. Maybe it's accidental, but her nail scrapes across my pectoral muscle, and desire shoots straight to my groin. Her lips find my right ear, and she whispers, "You're right, Andre. You are such a god among men. Which is why I need you to do exactly as I say if you don't want to end up a mere mortal like the rest of us."

Then, she firmly plants her hand on my chest and pushes her way into my house.

ZOE

*M*y heart hammers in my chest as I step inside Andre's home.

I hate the way he can push me to my limits within just five minutes of being in his presence. I hate the way he can turn my dislike for him into something that feels a lot more like lust. Want.

More.

All right, I'll be honest—I want more of Andre, more of the guy who stuck up for me in front of Walter Collins, more of the guy who makes me feel giddy with laughter. But he's not willing to open up, so wanting anything more really doesn't do much for me.

My gaze latches onto a photograph on an entryway table, and the sound of my stilettos beating into the marble floor quiets as I roll to a stop. Bright blue eyes blink back at me from within the frame. The kid is maybe two years old, more toddler than anything else, with a bright smile and messy brown hair.

"Your nephew?" I ask Andre over my shoulder. "He's cute."

Andre moves silently toward the table, his hand outreached. His long, tapered fingers pause mere inches from the black frame, before curling into a fist. "Yeah." His arm falls back to his side. "He is."

One quick look at his face tells me that he's uncomfortable with the direction of the conversation. I want to pry, to dig a little deeper into why his mouth has flat-lined, but I doubt I'll get anywhere.

Andre Beaumont is not a talker, something I learned quite well in his car the other night.

With one last glance at the young boy, I twist away and motion to the house's grand entryway. The ceiling is twenty-feet tall, and a wrought-iron spiral staircase winds up to the second floor. A decorative chandelier hangs about four feet above my head. "You sure decided to live in style when you came to Boston, didn't you?"

His house back in Detroit was a lot more modest. A historic Victorian that had seen better days, but it was cozy and sleepy, a perfect place for a man who spent the majority of his year on the road.

"It works for now," Andre tells me. He shows me his back as he heads into the room next door, which turns out to be the kitchen.

To hell with it—I can't help but pry, just a little. "Because this is your last season? And you have no plans to stick around?"

The look he gives me would probably cower a lesser person, but I know Andre, both as a person as well as in the biblical sense. So, I stand my ground and wait him out. He'll give in. He always does.

With a sigh, he runs his fingers through his messy, black hair. "You're annoying as all hell sometimes, you know that?"

I'll take that as a compliment, thank you very much. Out loud, I say, "Someone sounds cranky this morning."

His mouth pulls down. "I just worked out."

Against my better judgment, I let myself drink in his appearance. He wasn't lying when he said he was sweaty. His cheeks are still flushed from activity, his T-shirt damp with perspiration. As always, his jaw is unshaven, and I have the absurd urge to walk up to him and run my hand over the stubble. To see if it's as abrasive to the touch as it looks.

"If you only came here to ogle me, Zoe, I would have at least showered for you."

The sound of Andre's voice snaps me out of my (ahem) blatant perusal, and heat warms my cheeks. "That's not—I mean, I'm not ... "

"You are," he returns silkily, "and you did."

I wave my hand at his body, as if that's answer enough. Words, beautiful things that they are, have fled my brain.

Andre's mouth tugs up into a rare grin, and he kicks away from the counter to swagger over to me. And, yes, it's a swagger. Hips slung low, chin dipped down. At the look of intent in his dark eyes, alarm bells spring into magnifying gongs, warning me *to back the hell up and escape*.

I don't have the chance.

Before I can even recognize what's going on, his arm wraps around my waist and pulls me in close. My cheek ends up plastered to his hard-as-a-rock pectoral muscles.

"Oh, my God," I whisper.

His palms settle on my shoulder blades. "Say it with me now, honey—Andre, you are a god among men."

I don't know whether to laugh or to stab him with the closest sharp object. It's a tough decision, made even tougher because the longer that we stand here together, the faster my heart pounds and the *want* spreads throughout my body like an infestation.

An infestation that I doubt will ever be curable.

Confession: I miss him, in more ways than one.

One of his large hands moves south, just enough that I feel his palm skate the ridges of my spine. His other stays firmly planted on my upper back, keeping me tied to him, keeping me from fleeing.

Which is the ironic thing, as Andre Beaumont is the one who's in the habit of running.

Forcing steel into my voice, I say, "Are you done with pulling the macho act?"

His rich laughter rustles the top of my hair. "Not a chance in hell."

I inhale sharply, grappling with the decision to stay in his embrace or to push my way to freedom. Briefly, I let my eyes fall shut. Just for a moment. "You never used to hug me."

The words leave me on a shuddered breath, unintentional, and I know the minute they register in his brain because his chest flinches under my cheek. "It wasn't allowed."

"It's not allowed now either."

He doesn't answer, not right away, and I wonder if I've made a disastrous mistake bringing up our muddled past. Then, so quietly I barely hear him, he says, "You're smart for turning me away the other night, Zo. Trust me on that. We're better off as friends."

The word lands like lead in my belly. "Is that what we are?" I lick my top lip nervously. "Friends?"

His arms tighten around me. "I've been a shitty one."

"You did stick up for me in front of Walter . . . thank you for that."

"That's the thing, Zo, you shouldn't even be saying thank you in the first place. It should be expected that I have your back, always."

I'm struggling to find breath, because even though he's telling me everything I've wanted to hear for months now . . . the words aren't enough. *Because you want more.* So stupid, but yes, I want more. "What if . . . " Trailing off, I swallow past the lump in my throat, my nails digging into his back. "What if I don't—"

"I want to be friends with you again, Zoe. You calling me at two in the morning just to talk, us going for runs, that sort of thing."

Something in his voice doesn't ring quite right. My fingers find his shirt, and I push back just enough so that I can peer up at his rugged face. "Then why bother doing this? Why bother telling me that there's no way we'll have sex again, only for you to try and kiss me the other day? And now this."

"Would you believe me if I said that I have a hard time resisting you?"

"No, I wouldn't. I think you have a hard time resisting temptation, whether it's on or off the ice. No matter what you do, you're always aiming for the sin bin."

At that, the pads of his fingers tighten on my back before he lets me go completely. His expression is unreadable, so it's not much of a surprise when he rolls his big shoulders in a shrug, and says, "You're right. I guess I get a thrill out of the chase."

Do not react.

Do not react.

Do not react.

As much as I want to curl into myself at his words, I force a bright smile onto my face. *Stand strong, girl.* "Makes sense," I tell him.

His dark eyes meet mine, questioning. "Does it?" he asks, his voice low.

No, it doesn't. "Sure."

"Right."

I tear my gaze away from his, and seat myself at his kitchen island. We need to get back on track. Slipping my hot-pink bag from my shoulder, I place it on the table and rifle through the contents. Out comes my laptop, as well as my day planner. I find my hot-pink pen in one of the zippered side compartments.

Andre's brows pull low. "You came prepared."

Prepared for what, though? Prepared to feel desire twine through my limbs? To feel warm and secure and *loved* even when he's telling me that I'm better off without him?

Somehow, I don't think that's what he means.

"We have a lot to talk about," I say instead, opening my laptop and turning it on. "I have a plan."

He takes the seat opposite mine, his big shoulders bunching as he plants his forearms on the kitchen island's counter. "You mentioned that earlier."

Well, isn't he paying attention for once? With a few clicks on my touchpad, I pull up the document I worked on all last night. "How do you feel about kids?" I ask.

When he doesn't answer, I glance up and note his horrified expression. "Feel free to stop cupping your testicles, Beaumont. If I needed a sperm donor, you wouldn't be my first choice."

His frown cracks, just as I intended it to, but the weirded-out expression on his face stays in place. "I'd be anyone's first choice," he says gruffly.

I nod sagely. "Ah, yes, I forgot—you're a god among men." Rolling my eyes, I flip open my day planner to today's date, and then uncap my pen. All right, we're ready for business. "Like I said, I'm not after your little guys. I'm talking about in general. Are you okay with kids? I mean—your sister's little boy is cute."

"Yeah, I'm . . . " He coughs into a closed fist. "I'm good with them."

"Great!" I slide my laptop around, and then use the tip of my pen to tap on the screen. "Right there."

Andre's mouth moves as he reads the words to himself. One second passes, two seconds pass . . . by the time we're nearing ten seconds, I'm squirming in my seat with nervous anticipation. "So? What do you think?"

Dark eyes blink slowly. "You want us to hold a hockey camp?"

Nerves bundle in my throat, and I push them down and away. "It's the sort of event that most teams do," I say, trying my very best not to let my insecurities rise. "You did it with the Red Wings every year. The Boston Bruins do it, too. But the Blades never have, not once since the franchise started."

His teeth momentarily settle over his lower lip, and, boy, I wish that one look wasn't so potent. "This is a big undertaking, Zoe."

"Sure it is—but it's also brilliant. What better way to show the world that you're not completely heartless than by hanging with kids for the afternoon, doing what you do best?"

"Zoe, what I do best is an adults-only party."

My mouth opens, and I go so far as to lift a finger, only to realize that I have nothing to say to that, except for, "Get your mind out of the gutter."

"I'm just being honest."

"Stop being honest, then."

The corners of Andre's eyes crease when he flashes a smile. "I think you might be the only woman who has ever said that to me."

"Glad to be the first," I reply, before tapping my pen against the laptop screen again. "Really, though, if you think about it, this is great. We'll get the Blades together—the whole team—and invite the media. Instead of barking at them—"

"I don't bark."

"Okay, instead of *growling* at them, you'll have a nice,

polite conversation, just like you did at *Fame*. Maybe we can get the local news station out there, too. Get the whole thing catered."

"Will this be held at the Garden?" The panicked look has lessened a little, and unless I'm mistaken, he looks . . . intrigued.

Intrigued is good.

Intrigued is better than what I had expected.

In answer to his question, I shake my head. "No, I don't think so. If I have my way, and I'm fully aware that this might not happen, I don't want any of this taking place on Blades turf. It needs to be at a local rink, a place where kids can feel like they're really playing one-on-one with you guys. At the Blades' practice rink or at the Garden . . . it's too formal."

"I agree."

For the first time, I think he does agree. And, even stranger than that, we might even be on the same page for once.

"I know it's not a particularly innovative idea," I say quietly, wishing that I didn't sound so uncertain. "It's been done before plenty of times, and it really isn't re-inventing the wheel, but—"

Andre surprises me by reaching out and placing a hand over mine. "It's a great idea, Zoe."

I blink back my shock. "You really think so?"

"Yeah, I do," he says, nodding solemnly. Removing his hand from mine, he scrubs it over his face and then blows out a big breath. "What grades are you thinking?"

I want to know what he's thinking, what has him suddenly avoiding eye contact.

I slam the door on that want, and say, "Kindergarten to eighth grade. Both girls and boys. I want everyone to have the chance to take part, and I don't want anyone feeling excluded."

"Okay." Andre shifts on the barstool. "Let's invite the high school kids, too. They can run personal practices with some of the vets."

"Like you?"

His gaze meets mine. "You want me to stick around with the younger kids instead?"

Nodding, I say, "I think it'll have the most impact on the public's perception of you."

"Okay."

That's all he says, but after a week of arguing back and forth, and a year of silence before that, it's enough.

ZOE

SEVEN DAYS LEFT

"*T*hanks for agreeing to help me out today, Tia."

My younger sister flashes me a big smile from her seat on the metal bleacher. Her feet are stuffed into hockey skates, and there's a glint in her eye when she says, "Did I tell you that my crush is here?"

"Yeah?" I lift an eyebrow and peek over my shoulder at the group of kids standing around in skates. "Which one is he?"

Tia doesn't have a shy bone in her body, and she thrusts a finger forward, nearly bopping me in the nose with her enthusiastic finger-thrusting. "Kyle. See the boy wearing the beanie hat?"

Every single one of the young teens is wearing a beanie hat. "Uh, yeah." I pretend to consider him, even though I still have no idea which one is her actual crush. "Has he asked you to be his girlfriend yet?"

Tia jams her chin on her fist as she slouches down. "Nah, not yet."

"Maybe he will today?"

"Probably not. He really likes this girl Melissa."

Call me crazy, but I hate the idea of this Kyle kid choosing someone else over my baby sister. Though, to be fair, having an unrequited crush is par for the course of being a teenager.

Andre skirts into my line of vision, and my heart squeezes.

Maybe it's part of adulthood, too.

Over the last few days, we've surprisingly banded together to get the hockey camp ready in such a short amount of time. The Blades' administration thought it was a great idea, and between a small group of us, we managed to pull it together ridiculously fast.

Today, the Blades will be joined by one hundred local school kids, including my sister and her crush, Kyle.

"Zoe?"

I turn to my sister. "Mhmm?"

She squirms under my stare. "I don't want to be mean, but, like, would you go and do . . . something else? It's bad enough that Mom told me that she's coming to watch the second half of the day."

A burst of laughter escapes me. "What, am I ruining your game?"

"Well, I mean"—she glances away at the rink—"it's just that if you're hanging around, Kyle *definitely* won't talk to me. So, maybe you could . . . "

Message received, loud and clear. Planting my hands on my knees, I push to a standing position. Unlike most of the people in the ice rink, I'm not wearing skates. I may have developed a fondness for the game ever since working in Detroit, but I've never developed my ice-legs, if you will.

Nope, I am currently content to stand on something that isn't frozen over.

"I'll check in on you in a little bit," I say, "or is that still too much for you?"

Tia shrugs. "It'll do."

It'll do—so proper.

Tucking my binder under one arm, I climb down over the bleachers until I'm back on the first level.

Today's event is officially scheduled to begin in thirty minutes. After I discussed everything with Andre, it was relatively easy to pull Gwen in on the job. She knows countless media contacts in the area, and within three days, we had a waiting list for people who wanted to bear witness to the Blades' first youth hockey camp. Even Walter managed to drum up some excitement in the last few days leading up to the event. The man hasn't stopped singing my praises at the office, which is a major turn of events after the *Fame*-speedo debacle.

But it wasn't Golden Lights Media or my coworkers who turned out to be the most excited about today—one meeting with Andre, and his teammates were bursting at the seams with anticipation.

Then again, that might be because Andre left them little to no choice.

Either they showed up and made the day a success, or he threatened to take it out on them in practice.

With one glance around the rink, it's safe to say that they all showed up.

As I'm shuffling my binder into my bag, I sense Andre's presence just before I hear his rough voice. "You pulled it off, Zo."

My eyes close at the nickname. "No," I say, as he steps in front of me, "*we* did it. Seriously, I couldn't have pulled this off without you."

His fingers brush mine, and I lift my gaze to his masculine face. Hard jawline. Soft, full lips. High cheekbones. The man is too handsome for his own good. "How about we agree to disagree, then?"

I tilt my head. "Do you even know how?"

"How to what?"

"Agree with someone," I say with a smile. "I didn't think it was in your genetics."

He returns my smile, albeit his is a little rustier. "It's a learned skill set. Thankfully, my teachers have let me out of their evil lair."

Overhead, I hear the speakers kick on as the Blades' coach, Hall, takes to the microphone to introduce the players one by one.

"Shouldn't you go over there?" I ask. "Rejoin your brethren for the day's activities?"

Slowly he shakes his head. "I will, but not yet. First, I need you to do something for me."

Immediately, my brain goes to the direst situation. A kid has landed on a skate. A kid has thrown a puck at somebody's face. A player has accidentally whacked a kid with a stick.

Andre's hand touches my shoulder, then cups the curve of my neck with a deep laugh. "Slow down, Zo. You're already thinking the worst."

"Well, *yeah*," I mutter, "but look where we are. It's a liability waiting to happen, which is why we have insurance in case something happens."

"Nothing is going to happen."

At his confident tone, I shake my head. "You don't *know* that."

"I know it well enough." His hand leaves my neck to tug at my purse's shoulder strap. "I'm going to need you to put this somewhere. Preferably behind the front counter."

My nose scrunches. "Why?"

"It's a surprise."

"I don't do surprises."

"Sure you do." His big body corrals me backward, until my feet are moving on their own accord to the front counter.

Andre lifts my purse and gives it to the kid behind the desk. "Give me a pair of skates for her, would you? Size . . . " He glances down at me with an arched brow. "What size do you think you are?"

Oh, no. No, no, no. "I'm not skating," I say hastily. "You *know* that I don't skate."

His mouth curls into a sexy grin. "Just as I *know* that we've been talking about getting you into a pair for two years now. C'mon, Zo," he murmurs silkily, "don't let me down now."

My heart pounds in my chest. "Today is for the kids," I squeak out pathetically.

That sexy grin of his grows wider. "And it's also for you. You've never let me see you on the ice before."

"That's because I spend most of the time on my butt."

I see the devilry in his eyes just before he murmurs, "There are a lot of ways to make you feel better after."

He's a walking hazard, that's for sure. I eye a pair of black hockey skates, dreading the words that I know are about to trip off my tongue. "What if I say yes?"

"To putting on a pair of skates and getting out there?"

"Yes."

He steps close, so close that I can catch his delicious scent. "I won't let you fall."

My breath hitches. "That's good."

"I promise it'll be better than good."

And with that promise, he brushes his fingers against my lower back and steps away, leaving me wanting yet again.

ANDRE

*I*t's safe to say that Zoe sucks on the ice.

It's also safe to say that I haven't had this much fun in a long time.

"You gotta—" I break off at the sight of her legs wobbling like a newborn fawn's. Pushing off my heels, I skate toward her, wrapping an arm around her slim waist just before she would have gone down. "Zo," I say, glancing down at her beautiful face, "you can do better than this."

Her hands push at my chest. "I told you," she grumbles miserably, "I suck at skating. Just let me stay on solid ground and I'll be okay."

"We *are* standing on solid ground."

"It's frozen water."

"Which is solid, otherwise we'd be swimming up to our calves."

Her mouth purses, but I can tell she's holding in a smile. "Stop being so literal."

"Stop being such a worrywart." Squeezing her once, I set her free and retreat from her tempting-as-hell body. "You need to stop thinking that you're going to land on your ass."

"That's because I *am* going to land on my ass."

Rolling my eyes, I hold out a hand, palm up. I shouldn't be surprised when she doesn't immediately take it, no doubt worried that I'll pull a dirty prank and send her flying to the ground.

I wait her out.

One . . . two . . . three . . .

With a sigh of frustration, she gives in, dropping her hand into mine. God, it feels good. Holding her hand isn't remotely sexual, but after having no contact with her for months, it feels like everything I've ever needed.

My voice emerges, deep and gravelly. "You ready?"

"No."

"Zoe, didn't I promise that I wouldn't let you fall?"

At that, her dark eyes fix unblinking on my face, and I feel that one look like a sucker punch to the gut. Because I can see what she's thinking as if she'd voiced her thoughts out loud.

Why did you have sex with me, knowing that I'd already fallen?

Because I couldn't say no. Because I needed her like I needed air to breathe and water to drink.

Because I'd needed *her*.

The way that I still need her.

"I won't let you fall," I tell her. In more ways than one.

And then we're moving together. She struggles at first, no doubt because her ankles are weak. I order her to push with her thighs, to let her feet just be the vehicle that brings her forward. Her hand stays in mine until I grab two hockey sticks and hand her one. "Take it."

She does so with a worried grimace. "Weren't you ever told not to hand a weapon over to a woman?"

I laugh, loudly. "You gonna beat me with the stick, Zoe?"

"I've certainly thought about it," she grumbles. She stabs the hook of the stick into the ice like a pillar to ground

167

herself. But it has the opposite effect—the abrupt downward thrust has her legs shaking, her skates moving, and the next thing I know, Zoe has slid down the stick like a stripper on a pole.

But with less elegance, that's for sure.

"I think I need to call it a day," she says, staring up at the rink's ceiling as she lays comatose on the ice. "My vanity can't take another wipeout."

I crouch down beside her. "You didn't do half-bad."

"But it wasn't half-*good,* either." She sounds so miserable that I can't help myself. I touch her. My fingers brush her exposed collarbone, drifting up to the underside of her chin. Her breath stutters out against the rough pads of my fingers when I skim her lips, pressing my thumb to the center of her lower lip, tugging down.

Jesus. I want her.

I've *always* wanted her, from the very first moment we were introduced so long ago.

"Andre?" she whispers.

Does she want me? That's the question at hand here. I've told her no. I've told her that we aren't ever going to happen again. Less than thirty days later, and I'm willing to renege on all of that just for one single taste of her lips.

One taste will never be enough.

No, but it'll have to do.

I pull my hand away, more so because I don't need anyone thinking that we're doing something that we shouldn't.

"Tell me you want this, too." My voice drops. "Tell me that I'm not alone in this, Zo. That I'm not the only one going crazy with fucking wanting you."

Mouth lifting in a small smile, she says, "Language. There're kids around."

"What I want to do to you involves a lot of language."

Her brow arches. "And other stuff?"

"Hell, yes, and other stuff."

With her hair fanned out around her head, she's got to be cold on top of the ice. But all she does is watch me, touch the tip of her tongue to her bottom lip. I nearly come just at that. My body roars to life, demanding, wanting.

"As friends?" she asks. "Are we doing this as friends . . . with benefits?"

No. Being friends with her isn't enough, not for me. I feel like a starving man, willing to take whatever scraps she can give me. It's more than just the sex, though I want that too with her. I need . . . Fuck, what I want and need are two different things. I need her friendship, her smile, the way she looks at me as though she's the only person who can read me, the only person who truly cares to. But if friends with benefits is what it will take to warm her up to the thought of being with me—*really* being with me—then that's fine. I'll roll with it . . . for now. After everything, I don't want to spook her and send her running in the opposite direction when our relationship is already so fragile. "Yeah," I tell her slowly, "if that's what you want."

For a moment, she doesn't say anything. Just flicks her gaze away. Then, "Not here. I don't want . . . I don't want to do a repeat of last time."

I know what she means immediately. We aren't going to have sex again where someone could find us. That I agree on fully.

"After the event. I'll take you home, and I'll—"

Her eyes narrow playfully. "Language, Andre."

"Fine, fine." I pull back, my hands going to hers so that I can help her into a sitting position. "But the minute I have you alone, you're mine."

I just wish it could be for longer than a single night.

I never thought I'd say this, but friends with benefits just isn't enough for me. *Take it slow,* I warn myself, *take it slow.*

There's the root of the problem, though—at the end of the day, "slow" isn't a word in my vocabulary. But to have Zoe as mine? It's time to leave my impulsiveness at the door. I don't have another choice if I want her to look at me as anything more than a coldhearted asshole.

19

ZOE

I'd like to say that Andre and I are classy people when we leave the rink after the event. That we wave politely to people, and say our good-byes like normal humans.

Yeah, that's not what happens.

We hightail it to our cars, only pausing when Andre grunts, "We'll take mine. I'll bring you back tomorrow."

In surprise, I glance at him. "I'm spending the night?"

His laugh is low and husky and so many kinds of sexy. "I don't plan to let you leave the bed."

"The whole time?" I ask. "Don't you think we might want some food at some point?"

"Fine. Food, but that's it. Rule has been made." He swats my butt, and, for effect, I give a good little squeak. Andre rewards me with pushing me back against his car, his big body concealing mine from any spectators.

"I need to kiss you," he growls, his hands coming to rest below my breasts. "I've needed to kiss you for a goddamn year."

If he realizes what he's said, he doesn't give more information. And I'm too caught up in *him*, the him that's pinning me to a car, the him that is dragging his lips up my neck, to worry that he may have meant something else.

His lips finally claim mine, soft and coaxing. The opposite of that first, fiery kiss in a darkened bar hallway after a few rounds of drinks a year ago. *That* kiss was steamy and panty-dropping in its harshness. *This* kiss is heart-*wrenching*, like Andre is determined to pour every ounce of unnamed emotion into the kiss.

"God, I've missed this," he utters against my lips, sipping at the bottom one until I give in, opening, inviting, warming to the feel of his familiar muscular body under my hands. "I've missed *you*."

I tear away from his lips to crack, "You certainly haven't acted like it. You said this was a bad idea."

"It *is* a bad idea." His hand snakes up to my breast, squeezing the sensitive flesh over the fabric of my shirt. "It's a bad idea," he repeats, "and you should stop me right now."

"No."

He chuckles at my sass. "Get in the car, Zo."

At his demand, I hook my fingers into the waistband of his sweatpants and tug him close. "You like to boss me around."

His lips lift. "It's part of my charm."

"Is that what they're calling it these days?"

His palm collides with the side of my butt again. "Car, Zo. I have a surprise for you."

"Another surprise?" I ask, because quite abruptly, I'm thrown back in time.

Andre always loved surprising me. Never gifts, that wasn't our style. But tickets to the movies to see the latest blockbuster. A trip to a new local restaurant he discovered and wanted to try out. A puppy that he wanted desperately to foster, until I reminded him of his crazy schedule.

Funny how I didn't realize how much I craved this aspect of our friendship until it was gone.

"Don't hold out on me now, Beaumont." I twist a little so I can see him fully. "I'm ready."

He chokes out a laugh that sounds like he's dying. "Are you?" he murmurs.

Am I? Silly question. "Oh, yeah."

He slips me a side-eye glance. "Prove it."

I pause, realization sinking in when he starts to laugh. "You've got such a dirty mind, Beaumont."

"Because *that's* a surprise?" He laughs even harder, so hard that I'm not sure he can even drive.

With his legion of women, I suspect I shouldn't be shocked whatsoever. But I know he's bluffing. Him wanting me to check if I'm "ready" is nothing but a joke to him. Which means that I obviously just have to prove him wrong.

Jeans encase my legs, and I do a dramatic flipping open of the brass button to catch his attention.

And, do I.

Andre blinks, then blinks again, then his hands clutch the wheel like his life depends on holding it. "What are you doing, Zoe?"

"Seeing if I'm 'ready,'" I murmur sweetly, edging the zipper down to the base. "Isn't that what you said to do?"

His Adam's apple dodges south. "I . . . Hell, Zo, we're *driving.*"

As if to prove his point, he pulls up to a stop sign.

One Mississippi . . .

I shove the waistband of my jeans to my upper hips.

Two Mississippi . . .

My fingers slip beneath the silk of my panties.

"Zoe. Please."

Three Mississippi . . .

Home base.

The tips of my fingers dance along my clit, at the exact same moment Andre bites out a curse that'd give a sailor a heart attack.

"Andre," I whisper, playing up the moment. It's all too much fun to see the color infuse his cheeks.

A car honking behind us has Andre swerving as he bangs a right and hits the gas. "Don't you dare fucking come," he growls. "Not without me. Not without my tongue on your clit or my cock inside you."

His words spike my desire, and I give in, rubbing the center of my pleasure in tight little circles. A moan works its way up my throat. It's been *months* since I've allowed myself even this much pleasure, and I can't control it. My wetness causes my finger to slip, and even that little change in angle does it for me.

I come openly, as Andre takes to the backstreets like a maniac. The only time he slows is at the next red light. Unexpectedly, he snags my wrist, pops my fingers into his mouth, and tastes me. It's as hot as it sounds, trust me.

Then he mutters, "You're going to owe me for that," and I'm done for. Done.

20

ZOE

We barely make it through his front door before Andre is on me.

His kiss tastes like heaven when he flicks his tongue against my upper lip.

His kiss tastes like hell when he explores my mouth, driving me to insanity, making me beg.

He's paying me back for my climax in the car.

Little does he know that there aren't any complaints coming from me.

I shouldn't want Andre. It goes against everything I believe in—he abandoned me when I needed him most. He told me that we wouldn't have sex, and yet here we are.

But I do want him. Because on the other half of that coin is the Andre I know exists under the hardness. The Andre who pulls out chairs for me, that puts my safety above everyone else's. The Andre who cares about my stupid sprained ankle, and stands up for me when I need him.

The man is as complicated as a jigsaw puzzle, and I so hope to be the one to solve him.

No, no there is no solving.

That sort of thinking landed me in this mess.

I just need to enjoy the moment. Enjoy sex with Andre Beaumont for what it is. Uncomplicated, feel-good pleasure.

Needing to feel him, I urge his T-shirt up and over his head. Visually, I eat him up. Tangibly, my palms trace the hard lines of his chest. I pause over his flat nipples. "The piercings would have looked good on you."

His laughter reverberates through his body. "Yeah, maybe. Except that my nipples turned green for days, and I swear to God I thought I was becoming the Joker."

I giggle. "Sexy."

"Yeah, I thought so."

And then we're right back at it again. His arm hooks around my waist, drawing me up against him, so that my feet dangle off the floor.

"Where are you taking me?"

"My evil lair."

"The sin bin?" I quip in reply. "I don't deserve a stint in the penalty box."

"Zo," Andre says with a shake of his head, his fingers digging into my backside, "for that stunt you pulled in the car, you deserve to sit out the entire game." He kicks open a door with his foot, and my eyes adjust to the dim bedroom. He drops me on the bed, and I bounce with a laugh. "Luckily for you, however, I'm not interested in doing this next bit alone."

Large hands go to my jeans, stripping them off and throwing them to the floor. He does the same with my blouse, my shoes, my bra, my panties. Until I'm blessedly naked and he's . . . shirtless. That's it.

I nudge his hips with mine, biting back a moan at the feel of his cock through the soft material of his pants. "Get naked," I tell him. "Join the club."

"Oh, I plan to join the club."

"Which one is that?"

His brows lift. "The party going on between your—"

I clap a hand over his mouth. "Don't say it."

I can feel his lips moving into a smile against my palm, but the words are so jumbled, they're intelligible. Then—oh, my God—he flicks his tongue against my palm, and I yank back as if burnt.

"Dirty trick," I mutter.

"No, *dirty man.*"

And then his fingers go *there*, between my legs, and he's right—there *is* a party between my legs.

He plays me like he was born to pleasure me and me alone. As his mouth works mine with agonizingly slow thoroughness, his fingers send the lower half of my body into something I don't recognize. A tail spin. His thumb finds the hood of my clit, and I cry out. His middle finger circles my entrance, and without further prompting, thrusts inside, thrusting *up* to hit me just in the right spot. The keening moan I release doesn't even sound like it belongs to me.

He doesn't stop.

Not there.

He quickens the pace, adds another finger. Curls just *right*. Oh. My God. Oh. My God.

"No," he grunts, "not yet."

And then he pulls away. Out of their own accord, my fingers head south to the apex of my thighs. I *need* what he was about to give me like I've never needed anything else in my life.

He rolls a condom down his cock, then bats my hand away.

"I told you, Zo, you're mine."

His.

God, I wish that I was. I wish that I was with every fiber of my being.

With a hand to my hip, Andre guides me onto my side and then slips behind me. His lips land on the back of my neck. His hand urges my leg back and over his hip, which exposes the bottom half of my body.

I'm not given a chance to feel any embarrassment.

Andre dances his fingers over the most sensitive part of me again, and then I feel the round head of his cock line up at my entrance. Surprise hits me that this is how he plans to take me for the first time in so many months.

With my leg tossed over his, his hand clasped to my breast, his breathing rustling the hair on my neck, the position is . . . Sensual. Romantic. Things—*emotions*—I didn't expect from anyone, much less Andre.

He enters me in a single, smooth thrust.

I cry out from the intensity of the position, and his hand moves from my collarbone to the base of my throat. "God, you feel so good. So fucking tight."

He does, too.

Good, I mean. Huge, too.

I can't find the words, but my nails sink into his forearm, holding him to me. *Forever*, I want to say, *I miss you*. "Don't stop," I whisper, "please, don't stop."

His chuckle ruffles my hair. His hips pick up the pace. "I couldn't even if I wanted to, Zo. *Never*."

He doesn't stop, just as promised. His fingers tweak my nipple, rolling the sensitive nub between his thumb and middle finger, before traversing the lines of my body until they stop where I need him most. Just the slightest amount of pressure, the fast pistoning of his hips, and he makes me orgasm long enough that I still feel the tremors long after his have subsided.

"Andre?" I whisper against the inner part of his arm.

His cock twitches inside of me at the sound of his name. "Yes?"

Don't say it. Please don't say it.

I gather my courage. "For one night, can you pretend that there is no one else?"

Andre's hand tightens on my hip. "Yes, Zo. I can definitely do that."

He slips me onto my back, black eyes burning brightly, and then gently kisses me on the lips. "I can definitely do that."

21

ANDRE

SIX DAYS LEFT

"*T*acos."

That's all Zoe says when I give her a call after morning skate the day following the youth hockey camp. "Is there more to that statement or is this one of those times where I'm supposed to work it out for myself?"

Zoe's girlish laughter, so at odds with her tenacious personality, comes through the receiver. "I'm craving tacos, that's all. And since it's Taco Tuesday . . . I don't know, I thought maybe that—"

"I'd take you out for tacos?"

"I mean, you certainly don't have to." I can practically see her eyes slamming shut with embarrassment. "I'm such an idiot. You're probably calling to talk about what's next in the lineup for you, and here I am talking about tacos."

God, she's cute when she gets all worked up. I clear my throat as I toss my gear into my truck and then climb into the driver's seat. "Actually, I was calling because I wanted to see you."

Silence.

Great.

I drop my head against the seat. "You there, Zo?"

"Yeah, yeah, I'm here. I just . . . *I'dlovetoseeyoutoo.*" The last bit is rushed, but I hear the words loud and clear, and damn it, I feel my mouth curl up into what's no doubt a cheesy grin.

"So, tacos?" I ask, still grinning like a fool. "I'm down for that."

"Really?" she chirps in my ear with full-enthusiasm. "Oh, that's great! There's this little place by my new apartment, and I haven't had the chance to try it out yet . . . "

We plan to meet at the Mexican restaurant in thirty, not that it'll take me nearly that long to get there, before disconnecting. Putting my car into drive, I head out of the rink and into downtown Boston. To my right, the city's recognizable skyline reaches toward the sky and reflects against the Charles River.

I've been here for a year and yet I don't think I've paid any attention to my surroundings.

Not until Zoe came back, not until I spent my days looking over my shoulder just to see if she might be walking toward me.

I smooth my hand over the steering wheel, thinking back on last night. On the hottest sex I've ever had.

Friends with benefits.

I snort out loud because that right there is the *stupidest* idea I've ever had. I don't want to be "just friends" with Zoe Mackenzie. And maybe I'm going about this the wrong way, because it's been an incredibly long time since I've dated long-term, but I want more with Zoe. More than sex, more than friends.

I want it all—and, for a man who's more comfortable hiding behind the icy façade, I've got no idea how to tell Zoe this. Hell, I'm pretty sure I just boxed myself into the twenty-first-century version of the "friend zone."

By the time I pull up in front of La Cantina, the little Mexican joint Zoe's itching to try out, I've made a new mission, a new plan.

It's time to woo Zoe Mackenzie.

Does anyone still "woo"?

Fuck it, doesn't matter. It's happening.

I crank open my car door after I pull into a parking spot. From the outside, the restaurant isn't anything fancy, certainly nothing like Vittoria. But it's quaint and brightly colored, and I'm not complaining—at a place like this, there's a smaller chance of running into hockey-crazed fans. More family-friendly and less drunken puck bunnies.

More time for me and Zoe to be alone.

More time for you to open up about Hannah.

My lungs squeeze. Yeah, not yet. Zoe and me, our relationship needs to be a lot tighter before I talk about my ex, about . . .

"Andre!"

At the sound of Zoe's voice, I glance up and immediately feel the oxygen leave my body. She's wearing a trench coat and a pair of fuck-me heels, and sue me, but I'm a guy and my first thought isn't, *she must be cold*, but rather, *is she wearing anything under that?*

Like I said, sue me.

Her stride slows, the insecurity pulling at her features. "It's, um . . . " She coughs into one gloved hand. "It's good to see you."

She's nervous. I grin. Let the wooing begin. "C'mere, Zo."

Her dark eyes drop to my open arms. "You just want a hug?"

No. "Sure."

Tentatively, she slips her hands around my back. I don't let her move away. Instead, I cup the back of her head, mussing up her hair. "I lied."

Her cheeks bloom with color, and I like to think it has less to do with the cold weather and more to do with me. "Yeah?" she whispers, her fingers pressing into my back.

"Mhmm." My lips find her forehead. Her skin is smooth, hot. I drop my mouth to her ear, and murmur, "I want to kiss you."

"Yeah?" This time, she sounds breathless. "I'm down."

Her response makes me laugh. Classic Zoe. "That's good." I nip at her earlobe, then grin smugly when she leaps in my arms. "You've got three seconds to change your mind. Three . . . two—"

She doesn't give me the chance to finish. Her hands clasp the back of my head, and then she's dragging my mouth down to hers, nipping at my lower lip, and slipping her tongue into my mouth. Taking control of the kiss. Taking control of *me*.

Holy hell, it's hot.

I give in, letting her have her way. Maybe this wooing thing is all about letting the woman take what she wants— and if what Zoe wants is *me*, then I'm all for giving it to her.

Our tongues tangle, warring. The kiss isn't soft and it certainly isn't romantic, but that's what this wooing needs to be, and so I slow her down, smoothing my hand over her cheek, cupping her chin. Her arm wraps around my back, unwilling to let me go, and then I'm right back in it again.

Tasting the waters.

Drowning.

Willingly choking on seawater—isn't that what she'd told me that first day at Golden Lights Media?

It's only at the sound of ambulance sirens that I pull back. I stare down at her, noting her pouty, red lips and her flushed cheeks. "Damn, honey," I growl, "I'm not even thinking about tacos anymore."

She flashes me a pleased smile. "I'll think about tacos for the both of us, don't worry."

Glancing down at the hard-on my jeans are doing nothing to hide, I mutter, "Easy for you to say. You don't look like you've got a hockey stick in your pants."

And then, tease that she is, she follows the direction of my gaze and bites down on her lower lip. "Tempting as it is to go straight home with you, Andre, I want food."

You're supposed to be wooing her. Stop thinking about your dick.

That'd be easier if I wasn't seeing different colors in my peripheral thanks to all the blood being south of my hips. I blindly reach out for the door to the restaurant, pulling it open for her like a true gentleman. "Food. Tacos. Don't mind me while I sit here starving the whole time."

With an arched brow, she asks, "You're not going to eat?"

"Oh, I will."

Her expression darkens. "I'm so confused."

I lean down, brush her hair back from her face, and kiss the sensitive flesh next to her ear. "I'm starving, honey, but only for what's between your legs." I don't give her the chance to respond. Instead, I place my hand to her back, usher her inside, and tell the hostess, "For two, please."

Really, I should have said three.

At this rate, my erection might as well have a zip code of its own.

22

ZOE

I think . . . I think that I'm on a date with Andre Beaumont.

It's tough to say, really, because I didn't think that Andre *did* the whole dating thing, but there's no denying the fact that he's being . . . charming. Playful. Sexy in a way that makes my toes curl in my shoes and my heart beat out of control.

"Tell me something that happened to you in the last year," he says as he spoons salsa onto his al pastor taco. "First thing that comes to mind."

First thing that comes to mind? I take a sip of my soda, buying myself time. "Well, right before I left Detroit, I sold everything. Ended up living in a hotel for a few weeks."

Dark eyes pin me in place. "That's the best you can do, Zo? You lived in a hotel?" He sets his taco down, wiping his hands on a cloth napkin, and then drops his elbow to the table. "Let the professional go first." He says this with a sardonic tilt to his mouth, never letting me forget that he's still Andre Beaumont, the most feared player in the NHL.

But then he goes and spoils the image by chuckling softly. "First day with the—wait, what did Hunt say?"

"When?"

"At The Box—oh yeah, setting the scene. All right, let's do it right, eh?" He drinks his water—nothing less for his temple of a body—and then spreads his hands wide, like he's about to start wind-milling them.

Laughter threatens to let loose from my chest. "What the hell are you doing, Andre?"

His brow furrows, drawing inward. "Setting the scene."

Leaning back in my chair, I fold my arms over my chest. "Is that what you're doing?"

"I'm drawing the curtains . . . You know what? Forget the scene bit." His full mouth presses together. "Okay, so there I am in the locker room. We've just finished with practice, and I'll admit that I was being a bit of an asshole—"

I grin, just a little. "Nothing out of the ordinary, of course."

He returns the grin, along with a sexy wink that has my thighs clenching together under the table. "Exactly, honey. Anyway, maybe I'd ticked off some of my teammates, maybe they were already planning this shit, but I'm getting ready to put away my equipment." His dark eyes glimmer with the memory. "Now that I think about it, I should have known those bastards were up to something with the way they kept watching me. Anyway, I open my locker door and *bam!* Ice."

I clap my hand over my mouth to stifle the laughter. The image of Andre Beaumont, King Sin Bin, standing in front of his locker as ice cubes rain down on him is just . . . perfect. Utterly, absolutely perfect. "What did you do?" I ask between bursts of laughter.

"What do you think?" He digs back into his plate again, taking a bite of his taco before topping it off with more water. "I cleaned that shit up, griping and threatening anyone who came close."

"Am I supposed to apologize on their behalf?"

His foot touches mine under the table, then doesn't move. I suck in a deep breath and then meet his gaze. "Nah, honey. The ice was nothing. The fact that they spent the next week leaving plastic critters in my duffel bag was worse. Roaches, snakes, crickets, you name it. I think they got a sadistic thrill out of making me shriek."

"*No*, of course not," I say, pressing a hand to my chest in mock-surprise. "Making the league's most intimidating enforcer shriek? Utterly boring and *so* not worth their time."

But Charming Andre has come out to play. In response to my sarcasm, he puckers his lips and murmurs, "Kiss me and I'll forgive you for the sass."

"No way." The giggles threaten to take over. "The sass is here to stay."

"Perfect, just the way I like you." He pushes up from his seat, dropping his napkin to the table, and comes around to my side. "A kiss, honey. Just one."

Heart, stop doing somersaults. I lift my chin. "You *had* a kiss."

"One wasn't enough." His voice lowers, sucking me in. "A hundred will never be enough."

And that's when I realize—I'm pretty sure this is a date. He's right, too, about the kiss thing. A hundred will never be enough, not for me. I tip my chin back, silently telling him to go for it, to take his kiss and to stake his claim.

But he surprises me. His lips don't land on my mouth, as I expected, but my cheek. Then my nose. Then my forehead. *The forehead kiss.* Oh, God, this *is* a date. Heart squeezing with anticipation, I cup his cheek and bring his lips to mine. They collide, gentle, coaxing, so damn softly, and *that's* when I know that Andre is trying to open up. He's trying to be vulnerable. And that, more than anything, is sexy.

He withdraws with a wink, then retakes his seat opposite me again. "All right, so, you heard from me. One thing that happened in this past year that I wanted you to know about. Tell me yours."

Considering that my last year has been consumed by thoughts of this man, I go for blunt honesty. "You know that TV show, *1000 Ways To Die?*"

Slowly, he nods. "Yeah, what about it?"

Aboot.

So cute.

"Well," I say, playing with my napkin, "I may have put a new spin on it."

Andre sucks in a breath. "Damn. Zo, I mean, I don't really know any police officers but—"

I hold up a hand, cutting him off. "I didn't kill anyone. I *may* have just spent a lot of time thinking about different ways to . . . tie you up, and take my revenge for skipping out on me."

He doesn't say anything.

I don't say anything.

Welp, this just got awkward.

But then he breaks the silence, his voice as dark as sin. "How many ways?"

My shoulders jerk. "What?"

His black eyes warm, and I feel the reciprocal heat in my lower body. "How many ways did you think of to tie me up?"

Now you've done it. "Roughly one-hundred and seventy-five, if, you know, we're taking into account locations in the world that I envisioned doing so."

In less than five seconds, it seems, Andre has dropped cash onto the table, our remaining food has been boxed, and we're standing outside of La Cantina in the cold. Except that I don't feel cold. If anything, I feel like I'm burning with fever.

"Have somewhere to be?" I hear myself ask.

"Yup." Andre encircles my shoulder with his arm, pulling me to him, and plants a hot kiss on my lips. "We're going back to my house, and you're starting with the first item on your list. I have only one request."

My breathing is coming fast now, and I lift my gaze to his handsome face. "What's that?" I whisper.

His lips find mine again. "That you're one-hundred percent naked."

I grin. "Done."

23

ANDRE

THREE DAYS LEFT

I made a mistake.

What kind of mistake, you ask?

Well, the kind where I let the most beautiful woman I know into my bed for four nights in a row. The kind of mistake where I wake up early, just so that I have time to cook her eggs and bacon each morning. The kind of mistake where I text her throughout the day because I want to see how she's doing.

I stare down at my phone, ignoring the guys around me in the locker room. We're padding up, ready to pull our shit together so we can hammer it out against the Boston Bruins. A city with two pro-teams is practically unheard of, and the NHL only acquiesced to the decision made by the Blades when the board rationalized some years back that *two* major hockey leagues would result in more income for the repairs to the arena. Nowadays, the Blades are as much of a city pastime as the Red Sox or the Bruins.

I don't think I've ever seen a rink this active before! Zoe's text reads. *Have I said thank you for the tickets yet?*

Hunching my shoulders so that Zoe's words are for me

alone, I type out: **You did. But I do accept gratitude in other ways. Sex, kisses, massages. Pick your flavor.**

I can practically hear her laughing on the other side of the screen. *Is this where I tell you that your Manhood is exactly what I need right now?*

I laugh out loud at that, and the sound attracts the attention of my teammates.

"You good?" Harrison asks as he takes it upon himself to sit next to me on the bench. "You're laughing like a weirdo when no one is around."

I flick my phone off. "Just talking a bit."

"With Zoe Mackenzie?"

According to the Rules That Be, I shouldn't have even kissed her. But I can't regret it at all because she's like a drug. I need her smiles and her laughter and everything else that is unanimously Zoe Mackenzie. "Just discussing some logistical PR stuff. That's all."

"Like having sex with her?"

My stomach caves. "No."

Duke pats my shoulder. "You're delusional. The girl wants you. Go after somebody for once. Do the whole chasing thing that usually makes your dick shrivel up."

He's right. I never do the chasing. I'd like to say that it's in my DNA, but that'd be a lie. Once upon a time, I did the chasing. Haven't for a while, though. Until Zoe, who I'm *wooing*. Jesus, even the word sounds ridiculous.

Right now, she's sitting up in the nosebleeds, the same way that she always did back in Detroit. It's her favorite place, although I could have easily put her somewhere closer to the ice. Somewhere closer to me.

Even so, the idea that she's *here*, that she's up in the nosebleeds waiting for me to take to the ice is like a high I forgot I needed to survive. To Duke, though, I mutter, "It's not like that with us."

"Lies, dude. Lie to me, if you want, because I don't really care one way or the other. But I hope you aren't lying to her right now."

My gut clenches.

How the fuck does he know that the guilt is piling in? Because as happy as I am, I'm not telling her everything.

Fifteen minutes later, we're on the ice and I'm not ashamed to admit that I use hockey like a stress reliever. As much as I talk about giving it up and moving to the Caribbean, I know I'd be bored with that life.

For nearly a decade, hockey has been my identity.

At least, it was until it wasn't.

For three years, I was someone else. *Something* else.

The puck drops and I hesitate, my instincts lagging as the past threatens to pull me under.

"And he's *lost it!*" shouts the announcer into the arena microphone. "Jee-wiz, I can't believe Beaumont lost that huge opportunity."

The announcer's words are like a drill to my head.

Get your ass back in the gear.

For the rest of the period, I give everything that I have to the game. Adrenaline pumps through my body, and I soak it in. It's that rush that puts me in place to receive the puck from McDermott. It's that rush that allows me to angle my trajectory path to the net, seeing an opportunity between shoulder pads and ice skates.

The puck hits the five-hole and the crowd goes wild. My teammates swarm me, lifting me up, even though I'm one heavy bastard, as they thump their gloved fists against my back for a job well done.

My gaze hits the stands, climbing the rows in search of her face.

I don't see her, but I imagine her up there near the top,

decked out in my jersey (I bought her my current one), jeans, and her ever-present stilettos.

It's the image that I carry with me as I finish the game. The announcers off-handedly comment on my lack of trips to the sin bin. For once, the nickname isn't mentioned, and I'm beyond grateful.

The guys and I towel off in the locker room after slick showers, and I force my way through an interview with the media, so that Walter Collins will get off Zoe's case about revitalizing my reputation. She's doing more than her fair share of work, more than I even realized until recently.

I need to shape up, if for no other reason than I want to make her life easier.

"You wanna go to The Box?"

I glance up at Marshall Hunt, who's got his towel slung around his neck and not much else on. "Nah, I'm good; thanks though."

Zoe and I have a date with food, and as much as I like the guys, they can't win out over her.

"Something tells me that your decline has a lot to do with the hot brunette waiting outside the locker room," Hunt muses, a smile pulling at his pretty-boy features. "I don't blame you."

This time, I don't even bother with pretending that Zoe and I aren't currently sleeping together. I offer my teammate a secretive grin, then hook my duffel bag over my shoulder. "Have a good time tonight," I tell him.

"You too, Beaumont!"

I ignore his cackling and head straight for home base. As luck would have it, she's exactly where Hunt said she'd be. And, Jesus, she looks amazing in my jersey. The navy blue and silver material is a tad long, so she's tucked part of the hem into the waistband of her skintight jeans. Naturally, stilettos accompany the look. Her hair is down, wavy and full, and I don't bother to stop myself—I drop the duffel on the ground, sink my hands into her soft hair, and angle her lips for a deep kiss.

Her hand goes to my heart. "You played amazing tonight," she murmurs, pulling back from me. "That assist with McDermott? *So* well-timed."

Her enthusiasm makes me laugh. "Can you think of it now? Two years ago, you didn't even know *what* an assist was."

"Give me a little more credit than that, please."

"I'm sorry, baby, you're right. I saw the *Hockey for Dummies* book you carried around. You were a quick study."

She doesn't react to the endearment, and I suppose that's a good thing. Two weeks ago, she would have nailed me in the balls for daring to utter it. Now, she only hums in delight, slipping her hand into mine as we wind our way down the hallway of doom toward the parking garage.

As she launches into a story about Tia, her half-sister, finally gearing up the courage to ask her crush out, I can't help but think she's hinting that she wants more with *me*. I don't do relationships. Ever. But lately, that's what I want with Zoe.

To come home to her each night. To slip my arm around her waist as we settle in the bed. To kiss her in the morning when her hair is a mess and her cheek has pillow imprints all over it.

Fuck me, but I *want* that. I want all of that and more.

"Date me."

The words are out before I can stop them, and she halts so abruptly that I lose hold of her hand. Her beautiful brown eyes are wide with shock, her mouth pursed into an *O.*

"What?"

Jesus. I'm screwing this up.

With a glance over my shoulder to check if anyone has

followed us, I rake my fingers through my hair, and repeat, "Date me."

"I heard it the first time."

"And?"

"I guess I'm just a little shocked, that's all," she answers pertly. "Not to mention the fact that Mr. Collins will have my head if he finds out."

I tug at my earlobe. I would never ask Zoe to quit her job. The woman works way too hard just to give it up now. Which means . . . "I'll find a new PR agency."

This time, her brows fly up high on her forehead. "What?"

Warming to the thought, I nod my head. "Yeah, it's perfect, actually. I mean, I won't leave yet—you still have your trial run, and I'd never jeopardize that. But after, when they begin assigning you new clients, I'll go else-where. That way, your work ethic isn't being compromised—"

"Andre, do you even know how many times you've compromised me in the last few days?"

Her tone is wry, and I give it right back. My hands find her hips, as I gently push her back against the garage wall. I lean into her, giving her everything. "I'm all for compromis-ing, baby. You up for another run?"

She gives a startled laugh. "You're ridiculous."

I lower my head to her neck. Now that the idea of us dating has been firmly planted, I can't give it up. Everything else . . . I'll tell her that in time, when it's right. I shove those thoughts away and nip at her earlobe. "You know you want to say yes, Zo. Think of it now—late night trips to the grocery store to buy you your favorite potato chips. Days spent binging on *Game of Thrones*. Me in your bed . . . " I thrust my hips gently against her, so she knows how hard I am.

Her quiet hiss is like music to my ears, especially when

she digs her fingers into my hips to keep me in place. "You push a hard bargain, Beaumont."

My thumb brushes over her cheek. "I'm a man who knows what he wants."

I watch her eyes fall shut. "King Sin Bin is becoming respectable, Andre. I almost don't know what to think of that."

I kiss her. I stamp my mouth down on hers, and absorb her squeak of surprise. Her fingers dive into my hair, tugging me closer, as if we aren't already one. Hell, I missed her this past year. I rock my cock against her belly, and grin wildly when she arches her back and begs for more.

This. This is what I've been needing.

Zoe.

"Careful," she whispers against my neck, "if you don't stop, you might just fall."

I know what she's talking about. "Don't mind if I do."

And then I put my mouth back where it belongs, on hers.

Mine.

ZOE

ONE DAY LEFT

J've never been so happy in my life.

It's true.

It's crazy to think that a month ago, I hadn't seen Andre in a year. That we'd been on the outs completely. And now . . .

I clutch his hair as his mouth lands *exactly* where I need him to be. His tongue finds me, hot and insistent, lapping at my clit like it's his new job. From my precarious angle on the bed, all I see are his wide shoulders, his dark, messy hair. He woke me up this morning at the crack of dawn, his hands molding to my body, his scratchy stubble scraping against the curve of my shoulder as he nuzzled my neck.

Nuzzled.

Andre Beaumont.

I'd be just as surprised if I wasn't on the receiving end of the nuzzling.

But the two of us are insatiable—maybe because we have a year to make up for—and when he threw back the covers and slid down my body, there wasn't a single peep out of me.

"Oh, my God," I whisper now, curling my hands into his hair. "*Andre . . .*"

His gaze flicks to my face, his dark eyes like sin. He doesn't stop. He pushes my legs wider, slips his hands beneath my butt, and tilts me to him like a veritable buffet.

Oh. Oh, wow.

My fingers clutch the sheets. I need him.

And so I take action—I hike one foot up and plant it on his shoulder, pushing him backward. With a jolt of surprise, he teeters over the side of the bed and falls to the floor with a grunt.

Oops. Totally not my intention.

I clamber to the side of the bed to peek over at him, only to see his shoulders bouncing. With laughter. Oh, my God, he's laughing at me, and a grin has split his face, and he is the sexiest damn thing I've ever seen.

He catches sight of me, and holds out a hand. "Get over here, Zo."

"On the floor?" I ask, eyeing the carpet with a skeptical eye.

"You know that you want to."

I do, and he's right, and I slither off the bed and crawl over to him on hands and knees.

I don't expect his next move.

Andre swoops in, hauling me up against his body so that I'm seated on his lap with his back against the bed. My breasts are in his big hands, and it feels so fantastic that I drop my head back.

"Guide me inside you, baby," he rumbles, thumbs flicking my nipples. "Let me feel how hot you are for me."

I'm on the pill, something we discussed the other night, and so I don't need further prompting to do exactly as he ordered. I align his cock with my entrance, and then sink down onto him. Oh, God. He feels huge—just right. Using my knees as leverage, I slip up, up, up, before crashing back down on him.

He groans his pleasure, head falling back against the bed, as his hands go to my waist. Up, down, up, down.

With each downward thrust, I feel my heart open a little wider. Become a little less careful when it comes to this man who has been my closest friend and the only person I've ever truly despised.

"You feel so damn good," he whispers, eyes still screwed shut. "I'll never get enough of you, Zo."

Selfishly, I don't want him to. So, I make it good for us both. So good that he'll never want to walk away again. I twist my hips, taking him all the way inside me. He hisses, nails biting my skin, as he takes control of my movements. Each time that I come back down on his cock is a little harder, a little less controlled.

It's *wonderful*.

Because Andre is a man who *only* knows control, and the fact that I'm the one who can make him lose it?

Heaven.

My fingers go to his chin, demanding that he look at me. He does, dark eyes blinking open, fevered with lust and . . . something else. Maybe I shouldn't go for it; maybe I shouldn't read too much into something that's so new.

But I've known this man for so long, and the words tumble out of me as my climax lights a fire inside me. "I love you, Andre."

The only hint that he's heard my declaration is the momentary stalling of his hips. But then he picks up smoothly, turning us over, so his body is over mine, my legs locked around his waist, his elbows holding him up.

He kisses my forehead. "Say it again, baby."

I moan.

He kisses my cheek. "Zo, say it again."

My fingers shake with the force of my orgasm. "I love you, Andre."

His kiss lands on my mouth, a little off-center. He thrusts once more, and again, and again, until he comes inside me with a quiet roar.

WE HAVEN'T EVEN PULLED OUR CLOTHES BACK ON BEFORE THE doorbell rings downstairs.

Andre drops his head to my chest, his damp hair plastering itself against my skin. "Fuck, this is not a good time."

I laugh a little. "Why, you have something to say?"

He lifts his head and meets my gaze head on. "You know that I do."

My heart thunders in my chest. "Say it."

"Not yet." Sliding off my body, he makes a grab for his clothing, which has been discarded . . . Well, everywhere. "Get comfy on the bed, baby," he adds, as he slips on a T-shirt over his head. "I'll be right back as soon as I send whoever it is packing."

It's not quite a declaration, but I'll take it.

Hell to the yes, I will.

He gives me a quick kiss after tugging on a pair of shorts, then heads for the doorway. I want to call him back and tell him that I love him again. I never once thought that Andre and I would get to this place. Sure, there are speedbumps that we still have to get over. Lingering issues, like the fact that I've signed a lease on an apartment, and haven't spent a single night there. Instead, I'm here with him. It's probably too soon to move in together officially though.

Although I guess we are a bit of a special case.

It's not like we'd only *met* a month ago. That'd be different. I think.

Then again, Andre has a way of making me forget about

the rules. Although I do agree about Golden Lights Media. It'll be less difficult for him to find a new company than for me to find a new job. And, honestly, it's sweet that he'd even suggest it in the first place.

Raised voices steal my attention, and I quietly tug on my clothes. I know that Andre told me to wait upstairs, but I can hear the frustration in his voice.

Against my will, my feet carry me to the stairwell, and I glance down into the foyer below. Andre has his hands on the back of his neck as he paces. And . . . my breath catches at the sight of a pretty woman opposite him. Her hair is thick and blond, her body trim from exercise.

I shouldn't be standing here. I shouldn't be listening.

Tell that to your feet.

"You can't just swing by here," Andre is saying, his voice pitched low.

The woman takes a step forward. "Andre, honey"—*honey?!*—"I'm not trying to cause any trouble."

The man who spent all morning bringing me to climax laughs harshly. "Hannah, all you *do* is cause trouble."

"That's unfair."

"What's *unfair,*" Andre mutters with a retreating step, "is that you show up wherever I go, Hannah. You show up and you stir the fucking memories, and you just don't get it, do you? *You* left *me.* This wasn't the other way around."

I . . . I think I'm going to be sick.

Neither of them have noticed me standing up here on the second-floor landing, which I suppose is a good thing, because I don't want to be noticed. Andre had been in a relationship? The man who *refused* to do relationships had been . . .

The *Fame* interview. His request not to answer the question about a time that he'd had his heart broken. Oh, God, I am *such* an idiot. Idiot, idiot, idiot.

"Andre," Hannah says pleadingly, "it was a *mistake*."

"No. No, Hannah, a mistake is sleeping with someone else once and then never doing it again. A mistake is not having affairs with multiple men each time I was on the road for games. A mistake is not breaking up with me, leaving me for someone else, and then informing me later on that you'd given birth to my son and that *my* son had died without me even knowing he existed." Andre's voice cracks, and my heart does right along with him. "*Those* are not mistakes, Hannah. Those will never be mistakes, and I swear to fucking God that if you ever come around here again, I will get a restraining order on you so fast, you'll have fucking whiplash."

I must make a sound because Hannah glances up and spots me clinging to the balcony railing.

Her shoulders stiffen. "I didn't realize that you had company."

Andre doesn't even turn to look up at me. Instead, he moves to the front door and swings it open in silence.

Hannah gets the hint, this time at least, I suppose, and struts her way out without another word.

The door closes.

And then finally Andre meets my gaze. His cheeks are bright from emotion, more emotion than I've ever seen from him before.

Hannah.

The girl he loved.

The son he never knew.

I'm so stupid, and it hurts even more to realize that now after I just professed my love for him.

"We need to talk," he says softly, though his tone remains hard, and I don't think he's referring to his plan to tell me that he loves me.

I nod, sucking in a quiet sob because I *know* what's

coming, and then move down the steps to meet him in the foyer. It's then that I remember the picture of the little boy I'd seen a few weeks ago, when I'd first come to his house. The boy I thought belonged to his sister.

Not to his sister, though.

To *him*.

He doesn't ham around, waiting for the "right way" to tell me. In a way, I appreciate the forwardness of his speech, even though I want to know why he waited all this time to say something. I wouldn't have judged him. I wouldn't have looked at him differently.

If anything, knowing his past would have opened the door to his soul—all the crevices and the wounds and the shadows.

His Adam's apple dips with a swallow. "Hannah and I met in college at Northwestern. She was the sister of a buddy, and I'd be lying to you if I said that I didn't notice her right off the bat."

Although it stings to hear him say that, I nod anyway. Isn't this what I wanted? To learn everything he hid away? My fingers clench into balled fists. I guess I didn't think his "secrets" would be something as momentous as this.

"We started dating in my senior year, right before I got drafted by the Red Wings. She moved with me, you know, never even put up a fight about not wanting to live in Detroit. I was her home, she told me over and over again. She'd go with me anywhere."

I bite down on my lower lip, wanting to ask so many questions but not wanting to throw him off.

He continues softly, "Best years of my life and worst ones as well. Hannah had a way about her that kept me hooked onto the relationship, even though it should have ended in college. The more my career took off, the less she wanted to be seen with me in public. I didn't understand. It was one thing if she was camera shy, but the way Hannah acted . . . it didn't feel that way. We'd go to the movies, and she'd slip her hand from mine. We'd go to dinner, and she'd invite my teammates so it looked like we were one big party going out."

My heart breaks when his mouth opens and then clamps shut, his fist coming up to rub his chest. I want to touch him, to bring him comfort, but something tells me he doesn't want that. That if I touch him, the story will end and this is . . . this is something he needs to let out. Something, I suspect, he's never told anyone.

His caustic chuckle catches me off guard. "Eventually, I caught onto her game." He moves to the entryway table, picking up the picture of the little boy. "She didn't want the media knowing about us, because if they had, then all of her lovers would have known she wasn't, actually, single. In the house, she slept in my bed and rubbed my back and sat on my lap. In public, we were strangers. Friends, at most."

"How did you find out?" I ask, already dreading the answer.

"The usual way." He laughs again, lips turning up in a smile I know isn't real. "Came home early from being on the road to find another guy in our bed. After that, she came clean and I was done. She left without a fuss, didn't even try to fight for what we had . . . or didn't have, I guess. What I didn't know then was that she was pregnant with our child. She'd never mentioned anything."

My stomach plummets. This time, I don't stop myself from going to him—I *can't* stop myself from going to him. I press a hand to his arm, dragging it around me so that I can slip my hands to his back and pull him into a hug. His hands hesitate briefly before following suit, tugging me close.

His chest is rock-hard against my cheek, and I can feel the shiver that racks his body when I press a kiss to his heart.

"For two years, I didn't know a thing, Zo. How does

someone *do* something like that? She didn't call. She didn't message me." His big shoulders hunch around me, and I realize he's trying to get closer. Heart squeezing, I palm his big back, rubbing in circles. "And then one day, she shows up at my old house in Detroit. Tells me that we'd had a son and that he'd caught bronchitis and had passed away. I didn't want to believe her. It honestly seemed like just the sort of fucked-up shit that she'd do to get back at me, but she shared the birth and death certificates with me. Offered to have me do a DNA test before he was cremated, so that I knew she wasn't lying."

My breathing is rough when I ask, "Did you?"

"Yes." I feel his nod against the top of my head. "I got the results back the day that you and I slept together."

For a moment, the words don't register.

And when they do, I reel back in shock, disengaging from his arms. No. No. My gaze searches his face, looking for any hint of dishonesty, but there is none. If anything, he looks more exposed, more uneasy, than I've ever seen him.

"So you used me?" I whisper, and wow, it hurts. I'd always known that I'd just been a random hookup for him. But this . . . The urge to vomit returns twofold. "Did you know that I would be an easy lay? That I wanted you so badly, and it wouldn't take much effort on your part to charm me out of my pants?"

Andre lurches forward, his expression a mask of regret and panic. "No," he hastily exclaims, "Wait, yes. But not because of how you're thinking it."

I lift my brows. "How *else* am I supposed to think of this, Andre? You slept with me. You let me suffer the media alone when everyone found out from that stupid security footage. You *used* me."

The aftereffects of our night together have always stung, but knowing the truth is like a knife to an open wound. In that moment, when his large hands had been holding me up, and my nails had been digging into his back, I had let myself think that it was just the start of something new. That Andre and I had a future ahead of us. The words "I love you" had been on the tip of my tongue, and meanwhile Andre had sought me out because he *knew* that I'd give him what he wanted. Sex. Uncomplicated sex with someone he never planned to sleep with twice.

None of this is news, but emotions aren't rational and right now . . . right now my lungs heave in an attempt to yank in air.

Andre's fingers encircle my wrist, stilling me. "Please, Zo, baby, just listen."

I pull away from his grasp. "I listened, Andre. And I can commiserate with your pain. I can understand why you'd be upset and how your world quite literally turned upside down. But we were *friends*, and you used the fact that I *loved* you against me. And when the pieces fell apart, you didn't even bother to help put them back together. You walked away. Just like Hannah."

He flinches at the sound of his ex's name. "I'm *nothing* like Hannah."

"No?" I poke him in the chest, then plant my hands on my hips. "For the two years that I've known you, Andre, you've slept with women without thought as to how *they* might feel."

"It's not a crime to—"

I cut him off with a wave of my hand. "No, it's not a crime to sleep around. But you let what Hannah did to you turn you into a man who had no thought to other people's emotions. You slept with women. You barked at the media. You got *mean*, Andre. What Hannah did to you? Unforgivable. If she was still here, I'd yank her hair out. But none of her actions make *yours* acceptable."

Our heavy breathing fills the foyer, rapid and panicked because we both know that we're hurtling toward the end.

We can't come back from this.

"I don't know what to say," he rasps. "I did use you. I used a lot of women who didn't deserve it. I—"

"What was his name?" I ask. "Your son?"

His eyes squeeze shut before cranking open. "Aaron," he tells me. "Hannah named him Aaron."

Aaron. I don't ask if Hannah listed 'Beaumont' as the boy's surname. Something tells me that she did. But I do shift closer to Andre, so that I cup his cheek. His stubble tickles my palm.

I swallow, hard. My fingers tangle in his messy hair. "I think you need to ask what kind of man Aaron would have wanted as a father. A man who spends his days living in the sin bin, even when he's off the ice, or a man who greets life head-on, whatever it throws at him."

"Zoe—"

I shake my head and step back. "Just answer me this, Andre. The moment that you saw me while Hannah was still here, what was your gut response?"

From the way a tick pulses in his jaw and he tugs at his hair, it's easy to see that he hates my question. In a low, gravelly tone, he answers me anyway: "I wanted to be alone. I wanted . . . Fuck, Zoe, I don't—"

I refuse to let the tears stinging my eyes fall. "Just say it," I whisper, "it's fine."

His hands curl into fists at his sides. "Seeing Hannah, remembering everything with Aaron . . . " His eyes slam shut. "I need more time. Right now with us, I just . . . I'm not sure I'm ready to take that leap. I thought I was, I"—his dark eyes open and hold me captive—"I care about you, Zo, I do, but I just need . . . "

"Time." The word sounds hollow. He's had time. He's had

years. "You need time, and I don't—" I inhale sharply, struggling against the hurt. "I need someone who's willing to take that leap with me, Andre. I need someone who's willing to let me shoulder the hurt with them as opposed to asking me for space. I hope that you find what you need."

He steps forward, his hand wrapping around my wrist. "I'm sorry. You have to know that I didn't realize—"

The feeling of his hand on mine is wonderful and awful all at once. "You weren't ready for a relationship," I finish for him, pulling away from his touch. "I heard you and I get it, but this time? This time I know what I want, Andre, and that's to be more than friends with you. That's what I want, and I'm not going to hide from it. Unless that's something you can see yourself giving me, then I think . . . I think that maybe we should just stop."

I wait. God, I wait for him to say that he wants a relationship with me, that maybe not *today* but that he will soon. He doesn't. His expression shutters, taking on that icy mask that I loathe so much, and he steps back. Into his safety zone where women don't pose a risk to his heart. Into his safety zone where he doesn't have to expose himself to more hurt.

As much as it hurts, I get it, but that doesn't mean I have to live with it. His insecurities. The pain he's not willing to share. The fear he's not willing to let me ease.

"Stop living like you're stuck in the penalty box, Andre." I swallow past the lump in my throat, hands curling into fists against my belly. "For once, just try to take the same risks off the ice as you do on it."

With that, I gather my things and leave, thankful for the fact that I drove over last night. I hold myself together as I head home and pull into the driveway of my new apartment. I hold myself together as I climb the steps to my third-floor apartment. I hold myself together until I step inside and realize that the place is empty and devoid of life because I've spent every moment with Andre since I signed my lease.

That's when my knees buckle and I slide to the floor, my back against the door.

I should have seen this coming.

I should have—but instead I let myself fall back in love with the one man who will never let his past go long enough to love me back.

ANDRE

ZERO DAYS LEFT

*S*he quit.

I slam my locker shut with more force than necessary. I can't believe that Zoe quit on the last fucking day of her trial run with Golden Lights Media. It's ridiculous, fucking ridiculous, and I am in such a foul mood that I'm—

"Dude, Beaumont, untwist your panties."

Duke Harrison swaggers into view. His nickname, "The Mountain," is pretty accurate. I'm big, but Harrison is the sort of big that reminds you of the Great Wall of China. Impenetrable. No wonder we put him in between the pipes.

"I'm not wearing panties," I grunt, dropping to the bench so I can lace up my skates for our game against Tampa Bay.

"Your speedo, then," Harrison quips. "They're practically the same thing."

The goddamn speedo.

Thinking of the speedo makes me think of *Fame* which makes me think of Zoe which makes the frustration bloom larger. Fuck. Hannah popping up unexpectedly was the very *last* thing I needed, especially when I was just about to tell Zoe how much I loved her. Yeah. Talk about a turn of events.

One moment I'm naked and in the arms of the woman I love, and in the next I'm arguing with the woman who stripped me of my human decency and turned me into something despicable. More importantly, I let the fear rock me back. The blinding worry that if I hit rock bottom with Hannah, then I could only imagine the shape I'd be in if Zoe left me.

And then she did.

Because you gave her no reason to stay, you dipshit.

For no less than the hundredth time since Zoe walked out of my house, I deliberate on my next move. My next game play. Because I can't let her out of my life. I did it once and that was my mistake, my fault, but I can't do it again. She's right—I need to start living my life with the same force that I do on the ice. I need to—

"You aiming for a stint in the sin bin tonight?" Harrison asks, not getting the hint that I want to be left alone. "Everyone is taking bets on whether you'll beat your record PIM from last year."

My gaze cuts to my teammate's face. "My *what?*"

He shifts uncomfortably. "You know, your penalty minutes."

"I know what the fuck PIM stands for," I growl, "but what do you mean that everyone is taking bets?"

More with the shifting around. I've never seen The Mountain so uneasy. "Last year with Detroit, you racked up 131 minutes for the full season. You're at that now, and the season isn't even over. So the guys are betting whether tonight will be the night you tip past your record."

Surprisingly, I almost want to laugh. It'd be the first time since Zoe walked out on me yesterday. "What's the pot at?"

"Ten-k."

I whistle. "High stakes."

"I thought so," Harrison says, chuckling. "For the record,

I've got you penciled down for 131 minutes, even after tonight's game."

He doesn't give the chance to reply, and maybe that's a good thing because I don't have the proper words for what I want to say. But once again, Zoe pops up front and center in my thoughts—particularly her comment about me living my life in the penalty box off the ice.

Dawn of a new day and all that, but looks like Harrison is about to become that much richer, if I have anything to say about it.

ZOE

*E*veryone is crowded around the bar at Vittoria during my shift. Yes, I said that—shift.

I quit Golden Lights Media. Probably shouldn't have done that so impulsively. Make that Disastrous Mistake Number Five-Hundred, please, followed by every single one I've ever made with Andre Beaumont.

My gaze latches onto the TV again, where the Blades are up against Tampa Bay. I haven't stopped to watch the game, too busy slinging cocktails and bringing food out to tables while Manny, the restaurant's GM, watches me like a hawk.

I talked with my dad today. He was more than accepting of me coming to work at Vittoria, but he'd had something up his sleeve I never saw coming—he wanted me to work at his restaurant, but he wanted me to run the business's PR.

Tonight, I'm only helping out the staff because we're so jam-packed with customers that the extra help is needed.

I slide my hands down over my skirt, ultimately giving in to the draw that is hockey. If I hadn't quit my job, if I hadn't quit *Andre*, I'd be there now, watching him play up from the nosebleeds.

"Everything okay over here?" I ask Carol, the bartender I'd met from a few weeks ago.

She spares me a small smile as she stuffs tip money into her apron's pocket. "Yeah, we're good. Everyone is just on edge because of King Sin Bin."

My heart stutters to a stop. "What do you mean?"

Carol lifts a shoulder. "Guy apparently hasn't played so well in years, and he hasn't even landed himself in the box once tonight."

Good for him. Really, good for him.

I blink back the sudden stinging of tears. I'm glad he's doing well. Even if I feel like I might break apart any moment.

The buzzer announcing the end of the game sounds off on the TV, and I quickly check out the score. Blades win five to two. The camera pans to the Blades hoisting someone up, and to my surprise, it's Andre. His helmet is off, and he's laughing so hard that his eyes are nearly closed.

"That's great," I say out loud. Brilliant. Fan-fucking-tastic.

I think I need wine.

Turning on my heel, I head back toward the kitchen. I need to step away from everything, to get back into *my* groove, the same way Andre has done for himself in the span of twenty-four hours.

"You good, Zoe?" my dad asks from behind the grill. The restaurant has closed for the evening, though the bar is still open for another hour, so it's only him and a few of the dishwasher guys left. Dad sent the servers home thirty minutes ago. "You look pissed."

I laugh. "I'm good, Dad."

"You sure? Shelby's not around if you want to tell me how angry you are."

"I'm not angry."

"Sad?"

Yes, sad. I sigh, untying the apron from around my waist and dropping the fabric into the laundry basket. "It'll be fine, but thanks."

He rubs his chin. "Have I mentioned how happy I am to have you working with me, kid? Always thought you'd do well here. I know you miss your mom . . . "

I really do. First thing I did last night was call her and book a flight to visit Detroit next month. I don't mind Boston, I actually really like it, but I miss my mom's hugs and her sly wit.

"Thanks for giving me a few days off next month so I can see her," I say. "It means a lot to me."

Looking awkward, Dad comes around the grill, wiping his hands off on a towel. Without giving me a chance to move away, he wraps a hand around my shoulder and pulls me into a hug. "I don't say this enough, Zoe, but I love you. I wish . . . I wish I had seen you more when you were growing up, but I'm glad to have you here now. Anytime you want to visit your mom is okay with me." He chucks me under the chin. "Now, don't look so pissed, kid. It'll give you wrinkles."

I laugh. Same old Fred Mackenzie.

Some things never change.

The sound of catcalling from the front of the house catches our attention, and with a single glance, we're sweeping in to the dining area, expecting a fire.

No fire.

Instead, everyone has their eyes trained on the TV, and the moment I walk in, multiple arms point in my direction before pointing crazily at the TV.

"What the fuck is going on?" Dad mutters, striding forward.

"Language," I reply rather uselessly.

Because the minute I step close to the TV behind the bar, *I'm* the one cursing. Oh. My. God. It's Andre and . . . I clap my hand over my mouth to keep the ridiculous giggles under wraps.

He's wearing nothing but a speedo—the *same* speedo he wore from the *Fame* interview—and . . . his nipples are pierced. *Both* of them are pierced.

"Take the subtitles off!" someone shouts. "I want to know what the hell he's saying!"

Carol fumbles for the remote and does as requested. Then, Andre's rumbly Canadian accent greets my ears, and my toes curl in my non-slip kitchen shoes.

"I was recently told that I'm mean." He holds up a hand, chuckling to himself. "Not everyone rush to my defense at once now. I get it. I know it's true. I've been a mean, cold-hearted bastard for a long time. I treated women like shit. I treated my teammates not much better. Hell, I'm pretty sure that every single one of you in this room has imagined me dead at some point or another."

This time, laughter echoes, and the camera pans to the journalists laughing quietly to themselves.

"Don't worry," Andre continues, "I get it. Thing is, it took a special person to tell this to my face. A special person to force me out of my comfort zone and put on this damn speedo for a magazine interview." He pauses, his lips curling up in a sexy grin. "Anyone in here see it yet? They've got me strutting around to Justin Bieber. Fucking great stuff—also, I apologize for the language. Baby steps, eh?" His audience laughs again, clearly charmed by a man who never plays the charming card. "Anyway, this special someone didn't let me get away with anything. She called me out on my shit. She forced me to realize that I've been miserable for way too long because I *chose* to be."

Is he really . . .?

"Let me tell you all something," Andre says on the TV. "Get out your notepads or your recorders or whatever it is that you stalk me with. Up until a month ago, I planned for this to be my last season. I've experienced a lot of heartache in the last few years, for reasons I won't disclose, and I wanted nothing more than to plant my ass on a beach somewhere and drink myself into oblivion."

"Are you really retiring?" one voice calls out.

"What about your contract?" another one shouts.

Andre waves them all away, his metal nipple piercings twinkling under the florescent lights. "Yeah, that's not happening any more. Sorry to everyone who thought they were getting rid of me. Because for the first time since I can remember, I'm going to live. Hockey is what I live for, but I live for something—*someone*—else, too." His dark eyes focus on the camera, and I swear, I can feel him staring at me as though we're in the same room.

"Baby," he murmurs, his voice pitched low, "if you're watching this, and I hope to hell that you couldn't resist doing so, I'm ready to live for you too. I'm standing here open, fucking vulnerable in nothing but a bathing suit and piercings. I'm yours. Now and forever. The only time I'm landing in the sin bin after this is on the ice—but off of it? Not a chance."

I don't even realize that I'm crying until Carol is shoving beverage napkins in my hand and telling me to pull myself together.

"If you love me at all," Andre adds, "meet me. I'll text you where so we don't have *you know who* stalking us down. I love you, and I fucking hope I'll see you there."

I don't wait for the clip to end. I run. I run for my phone, which I left in the beverage station.

He can't text me fast enough.

ANDRE

*L*et me tell you, wearing a speedo in public is embarrassing. Getting my nipples pierced at the butt crack of dawn at a random tattoo shop is also embarrassing. Appearing in front of millions of people like this on national TV?

Embarrassing.

What's not embarrassing is the way my heart threatens to beat out of my chest on my drive home after the game. What's not embarrassing is the way my hands turn slick with nerves, anticipation, *worry* that Zoe won't be there waiting for me when I arrive. What's not embarrassing is the way I rehearse my speech so that I can tell her how I feel—if she's even there. If she even heard me on TV.

All of that emotion proves that I'm living. It's real.

She's waiting for me on my front stoop when I pull up to my house, and, fuck it, I'm *not* embarrassed about the not-quite-sob of happiness that clutches my chest.

I throw the car into park and jump out within seconds.

It's dark out, but streetlamps provide all the illumination I need to see her face.

To see that tears have carved their way down her cheeks.

Fuck, fuck, fuck.

"Zo," I whisper brokenly. "I'm so fucking sorry." I edge closer, uncertain if she'll be receptive to a hug. "Please don't cry."

At that, she gives me a watery smile. "Where's your speedo?" she asks.

I flick the button of my jeans. "Under here. Didn't want to be arrested for public indecency."

Her gaze goes to my chest. "And your nipple rings? Have they turned you into the Joker yet?"

I laugh loudly. "I'll be honest, my nipples are hurting like a damn bitch right now. But I once heard you mention that they'd look good on me . . . "

"So, you went and got them?"

"A man named Twinkle did them for me," I tell her. "He had so many tattoos that I couldn't even tell where his mouth was, but he had a voice like an angel."

It's her turn to laugh. She claps a hand over her mouth, her shoulders bouncing with mirth.

"Laugh it up," I say, chuckling along with her. "I'll love you anyway."

That stems her laughter, and . . . this is my chance. I swallow past the nerves, running my sweaty hands against my shirt. "Zoe, I'm sorry for what happened. I don't have . . . " I hold my hands up. "There isn't an excuse for what I did. You walked into my life and turned everything upside down. You started as a friend, yes, but you quickly became my best friend. The only person I sought out regularly. The only person that I allowed to catch a glimpse behind my emotional walls. But I still didn't tell you everything."

"Andre—"

I shake my head. I need to get this out, for her, for us. "Not telling you about my past with Hannah is a regret that I had even then. But the thing was, you pushed all the hatred away. Being with you, in whatever capacity, allowed me to just *live*. I didn't want to drag her into our relationship. By the time I learned that Aaron had even existed, I was in too deep with you. I didn't just want a friendship with you. I wanted more; I always wanted more."

I take a risk and step close to her. Light slips across her features, and I brave a touch to her cheek. To my surprise, she nuzzles my hand, clasping it and keeping it close.

"That day that I found out Aaron was my son . . . I needed you. I wanted to lose myself in your warmth. I wanted to lose myself in the feeling of you. You were right, I *did* use you, but I wanted to remember what it felt like to be *loved*."

Her breath crashes against my palm. "Andre, it's okay. We don't have to—"

She needs to hear this. If we're ever going to move forward, together, it needs to be out in the open. "I didn't look back after that night because I knew you loved me, Zoe. I knew it, just like you told me the other day, and as much as I craved it, I also feared it. The hate was festering and I . . . Fuck, Zo, I knew right then and there that we needed to stop. No contact. You loved me and I was a shell of a man, using you to feel alive again. That wasn't fair."

Her nod is slight, small, but she surprises me again by pressing a kiss to my palm. "And what of now?" she asks. "What's different now?"

Trust Zoe "the Barracuda" Mackenzie to put me on the spot. "The difference now is that I want to live. I want to live for myself, just as much as I want to live for you. I want marriage and kids and an entire life with you. I want it all." Swallowing, I add, "That is, if you still want the same."

She slips a knuckle under her eye to wipe away a tear, and my gut clenches. "Are you proposing?"

Moment of truth here. "I hadn't planned on it," I tell her

wryly, "but now it's out there in the open, and so if you *want* to put me out of misery, feel free to do so."

"Yes."

"Yes?" I squeeze her hand. "Is that a yes to putting me out of my misery or . . . ?"

Her tinkling laughter is like music to my ears. "It's a yes to everything, Andre." Feminine fingers clasp my neck and pull me down for a hot kiss that has us panting within seconds. She pulls back. "It's a yes to loving you. It's a yes to waking up next to you every day, even when you hog the covers. It's a yes to your nipple piercings and the way that you like to boss me around." She taps my chest. "Be glad I find that domineering side of you sexy."

"Thank God," I tease, stealing another kiss from her lips. "We'd be screwed otherwise."

"Exactly." Stretching up on her toes, she kisses me again. "I love you, Andre. I loved you a year ago, when you sexed me up in a damn laundry closet and everyone learned that I have a banana-shaped birthmark on my ass. I loved you during all these months, even when I cursed your name and thought of one-hundred and seventy-five ways to tie you up and make you pay. I loved you when you walked into Golden Lights Media, and then later the next night, when you goaded me into telling you that you have a big dick."

I lean forward, thrusting my hips to her. She releases a moan at the hard line of my cock. "It's only the truth, Zo. I can't have you lying like that to yourself."

She shakes her head, reaches down, and cups me. I swear to God my eyes roll to the back of my head. "You're right. No more lying."

"Exactly," I repeat, mocking her, before I groan at her touch. "Please don't stop."

Her hand skates up the length of me. "Ask me again if I'll marry you."

Whatever she wants. "Marry me, Zoe?"

"On one condition."

I grasp her hips and yank her close. "On what?"

"On whether you make me dream about sex with you tonight."

A burst of laughter escapes me. Because damn it if she hasn't thrown my own words back at me from the beginning of the month when we sat at her dad's restaurant. "Well, I'd say that it's game on, then, Mrs. Future Beaumont." I swoop down low, hook my arm around her legs, and haul her over my shoulder. "Just resign yourself to saying yes. You know you want this hard stick."

"Andre! So cliché!" she laughs, striking my butt with a fist.

"I'm a hockey player, baby. Puns are included with the package deal."

"I'm rethinking saying yes to this proposal."

I slap her butt playfully, taking away the sting with a rub of my palm. "You'll be thanking me after I score a hat trick tonight."

And then I kick open my door, cross the threshold with my future wife over my shoulder, and proceed to do just that.

EPILOGUE

ZOE

Three-Hundred and Forty-Two Days Later

"Marshall Hunt's laying it on extra thick, don't you think?"

I lean forward, my hand clasped in Andre's, as I watch the Blades' hottest new first-stringer dip his dance partner so low that her hair brushes the floor.

Waving my hand at the couple, I add, "I mean, look at him! Supermodel after supermodel. You'd think that—"

Andre's big body presses me against the balustrade of the balcony. "I thought we went over this, baby." His fingers trace a path from my hip up and over to my elbow. "Leave poor Hunt alone."

My breath hitches when Andre dips his head to kiss my neck, and all thoughts flee. Because that's what happens when your fiancé has the ability to make love to you with just his voice—a voice that grows only deeper, more gravelly, when you fake a fascination with his teammate.

I tip back my head, running my hands up his arms and

223

then back down again. "What's the matter, *Sin*, not feeling pretty tonight at your own charity event?"

Dark eyes spark with mischief. "You know how I feel about that nickname."

"Well, you know how I feel about *you*."

Because my fiancé is sex on a stick, his next move leaves me in a pool of desire. He skims his hand up to my chest, over to the strap of my ball gown, and slips the material to the side. Masculine lips find the curve of my shoulder blade, and a shudder works down my spine. He peers up at me, his gaze hot. "How's that?"

I have no thoughts. Except that I wish we were home so that he could strip me naked and fulfill the promise in his eyes. "I love you, of course."

The grin he gives me is so boyish it hurts. "Well, that's good."

"I hope so."

Something in his tone has me raising a brow. "You're hiding something."

He presses another kiss to my exposed shoulder. "Maybe." Another kiss, this one farther up, closer to my neck. "I have a surprise for you tonight."

Sucking in a deep breath, I tilt my head to the side to give him better access. I know, I'm utterly shameless. "You know how I feel about surprises."

His next kiss is just beneath my jaw, his warm mint-flavored breath fanning over my face. "You love them, baby. And you're going to love this one, too, but first you have to promise me two things."

If he keeps kissing me I'll promise him whatever he wants. I say as much, my fingers clutching at his hard stomach.

He chuckles softly, prying my hands from his body and lifting them to his mouth to kiss my knuckles. Swoon, honestly. Is there anything hotter than a guy who loves the woman he's going to marry?

"If given the option between me and your boy, Marshall Hunt," he tells me, "you'll always choose me."

I gape at him a little. "Is that even a question?"

One big shoulder lifts in a half-shrug. "Figured I'd put it out there."

Eyes narrowing, I throw my arms around his waist, just as I always do at home when it's the two of us. I don't care that there are people watching: those who have come for the joint charity for Boston's first responders, hosted by the Boston Blades and Vittoria. Nope, I only care about Andre, and as I snuggle up against his chest, delighting in his rough laugh, I say, "Next promise please—I don't put up with silly ones."

"Well, you see, the next promise comes into play because of the first . . . "

Thirty minutes later, I find myself standing in the crowd next to my former coworker-turned-friend, Gwen James. Everyone is gathered around a makeshift stage that was intended for a band but is now being put to use for something else.

An auction.

A *date* auction.

Apparently, I've been tasked with convincing Gwen to vote on one particular man—Marshall Hunt.

When the first player struts out onto the stage in nothing but his hockey pants, the crowd goes wild. Gwen, in particular, sticks two fingers in her mouth and whistles. "His abs?" she says, nudging my side. "I could eat off them."

On my other side, Charlie leans around me to say, "You're insatiable."

Gwen shrugs. "How is that my fault? You're in a

committed relationship, *Zoe's* engaged, and I'm rocking singlehood like it's the new Prada."

I hold up a finger. "To be fair, I've never heard you say that you *want* a relationship."

"Well, no." Gwen grins slowly. "But that's not to say that I wouldn't want to get one of these players into bed."

"Clearly she's learned nothing from us," Charlie says with a boisterous laugh. "We're both cases of breaking professional boundaries, and here's Gwen with not a care in the world if she sleeps with a client."

"I *care*." After taking a sip of her cocktail, Gwen adds, "It's just that I like sex more. Plus, if I just make sure not to sleep with someone who *is* my client, problem solved."

The next player comes out and I realize that it's Marshall. Just like the guy before him, he's in just his pants and shoes. Engaged or not, I give a low whistle because the man is dangerously sexy. Something that Gwen fails to notice, if the way she checks out her phone is any indication.

Marshall turns around at the end of the stage, blows a kiss to the crowd like a damned Victoria's Secret Model, and swaggers back toward the rest of the guys who are all lined up, waiting for their turn.

"Gwen."

"Hmm?" She doesn't look up from her phone.

"Did you not see Marshall Hunt just now?" I point at the stage. "He's your type."

"He's too young."

Too young? "Girl, the man is ripped, funny, and fifteen different shades of sexy; I don't think his age is an issue." Time to go for broke. "I think you should bet on him."

That gets her attention. "Absolutely not."

"It's just a date." I give her a little nudge. "Dinner. Hell, you can even just grab coffee if you don't want to spend that much time with him."

"He's not worth the money."

Beside me, Charlie lets out a whoop of laughter.

I don't know *why* Andre asked me to get Gwen to bet on his teammate, but all I know is that he did. Time to pull out the big guns—guilt. "Your bid goes to charity. You're helping people."

Gwen's blue eyes dance away from me. "I didn't say that I won't bid on anyone; I just won't bid on *him*."

Hold on here a second . . . "Did something *happen* between the two of you?"

Her cheeks bloom red, and I know for a fact that it's not her expensive blush doing the trick. "Absolutely not," she mutters, eyeing her phone again. "Absolutely not. I wouldn't touch Marshall Hunt with a ten-foot pole. I'd be likely to catch herpes."

Considering that Gwen is a wild bird herself when it comes to men, I opt to hold my opinion to myself.

But then the announcer, Coach Hall, steps forward to start the bidding process. McDermott comes first and, surprisingly, a few hands swing up as numbers are called out. He promptly goes for two hundred dollars to a man in the back of the room. Figures.

One by one, the Blades members step forward. When Duke does so, his gaze immediately searching for his girl-friend, Charlie flings her hand up in the air and shouts, "No one bother! I'll outbid every single one of you."

The Mountain sells to Charlie for a grand, after a few of his teammates throw out random bids just to mess with Harrison.

Charlie smiles into her drink, and murmurs, "Best one thousand dollars I'll ever spend."

Then it's Marshall Hunt's turn. I haven't seen Andre since he left me to go meet with the guys, but I search for him now. He's not up with the team, and a seed of disappointment sinks into my belly. Call me crazy, but I *wanted* to bet on him, to mark him as mine in front of everyone.

"Bids for Marshall Hunt?" Coach Hall calls out. "Lemme hear those bids!"

I elbow Gwen. "Now's your chance."

Her expression freezes. "No."

"Do it, girl. He's hot and, yes, young, but I'm sure he'll rock it in the sheets."

Charlie points her drink toward Gwen. "I've heard that he can make a woman come in twenty seconds."

Gwen snorts. "Fucking unbelievable. Listen up, there is no way in a million years I would bet on a man who can't even—"

"*Two thousand dollars!*"

Oops, that was me.

Coach Hall thumps his gavel down on his podium stand. "Going once for Marshall Hunt at two thousand! Going twice!"

"If Coach ever loses his job, he's got a calling as an auctioneer," Charlie says with a laugh.

"*Sold!*" Hall shouts. "Marshall Hunt for two thousand dollars to the future Mrs. Beaumont."

I sigh a little at the anticipation of my married name before thrusting a hand in the air. "Actually, Coach! My bid is an honorary one . . . for Gwen James."

Gwen gasps beside me.

A seductive grin curls Marshall Hunt's mouth.

And then I feel masculine arms, *familiar arms*, wrap around my middle and tug me back against a hard chest. Andre's lips find my ear, and his breath rustles my hair. "What did I tell you about choosing Hunt?"

I can hear the laughter in his voice, though, and I know he's just teasing me. "I had to take drastic measures. You tasked me with getting Gwen to bid on him and that's what I did."

He kisses my neck, then my cheek. "You did well."

I turn my head to look back at him. "Where did you go? I was hoping to have the chance to bid on you."

Dark eyes meet mine, and I melt. I'm not kidding. I melt in his arms right there because I can see all of the love there. "I had to go help your dad with moving some of the buffet tables. Also, I never planned to join the auction."

"There's no fun in that."

"Sure there is." His fingers brush back and forth against my belly. "You get to bid on me every night. Which position you want me to take you in. Which trashy TV show I'll cave and let you watch. How many times I'll tell you that I love you."

"If you get to wear clothes that day or not," I tease, already reaching up to sink one hand into his thick hair. "Tell me again."

He doesn't need further prompting. It's a tradition we started soon after getting engaged six months ago. "You're a goddess among women, Zo." His lips curl up in a sexy smile. "And I love you more than fucking anything."

I pull him down for a kiss. "You're a god among men, Andre, and I'm so glad that I slept with you in that dirty laundry room."

His laughter is rich, throaty.

A sound that I adore.

A man that I adore.

Someday we'll tell our future children about the time that King Sin Bin married the Queen of Bad Decisions and lived happily ever after. But tonight, I just let my fiancé hold me. Kiss me. And prove, once and for all, that real-life happily-ever-afters come as a result of a healthy dose of bad decisions, one ridiculously hot hockey player, and multiple stints in the penalty box.

Turn the page for a sneak peek of the upcoming Blades Hockey novel, HAT TRICK ... featuring Gwen James & Marshall Hunt. Trust me when I say that their romance is one you won't see coming!

PREVIEW OF HAT TRICK

Hat Trick is now available! Keep scrolling to read an excerpt from the next Blades Hockey novel, featuring Gwen James & Marshall Hunt. It's a steamy second chance, mixed in with a dash of unrequited-love that will heat up your e-reader!

WHAT THE HELL IS GWEN DOING HERE?

My stride slows, and she must hear the tread of my heavy boots because she glances up from her phone with a strained expression. The loose curl of her hair is frizzier than normal. Even her clothes, which are usually perfectly tailored, look disheveled today.

Her slim, knee-length skirt is off-center, the row of buttons not aligning with her belly-button. Her flouncy shirt is half-tucked into the skirt. And, hell, the woman is wearing flats.

Gwen James is a stiletto kind of girl.

I haven't seen her in anything else since Accounting 201.

Be casual, man.

Right. Be casual. How's that even possible when all I want

to do is muss Gwen up even more? With my fingers. My tongue. My cock.

I purposely slide my gaze down her trim frame, taking in my full, before slipping my phone into the back of my jeans and cocking my head to the side. "Fancy seeing you here, Miss James."

Her blue eyes flick away from my face, but I suspect the aversion has less to do with checking me out and more to do with hiding her flushed cheeks—a blush that I doubt has anything to do with the chilly weather.

"Marshall," she says somewhat stiffly, sliding her hands down the length of her skirt. "I was hoping to run into you."

Had she? I squelch down a burst of pleasure, stomping the bastard hard into the ground. I'm done with the hope. I meant what I said last night. Sliding my hands into my jeans' pockets, I tilt my head toward my truck. "Looks like you found me."

The flush burns even brighter, and this time I know damn well the freezing temperature isn't responsible.

"Yeah, I . . ." She visibly swallows, and I realize that I've never, not once, seen her so at odds. Gwen is the epitome of ice and class, a concoction that keeps her nose in the air and her true feelings wrapped up in steel walls.

But this Gwen . . . the messy, uncertain Gwen standing before me? Well, color me intrigued.

Wanting to push her a little more, I lift my brows in a show of deliberate patience. "You are . . .?"

Her red hair is shoved indelicately behind one ear. "I'm here."

She's pretty much told me nothing. I nod slowly. "Congratulations. You lookin' for a trophy or something?"

White teeth sink into her bottom lip. I suck down a groan and force myself to stop thinking about those lips wrapped around my cock. Never gonna happen, that's for sure.

"I, um." Gwen shifts her weight, tucking one foot behind her opposite calf like she's nervous to have me see her this way. "Listen, I . . . So, this is officially a lot harder than I thought it would be."

I watch her expectantly, giving her nothing. Oh, how the tables have turned. Plus, I doubt she's here for anything *us* related. If anything, she's probably here on her boss's bidding. The man has been trying to lock me down into hiring Golden Lights Media for a year now.

I'm not interested.

I've already signed on the dotted line for another firm; a firm, I might add, that took me on even when I was still on the farm team, when the Blades had yet to pull me up onto their official roster.

"Okay, okay." Gwen shoots me a glare, like I'm the one at fault for her halted speech. I hear her mutter something that sounds *suspiciously* like, "I can do this," and then she's straightening her shoulders, thrusting her full breasts up and out, and announcing, "I'd like to take you up on that offer for our date. The date that I won from the charity auction last spring."

Shock clamps my jaw shut.

But now that Gwen has opened the gates, proverbially speaking, she doesn't stop. She steps to the side, head down, tucking her hair behind her ears. "I know that I sort of . . . you know, turned you down rather harshly. I'd told Zoe I didn't plan to bet on you, and I know the money was going to first responders, but I just couldn't . . . I mean, it's never been about your looks." She offers an awkward *ha-ha*, her blue eyes skirting up to my face before swiftly darting away again. "You're handsome. And young. Oh, God, what I *mean* is—I already said that. The *I mean* thing, I mean. I just did it again." Her eyes go wide as though begging me to end her misery.

I don't.

Let the misery continue.

I fold my arms over my chest and keep up the mute act. I like this Gwen. Hell, I really like this Gwen.

She huffs out a heavy breath, repeating the tuck-the-hair motion again. There's no more hair to tuck. It's already been plastered behind her ears. But she's nervous. For the first time in years, I think I may be witnessing Gwen James come undone.

Over me.

Does sweet justice actually exist? I think it does.

"So, yes, I turned you down repeatedly. That's on me. I was going through . . . life? Yeah, we'll go with life. But I listened to what you said last night, Marshall, and I realized that I'd like to go on a date with you. It'd be nice. I mean, I *think* it would be nice. We won't know if we're compatible until we go out or whatever. To be honest, I'm not even sure a relationship is the best thing. Does love even really . . . it doesn't matter." Her shoulders hike up, her flouncy shirt fluttering around her breasts.

Blue eyes meet mine, hopeful and nervous.

"Will you go on a date with me, Marshall?"

I stare down at her—the woman I've crushed on like an idiot teenager for half my adult life—and say the one word I never anticipated telling her.

"No."

Can't wait to find out what happens next? HAT TRICK is now live on Amazon/Kindle Unlimited!

Swipe right to the next page to get a freebie goodie for SIN BIN.

DO YOU WANT TO KNOW WHAT HAPPENED IN THAT LAUNDRY ROOM?

Besides the dirty laundry, of course? If you do, you're just in luck! Maria has created some extra bonus content goodies detailing that particular scene (just *how* did Andre prove to Zoe that multiple orgasms were a thing, after all?). All you have to do is follow the link below, and sign up for her newsletter, and you'll be sent the goods! Enjoy!
Copy this link into your internet search bar: http://www. subscribepage.com/sinbin-signup

DEAR FABULOUS READER

Hi there!

Thank you so much for joining me on this wild journey with Andre and Zoe. For those who are new to my books, welcome and thank you for giving my stories a try! I so hope you enjoyed SIN BIN.

If you're wondering what this space is . . . in every single one of my books, I love to give a little behind-the-scenes glance at the book. When it comes to SIN BIN, funnily enough, this book was never supposed to exist! I had written the first in the series, POWER PLAY, after hearing an amazing song that sparked everything for me. It was meant to be a standalone, but on the morning of POWER PLAY's release, inspiration struck in, of all places, the shower.

The title came to me first. Then the plot—what would happen to a couple if they allowed lust (and love!) to get in the way, so much so that it ruined their friendship *and* their careers? Immediately, the plot for SIN BIN took root. But, I needed characters.

So, I thought of the (somewhat) terrifying Andre Beaumont who had only a few lines in POWER PLAY. I was immediately intrigued by him . . . could I take such a man and show him to have a heart? To allow him to be vulnerable under all that icy veneer?

The rest, as they say, is history. So, while SIN BIN was not originally in the plans, it soon became the story I stayed up at all hours to write, to reread, to tear apart until Zoe and Andre's love story was one that even made me, the author, swoon.

There are a few aspects of SIN BIN that I couldn't help but throw in, the first being the IHOP that Zoe and Andre visit in Cambridge, Massachusetts, one city over from Zoe's Somerville. I've been to that IHOP one too many times, and couldn't resist having them eat there. Vittoria, as well, is loosely based off a family restaurant in my hometown. While the original restaurant is Greek (and not Italian), the interior design, the feel, and, yes, the singing, are all at the heart of dining there.

As for the next book in the Blades series, fear not, it's definitely coming your way!

You may have a guess as to who the couple will be after reading SIN BIN's epilogue?

Again, thank you so much for giving SIN BIN a go, and I hope you'll enjoy my other books! On the next page you'll find a little sneak peek of the first book in my NOLA Heart series. Hot detectives against the backdrop of sultry New Orleans? If this tickles your fancy, then you're in for a treat!

Enjoy!

Much love,

Maria

PREVIEW OF SAY YOU'LL BE MINE

The NOLA Heart series is now complete! Keep reading for a sneak peek of Say You'll Be Mine, the first book in the series—featuring a hot cop and his high school sweetheart.

"Need help with those?"

Shaelyn jerked at the familiar masculine voice and nearly pantsed herself. Picking a wedgie in public, while sometimes necessary, was embarrassing, but losing her shorts in front of Brady Taylor, strangers, and the all-seeing eyes of her parish church might actually spell the end of her.

Then again, problem solved. Meme Elaine would have to find someone else to inherit their ancestral home, of course, but Shaelyn could work some serious magic from Upstairs.

"Nope, I've got it," she bit out. She didn't look at him. One glance and there was a decent chance of her good sense going MIA.

"You sure?" Black Nike tennis shoes entered her peripheral vision. "Looks like you might need a hand."

His toned calves were dusted with short, black hairs. It was a sign of weakness, she knew, but Shaelyn couldn't stop the upward progression of her gaze. Settled low on his hips were maroon basketball shorts with cracked-gold lettering running up the side. The first and second O's were missing, so that instead of Loyola, it read "L Y LA." She wondered why he wasn't wearing his alma mater, Tulane University, and then reminded herself that she didn't care. Her gaze traveled up to a faded-blue NOPD T-shirt that—

Shaelyn inhaled sharply as she realized just how awful *she* must look. Boob sweat was the least of her worries when her underwear had officially integrated itself between her butt cheeks. She reached up to smooth her short, curly hair, which she'd tamed with a headband straight out of the '90s. Her bedroom was proving to be a treasure trove of forgotten goodies.

"You've got something . . . " Brady reached out a hand toward her butt.

"Hey!" She swatted at his long-tapered fingers. He wasn't wearing his hat today, and she finally had her first glimpse of his blue-on-blue eyes. She'd once compared them to the crystal blue waters of Destin (where their families once vacationed together in Florida every summer), and she was annoyed to find that time had not dampened their appeal. Straightening her spine, she snapped, "Hands off."

Holding both hands up, he dipped his chin. "You might wanna check out your behind then." Those blue eyes crinkled as he grinned, with small laugh lines fanning out from the corners.

Shaelyn twisted at the waist. Three leaves were stuck to her butt, suctioned to the fabric of her shorts as though hanging on for dear life. Sweat, apparently, was the proper glue foliage needed for attachment.

She was never working out again.

"You got it?" Brady asked, humor lacing his husky drawl. "I'm good with my hands, if you need help."

An image of Brady's large hands cupping her butt snapped her into action. She swiped at the offending leaves, sending them fluttering to the ground. "I'm good. Thanks."

His sweeping glance, one that traveled from her tennis shoes all the way up to her face, left her wondering if he liked what he saw or if he was glad he'd dumped her years ago. Finally, he murmured, "I can see that."

The key ring came loose from her belt loop with an extra hard tug of desperation, and she started for her car. "Right. Well, nice to see you."

Brady effectively ruined her escape by leaning against her car door with his arms crossed over his hard chest. Hadn't she suffered enough today without having to deal with him, too? Boob sweat, wedgies, and leaves suctioned to her ass were all a woman could take, thank you very much.

She gestured at him. "Do you mind?"

His answering smile was slow and easy. "Not at all."

Her fingers curled tightly around the car keys. "I've got somewhere to be."

"Yeah?" His tone suggested that he didn't believe her. "Where are you going?"

She toyed with the idea of blowing off his question, but if there was one thing she knew about Brady Taylor, it was that he was annoyingly persistent. "I've got a bachelorette party tonight."

"Oh, yeah?" He said it differently this time, as if intrigued, perhaps even despite himself. "Didn't realize you had many friends left in N'Orleans?"

She scowled, placed a hand on her hip, and then realized that she must look about five seconds away from throwing a good ol' Southern princess tantrum. Hastily she folded her arms over her chest to mimic his stance. With determination she ignored the way her sweat-coated skin fused together.

"For the record, I do have friends." She didn't, not really, but he didn't know that. "And secondly, my job is hosting a bachelorette party."

He seemed to digest that, his full mouth momentarily flattening before quirking up in a nonchalant smile. "Where do you work nowadays, Shae?"

The bells of Holy Name chimed again. She really had to be going, but something stopped her from walking around the hood of her car, climbing in, and speeding away. She didn't want to think about what that *something* might be.

"I work at La Parisienne in the French Quarter. On Chartres."

One of his black brows arched up in surprise. "The lingerie joint?"

Only a man would call a business that sold women's underwear a "joint." Rolling her eyes, Shaelyn let her weight rest on her right leg. She bit back another moan of pain. "It has a name, but yes, I work at the 'lingerie joint.'"

"And they host bachelorette parties?"

She shrugged. "Sometimes. Tonight we're cohosting it with The Dirty Crescent."

"The sex toy shop?"

"Yes."

His blue eyes glittered, and when he asked, "Can I come?" his voice slid through her like that first shot of whiskey she'd downed in his grandfather's office years earlier. Shocking at first, and then hot and tingly as it heated her core.

Then he ruined everything by laughing.

Nothing ever changed with him.

"You're such a jerk," she snapped. She stepped forward and pushed at his chest to urge him away from her car. He didn't budge, which only infuriated her. How dare he tease her like he hadn't broken her heart? So what if she'd been young, naïve, and fifty shades of stupid? Being a gentleman was not overrated.

244

He was still laughing when he caught her by the shoulders. "I could arrest you for harassment." His hands were warm on her exposed skin, hotter, maybe, than the late afternoon sun toasting the back of her neck.

Shaelyn glared up at him, not the least bit pacified by the mischievous glint in his blue eyes. His thumbs stroked her collarbone. Once, twice. If she'd been a weaker woman, she would have curled into his embrace. "You should arrest yourself."

"For what?"

"For being an ass."

His head dipped, his breath a whisper against her ear. Goosebumps teased her flesh. "You gonna do it yourself? Maybe buy a pair of new 'cuffs from that party tonight and put them to good use on me?"

Want to keep reading? *Say You'll Be Mine* is now available on Amazon!

ACKNOWLEDGMENTS

Once upon a time, I once thought that a book could be successful on its own merit.

…We don't really need to mention how ridiculous of an idea this is, right??

I cannot even stress how many people I owe thanks to for helping me to pull together SIN BIN into what it is today.

Viper, you are kickass. I can't even stress how thankful I am that you agreed to be my beta reader. For as long as I'm writing, you are more than welcome to stare over my shoulder and watch me type, creepily or not. You don't even have to ask. You are amazing!!!

So much thanks goes out to Najla, my cover designer, of Najla Qamber Designs. I may be able to write a book, but I have no talent when it comes to book design and I never want to try. Thank you for always taking my jumbled requests and giving me a product that was *exactly* what I wanted. Even more, thank you, thank you, thank you, for making the girl's hair on the cover brown and making her into the perfect Zoe!

Kathy, you are such an amazing editor and I cannot stress enough how grateful I am to have found you. I'm not kidding when I say that I need to make a 'What Would Kathy Do?' t-shirt. When I write, you are constantly in my head (in a non-creepy way, of course), so that I always keep in mind your words of wisdom. Also, one day I promise I will get colloquialisms right on the first round. Thus far, I've failed epically, but I'm sure I'll get there at some point! LOL.

Tandy, you are a proofreading goddess. Thank you for taking the time (and speed) to get through SIN BIN, and to make the experience painless.

To my author friends-turned-family…you're everything. Terra, Emma, Natalia, Joslyn, Roberta—where would I be without y'all? Honestly, I don't want to know! I love you guys to the moon and back!

To my VIPers, I bow down. Thank you for taking the time out of your lives to read my books and to review them. I would be nothing without you—and I'm not exaggerating in the slightest. Thank you for all that you do; your words of kindness, love, and support. When I started this author journey, I never expected to find my tribe—and then I met you all, and now I fear you're stuck with me for good

To my family and friends (especially to my mother and Michael), who put up with me when I'm in the writing cave, revisions mode, hanging out on livestreams on Facebook, and am not always present in the real life . . . thank you. Thank you for always encouraging me to reach for my dreams, and for never letting me give up, even when the road grows rocky.

And, most of all, thank you to my readers, my ride-or-die fans. Without you, my dream of being an author would be nothing but a figment of my imagination. Thank you for taking a chance on me, my characters, and my work, and allowing me to reach for my dreams. As Zoe once said, *believe it and you will achieve it*. Well, without you, the "achieving" bit would be a lot more difficult. You rock.

Much love,

Maria

ALSO BY MARIA LUIS

ABOUT THE AUTHOR

Maria Luis is the author of sexy contemporary romances.

Historian by day and romance novelist by night, Maria lives in New Orleans, and loves bringing the city's cultural flair into her books. When Maria isn't frantically typing with coffee in hand, she can be found binging on reality TV, going on adventures with her other half and two pups, or plotting her next flirty romance.

Stalk Maria in the Wild at the following!
Join Maria's Newsletter
Join Maria's Facebook Reader Group

Made in the USA
Middletown, DE
15 November 2020